THIN PLACES

A NOVEL

Diane Owens Prettyman

****

Author's Photo by Ed Prettyman, Psy.D.

http://www.dianeowensprettyman.com/

Cover art by Jim Gingerich. www.jimgingerich.com

****

To those saints who dwell in the thin places.

For Ed, Lee, Cassie and Maddy.

****

Heaven and earth are only three feet apart, but in the thin places the distance is even smaller.

Celtic Saying

Chapter One

Polunsky Unit, Huntsville, Texas

The way I see it, it's the people you least expect, the people the rest of the world walk right by, maybe even turn away from, who know about the meaning of life, and by that I mean the world beyond this one and all those strings that connect us to it. I know now that Calvery was one of those people.

I was an addict and a liar, but Calvery entrusted me with his dying wish. Me. A guy so lost a bloodhound couldn't find me. At the time, I thought he was nuts. Now, I think maybe the Divine did have something to do with it.

While doing time for one too many parole violations, all drug offenses, I mopped floors all over Polunsky, including death row. Each time I headed over there, good ol' Spud, the Boss responsible for setting me up with my job as porter, gave me a cursory pat down. I could have packed a blade in my sock, green money in my shoe and a cell phone in my boxers, but we both knew I wasn't that kind of convict. What I did was mule sugar.Calvery lived on the row, and we'd become friends.

For the past year, I had slipped him a pound of sugar every couple of weeks. It took eight cups to make a gallon of wine. In return, he always gifted me some of his homemade wine. This ended up a little risky for me, but in his situation, I figured he deserved a little hooch to wash down his bread and beans. He bought his fruit juice in the commissary just like the rest of us, but he needed sugar to ferment the juice into wine. To get sugar, you needed to know someone who worked in the kitchen. Being a porter, I had connections. It was easy enough for me to do him the favor of dropping a pound of sugar in his bean slot every now and then.

When I reached Calvery's cell, his house as we called it, I pushed my trashcan up close. He dropped a plastic Sunkist bottle full of his wine into the trash. I covered it with the Houston Chronicle and started to slide some sugar through the slot. Talking to death row inmates was forbidden, smuggling sugar, even more serious, so even though Spud seemed to like me, I kept everything on the down low. First and foremost, I wanted to get out of this place.

"I won't be needing that," Calvery said. He stood behind the braided wires of his tiny window. I never got to see his face in plain view, but no matter when I saw him, his eyes beamed at me beneath raised eyebrows. In short, he always seemed lit. He lifted a cup to the window and said, "I got plenty to last me."

This struck me as a strange thing to say given our arrangement with the sugar. "You attending AA meetings?"

But Calvery only smiled and said, "This is it."

"What're you talking about?"

"Tomorrow's my last day."

I knew this was inevitable, but we never talked about it. Why couldn't this happen after my release? I looked stunned, I suspect. Shouldn't I have felt something? But with the deadly heat of summer stuck to my skin and my teeth clamped tight, I felt empty as a well in August. "I can't believe it."

"It's true," he said. "How would you say it? I'm starting my descent." After his comment, he paused waiting for his audience of one to laugh. Calvery had always liked my sayings and tried them on whenever he had a chance. When I just stood there mute and tight-lipped, Calvery added, "I'm in my final approach."

"Stop." I raised my voice. What do you say; what could I say?

"I can see the runway."

"Stop it, I said." I glared at him, and if a three-inch, steel-reinforced door hadn't separated us, my hands would have been on his shoulders, shaking him, telling him to shut up. "It's not funny."

He put a finger to his mouth and hushed me in the same fatherly way I used to comfort Lacy, my daughter. That got me to thinking about Lacy. We used to walk along Galveston beach with her lime-green bucket and shovel until we found a spot to dig and watch for freighters entering the ship channel. I liked the shells; she liked the freighters. Once she found a sand dollar the size of a dime, perfect as a button. I still have it stowed away in my treasure box. One day I will give it to Lacy, maybe put it in glass and hang it on a gold chain.

Calvery would never see his little girl again. What little hope I had for the future depended on Brooke and Lacy. I had nothing to give Calvery except pity, a listening ear, and an honest look in the eyes. That day, while we locked eyes in that tier with its shiny floors and blinding white lights and inmates shouting at each other like men with nothing to lose, with my mouth dropped open in shock, and the look of happiness on his face—a look even the certainty of death didn't chase away—I think maybe something passed between us.

"You promised you'd talk to Chloe, Finn," he said. "Tell her I'm innocent."

I had promised this about a year ago because Calvery couldn't tell her himself. His family didn't want anything to do with him, and he didn't want anyone to know Chloe existed. That meant Calvery was doing the hardest kind of sentence—time with no visitation.

Calvery asked me because he figured no one could connect me to him. I was a safe bet. I made the promise to Calvery thinking I'd never have to make good on it—not that I'm the kind of guy that doesn't keep his word—I just figured a guy doesn't really expect you to follow up on something like that.

"I guess I never thought—."

"They'd execute me?" Calvery laughed. He ran his fingers through his grizzled black hair.

For the last two years, I had selfishly repressed the idea of his impending death. He refused to be bothered by it; I followed suit. But now, the day had come, and I would have to make good on my promise.

"You forget, I've got a wife and daughter," I said, keeping my eyes off him.

"They won't suspect you. You don't have any connection to me."

"There's money in it for you." Behind the wire, Calvery looked every bit the priest in a confessional. "When you see her, ask her where her grandfather was buried."

"And?"

"That will lead you to the treasure."

Calvery always talked about the treasure, and I indulged him. I knew better than to scoff at a dying man's fantasy. But I didn't believe a word of it. If there were a treasure, surely Calvery wouldn't have ended up on death row.

"I'm not expecting a treasure," I said. Then I added, "Thanks anyhow," because I might have sounded a little dismissive.

"Just the same, you'll find it. I know you will."

"I don't get you," I said. "You've got a good attitude for someone in your position."

"I feel like I'm on the last leg of a long road trip and about to get home to a nice meal, a warm bed and a beautiful wife," he said. "Besides, I know that God sent you to help me. I'm sure of it."

"God wouldn't send me to the mailbox." I tapped the mop bucket with the toe of my shoe.

Any other guy talking like that I'd think he was crazy. But over the last couple years, I had learned Calvery knew the secret to survival, and it wasn't the homemade wine.

"The truth is always unbelievable."

That made sense to me. All the big moments of my life, marrying Brooke, seeing Lacy in her arms, were unbelievable. I turned it over in my mind until across the hall an inmate screamed and startled me. I over-balanced and ended up with the mop handle stabbing my throat. "Poor guy's a taco short of a Mexican plate."

"Solitude does strange things to a man. When it's just you and your soul, you better be friends, " Calvery said.

"I know about that, I guess."

"Look in here." He thumped on his chest.

"I don't imagine I'll find my soul there, either. Not in this godforsaken place," I said, looking down the hall toward the way out.

"You'd be surprised at the places God turns up."

Behind the wire, Calvery's face glowed like a pastor's on Easter Sunday. Was he crazy, or was there something real and true inside him that kept him going? I wasn't sure which answer frightened me more.

Sure as I am here to tell this story, it was the fear of missing out on what Calvery had inside that stopped me from picking up my mop bucket and hoofing it to the guard station. And I counted Calvery as my friend. The number had dwindled over the years, drugs and jail do that to you, and I'd found myself in the regrettable position of having only three—my cellmate, aka Cellie, my pal Jacob in Galveston, and a death row inmate.

Down the hall, a gate rammed into place, the metal clanging like a rear-end collision in downtown Houston. Spud headed toward me. Our conversation had gone on a little too long. I shoved the mop against the baseboard and scrubbed, nonchalantly edging away from Calvery's cage. When Spud was in ear shot, I started whistling "Thirty Days in the Hole."

Spud looked over at Calvery, then at me. "Tully, you have a lot of space to cover."

"And I have miles to mop before I sleep, sir," I said, glancing at Calvery who grinned at my joke.

The bulk of Spud disappeared down the hallway.

Calvery reached a few fingers through the wire. "She lives in Washington State, in a little town called Clam Harbor."

I put my hand against the wire. His nails were clean and short, his skin smooth and pale. As his fingers closed over mine, a warm charge of electricity pass across my palm and spread through me. The memory still gets to me. I will never forget it, nor the peaceful feeling that passed through me that day in the middle of Texas death row.

"All right then," I said.

"It was nice knowing you, Finn. Thanks for sharing the cup with me. I think this batch is my best ever." He nodded to the trashcan.

His voice sounded distant and garbled. I felt lousy, like I had just dropped off a dog to be put down. In a few minutes, I would be out of this hall, back in my cell, shooting the breeze with Cellie. In a few months, I would be back home in the arms of my wife, my little girl on my lap. Tomorrow Calvery Thomas would be dead.

"Stay cool." I moved my waving hand to my forehead and saluted him. It was a corny way to say goodbye. "See you…" My voice faltered before I could say, on the other side.

"Yes, that's right," Calvery said. "I'll see you in the thin places."

***

On the day of Calvery's execution, my cellmate, Jesús, a Catholic from South Texas, chalked our cinder block with the final touches of his latest Saint-of-the-Month—Joan of Arc. We had been through many saints over the last couple of years. I always looked forward to the next one.

Early on in my time, I had nicknamed Jesús, Cellie. I wasn't about to call anyone mortal Jesus, even if it was a common Mexican name and even if it was pronounced

"Hey Soos." Cellie was doing ten years for smuggling a ton of smoke under a truckload of Rio Grande Valley Ruby Reds. He was on the last leg of his sentence.

It had been a few weeks since Cellie had shaved his head. His black hair stood straight up, giving his skull that prickly, nerdy-dude look of a football coach who wears beltless knit pants. I am fairly certain it was not the look Cellie was going for.

I wore my hair as long as they allowed me to, about four inches if I pushed it. With a little gel to slick it back, it looked as dark as Cellie's. He stood five-six to my six-two and kept in tip-top shape. So did I. Not much else to do here. Besides, it was a matter of survival if you wanted to make it through the inevitable fight-of-the-week. I was still skinny, though. If Cellie and I were dogs, he would be a pit bull, and I would be an underfed Great Dane.

For me, Calvery's last day drug on like a Sunday sermon. In fact, everyone seemed on edge, maybe even reflective. Showing respect for those about to be executed was part of our unwritten code—a code that included other universally accepted mores such as smashing on pedophiles and shunning anyone who would dare hurt or con the elderly.

As the execution hour approached, Polunsky geared up for the execution. At five-forty-five, the guards ordered a lockdown. The gates slammed shut, and along with them, the doors to our cells.

"This is it," I said. "You think they'll stay his execution?"

Cellie turned from his drawing and shook his head. "Lo siento."

"Sorry is the word for it all right." I stepped over to my bunk. When I pulled Calvery's wine from beneath my mattress, Cellie's face lit up. "This is the last of it," I said. "It's too bad. His is always la mejor." Cellie thrust his cup my way.

The wine splashed into his cup. After inhaling a full nose of toilet water—all prison wine is fermented in the toilet tanks—I smelled a hint of oak and blackberry. Calvery was big on Oregon Pinot Noir and always tried to emulate it. I took a sip. For a moment, I thought I was on the outside at some fine steak place, chowing down on a T-Bone with Brooke and Lacy. Somehow, this time, by mixing just the right blend of dried cranberries and fruit juice, Calvery had managed to come up with a wine actually resembling an aged red. Cellie raised his glass to me. I gave him the thumbs up.

Cellie had a little black old school clock with bright red numbers that flipped over as the minutes passed. They hadn't sold those in the commissary for years. When it turned to six o'clock, The Unit quieted down from its usual roar. At least this tier full of no-accounts cared about Calvery's death. That was impressive.

At 6:01, Cellie brushed off his hands, sending a shroud of black dust into our cell, and stowed his chalk under his bunk.

I pictured Calvery sitting there, his arm strapped to a board, the blue-white glare of fluorescent bulbs blinding him, a needle stuck in a vein, as I had done so many times.

Cellie knelt before his altar—a tattoo of the Virgin Mary on one bulging bicep, a tattoo of a topless senorita on the other—praying for a man he had never met. Except for the tattoos, he looked like a bona fide saint.

I turned to the clock—6:04. Was this about the time Calvery said his last words to a sea of unsympathetic strangers? Was there even one friendly face to look at? His last words to me came to mind. See you in the thin places, Calvery had said.

The numbers of the clock flipped over with a sound like a tongue clicking. It was already 6:07. Downing my cup of wine, I wondered about Calvery's daughter and how she coped with all this. "It was a raw deal," I said. "Someone should stop it. He was a good guy. I know he was."

Cellie ripped his St. Christopher's medal from his neck and threw it at his icon of Mary. "It's God's will."

"Cheers to our friend," I said as I filled his cup.

He took it, and when the tension in his bicep released, he somehow passed it to me. He sipped the wine, then gulped it, and his features slowly softened and shriveled like a child's blow-up toy losing air.

It was 6:10. "My friend's dying." I said the words just to see if they sounded true. They didn't. A surge of panic and worthlessness flashed through me; I buried it with a deep breath, thinking of all the times I had come off heroin, thinking of the trouble I was in, knowing I had pissed off every person in my life that had ever given a shit about me.

With my head in my hands, I let things settle in my mind until I heard the snap of the clock again—6:11. Cellie crossed himself. It was too late, I was sure of it. Too damn late. I ran to the bars and yelled out, "Spud! Boss! Somebody!"

The tiers shouted back with a deafening chorus of profanity. And all the shit of my life came back to me. I was younger then, and jolted awake by the skidding of my Ford 150, the hard stop of the front end against a live oak, mesquite brambles scraping at the windows, Lacy howling from her car seat, the blackness of the night setting in on us—a darkness I've lived with ever since.

Just as the deplorable shame of my life elbowed its way toward me through the pitchy gloom, as I recalled the heart-broken look on my mother's face when she saw the police car pull into her drive, as I remembered the hate-filled eyes of Brooke when I walked past her in handcuffs, as I relived my stammering explanation to all of them, Mother, Brooke, little Lacy, trying to explain why I couldn't keep away from the heroin, why it meant more to me than living another day; just when I couldn't stand it any longer, the picture of Mother crying, of Brooke's disgust, and the mask of fear forming on Lacy's face, a warm breeze blew in from the tier. It brushed across my face, raised the hairs on my arms and left through the window carrying my vexation along with it.

At the same time, a bell sounded. The pure tones

poured through the bars on our window and vibrated in the superheated air until one after another the notes collected, one on top of the other, saturating our cell with a sweet noise that lifted me far away from this place, and now I wonder if somewhere a handful of bell ringers had pulled a quarter peal for Calvery.

When the chimes of the bells stopped, something like a hand, heavy and reassuring, patted me on the shoulder. I reached for it and felt nothing except an odd sense of serenity settling down in my chest. Across the room, Cellie sat on his bunk with his knees folded and the last cup of Calvery's wine between his palms.

Chapter Two

Clam Harbor, Washington

The morning of the execution, Chloe peeked under the window shade to examine the weather. Red sky at morning, sailor take warning. What a bunch of bunk. She'd been operating a small fishing charter for almost a third of her life, and at twenty-five, she'd never once seen a red sky, not here, not in Clam Harbor.

She'd seen more than her share of gray—slate gray clouds on a bad day, pearl-gray mist on a good one. The rest of the days fell somewhere in between, just like this one.

Jazz, her Airedale, stuck the tip of his muzzle against her belly. Chloe jerked away.

"I know, I know," she said, scratching Jazz's neck. "Let me just rest one more minute." She let her head sink into the pillow. Jazz stuck a paw on the bed and whimpered. "I'm all right," Chloe said. "Just a little sick to my stomach."

Jazz licked on her free hand and had moved to her forearm when she finally lifted her head. With just that tiny bit of effort, she felt the effects of last night's wine. Coffee, that was what she needed.

On auto-pilot, Chloe stumbled into the kitchen, failing to reach the coffee pot before catching sight of her father, rather, the unflattering view of his mug shot. He was staring at her from the front page of last night's Clam Harbor Gazette—Clam Harbor Resident Slated for Execution. The newspaper had started last night's binge. When she had seen her father's photo, she opened a bottle of Pinot Noir. Normally, she wasn't a drinker, nor was she the type to chase after men. She wasn't much of anything really—a cash-strapped boat captain with no one in her life but a mother in the nursing home, a dog and a soon-to-be dead father who she never really knew. But last night, it had seemed appropriate to toast his life with his favorite wine. It was the only vice she could manage.

This morning, the sight of the picture prompted a different reaction. With one jerk of her right hand, Chloe ripped her father's picture from the paper, and along with it, the entire bottom half of the Clam Harbor Gazette. She squeezed the newsprint into a tight ball, wound-up for a pitch and slung it against the window. Nothing happened. She had wished for a crash, the accompanying shatter of glass, her window destroyed, some lasting destruction to signal the end of father's life, but she was exhausted, wine-fogged, and in shocked disbelief that she cared about this man who had caused her such shame and pain.

To the average Clam Harbor resident—aka Clam Harborite—who had watched her load up her charter each day, she was respectable, well within the wide range of normal typical to Clam Harbor. For the most part, this distinction held up to scrutiny despite the fact that she was the only female charter boat captain in town and a single woman whose only companions were a dog and the town drunk. And despite the fact that she'd broken it off with Scooter McCoy, the most eligible bachelor in Clam Harbor.

So on the outside, Chloe was a typical girl. But inside, after she had discovered her father was a murderer, she walked the wharf everyday wondering who knew the truth about her, who knew her name had been changed twenty years ago, who knew she was Chloe Thomas not Chloe Gallagher, and who knew her father was on death row.

Today she felt certain they all knew. Inside she was light-headed as she passed by the whale-watching kiosk, nauseous when she reached the coffee stand and completely weak-kneed by the time she stepped on the dock.

This is the forest primeval. The murmuring pines and the hemlocks… She repeated Longfellow's verse to calm herself as she struggled with her rolling ice chest filled with today's lunch.

"Can I give you a hand?" The baritone voice of Scooter sounded in her ear.

"I've got this," she said. "Perfectly balanced as is. Don't need any help."

"You all right?"

"Like I said, everything's fine." She repositioned the ice chest, then flashed an exaggerated smile at Scooter.

"Don't."

"What?"

"You know what."

Scooter was the one person who knew her every thought. The day she found out her father was not dead after all, she told Scooter—Scooter, her perfect boyfriend from a perfect family, her happy-go-lucky Scooter whose worst tragedy in life was missing a free throw in the state quarter finals. They won the game anyway.

On her deathbed, Chloe's grandmother finally told Chloe the truth just three years ago. Minutes later Chloe called Scooter. While Chloe and Scooter hiked up the hill behind her house, she told him everything—her father was on death row for murder, her mother had disowned him twenty years ago, Chloe's last name was not really Gallagher. Her mother had picked Gallagher out of a book of Irish names. She hadn't wanted Chloe to grow up with the shame of knowing her father was a murderer.

Meaning her father had been involved with the wrong sort. What else could it mean?

Chloe even told Scooter that she wished her father were dead. He had no right to be alive after all these years. The minute she said it, Scooter said, “You don’t mean that,” and Chloe wanted to take it back, but it was too late.

Her horrible thought had always been out there between them. Now, today, her horrible thought was a reality.

“Thanks. I’ll be fine,” Chloe said. She looked down the dock hoping to see a friendly face. “Well, I’ve got to get to the boat. Got these bankers from Seattle coming in today. You know how that is.”

Scooter put his arms around her, and she was reminded of the physical connection they had once shared. He put a finger under her chin and lifted her face to see his. He is so going to see right through me, she thought.

“I love you,” he said. “No matter what.”

She turned away, felt the heat rise to her face, and the roiling in her stomach turn into high tide. A normal girl would have stayed in their relationship. She had wanted to love Scooter, and maybe she had. But something told her he couldn’t handle her. What would happen when her father was finally executed and the reality of her life finally set in on him?

Chloe knew that after awhile Scooter would wonder if Chloe would follow in her father’s footsteps. Gradually the knives and guns would disappear from the house. Scooter would tense anytime she raised her voice. In the back of Scooter’s mind, she was sure of it, he would wonder if this tiff, this fight, this argument, was the one that turned her into her father—the one that turned her into a murderer.

Pulling out of Scooter’s arms, Chloe straightened her back. “Good to see you,” she said. “Gotta run.” Chloe tugged at her ice chest and hustled away.

Chloe docked her boat, Perpetuity, midway down Pier 6. On the stern, her father had mounted a wooden carving of a Celtic knot. Below it hung a brass bell, at least a foot in diameter, with a shine so bright she could use it as a rear view mirror. Chloe rang it every time someone pulled in a fish. She kept the bell polished with

Barkeeper's Friend, and when clients brought their kids with them on the boat, she let them ring it just for fun, knowing they'd get their fingerprints all over it, and later she'd buff it again.

Chloe climbed below to check the drinks in the refrigerator. The bankers would bring their own liquor. She stocked water, coffee, and tea. For Butch, her father's partner in the fishing business, she kept a stash of Mountain Dew and rum. If she paced him just right, he lasted a good twelve hours.

"How about a little drink on account of—," Butch said, stopping short when he saw the look in her eyes.

Chloe wouldn't break the rules no matter what, and he knew it. They had a system. The first drink after they cleared the harbor. She considered Butch as the father she never had, until she turned eighteen. Then, as if they had always planned it, he turned the boat over to her. He stayed on to help; he started drinking more.

She heard the tromping of heavy feet and the squeak of the dock against Perpetuity's bumpers before she caught sight of the bankers, Brian and Phil. They drove in from Seattle twice a month during peak season—July through October.

Phil, clearly more brain than brawn, strained to lift their ice chest. He dropped the chest on the bench. She heard a crack and cringed, forced a smile and said, "Really?"

"Sorry," Phil said.

Chloe shrugged it off and started Perpetuity's motor, all the while wondering how much longer the boat would hold up. Perpetuity needed a good going-over. Butch had promised to redo the rotten wood. But that would never happen. Chloe barely made the boat payments as is, forget about buying teak. It was ten o'clock Texas time. Her father had eight hours left.

When Perpetuity reached the Japan Current, Butch idled and set anchor. They had fished this spot before with good luck. Brian tossed in his bait—a sockeye head. It plopped in the ocean and splashed up a crown of water.

He reeled the line until it was taut, just as she had instructed him a couple years ago.
Brian called up. "You having a good year so far?"

It was nice to be around someone who didn't know about her father.

"It's been all right."

"You ought to fix up the boat, maybe sell beer and wine. You could make a lot more money." He pulled on his rod and then relaxed it.

"I'm pretty much busy during the tourist months. That's all you can hope for."
He thought a moment. "There's got to be a way to make some more money off this business."

Phil suggested offshore gambling. Brian dismissed the idea, since a big Indian casino was nearby.

"I'll loan you the money to fix this tub up," Brian said, gently reeling his line.

"At what interest?" She asked, thinking of her current debt and the number of times Brian had offered his help. "We'll be all right."
She looked at her watch: high noon. Four more hours.

Brian's line bobbed, a couple quick dips, and then stopped. He started to pull. "Hold on." Chloe motioned for him to wait. A minute or so later, the line bobbed again. Chloe shouted, "Pull!"

The pole bent into a horseshoe. She had hoped for a big catch today; some part of her was convinced she deserved a big fish on today of all days. A halibut would be nice, but she would settle for a good-sized salmon. All eyes watched the line as Brian tugged and reeled.

Butch cried out, "You've snagged her." He rushed to port and pointed, "It's a halibut."

Chloe felt the weight of the day lift from her shoulders. The diamond shape skidded across the surface of the Pacific, its tail swatting at the waves while Brian worked the pole groaning and huffing with his labor. The halibut surfaced again, one jet eye glaring at her.

Thirty minutes passed, then forty, and all the while, Chloe coached Brian and blotted his brow. She felt the thrill as keenly as she imagined he did.

At last, Brian pulled in the best halibut of the season. She guessed the fish weighed a good one hundred and fifty pounds. When the fish was safely aboard, in honor of the catch, Phil hurried over to the bell and rang it with such excitement that Chloe couldn't help but laugh.

It was after two before Chloe went below to set the lunch table. The bankers stayed up top toasting their success with tequila shots and admiring their prize fish.

She had started serving gourmet lunches when her finances hit an all-time low. A little advertisement: Chloe's Charters—Fine Fishing, Fine Food—doubled her cash flow. Unfortunately, it was still barely enough to keep things going.

Chloe placed an appetizer plate of country pâté, gherkins and dark grain bread on the table. In the movies, death row inmates chose their last meal. Would her father eat fish or steak? Did they allow alcohol? She thought not. Chloe uncorked a bottle of Pinot Noir from Oregon's Umpqua Valley and poured a sample. She swirled the glass, then inhaled deeply to catch its nose of mushroom and cherry cola. Her mother had once said the wine was her father's favorite. Once she sipped it, Chloe understood why. The Pinot Noir tasted like a liquid silk spun from forests and orchards.

After Chloe served the bankers their lunch of salmon with dill and caper sauce, a purple fingerling potato salad and a succotash made from locally grown green beans and corn, she excused herself and ascended the stairs to find Butch.

From the wheelhouse, she heard, " 'I've got to walk this lonesome valley….' "

Despite the bright sun, Butch wore his Mariner's windbreaker and sat hunched over the wheel staring intently at the sea, as if navigating through the Strait of Juan de Fuca rather than the open sea where Perpetuity was the only boat in sight. She had interrupted his thoughts.

Poor guy. Somehow, on this weird day, it is worse for

Butch; he is about to lose his best friend. As for me, I am only losing something I've never had.

"You want me to take over?" Chloe settled onto the bench behind Butch.

"No. I've got it," he said. "Any chance the governor will call it off? I've seen that in the movies."

"He's in Texas, remember? Their governor wouldn't stay the Pope."

Over the years, Butch had tried many times to convince her of her father's innocence. More than anything, Butch wanted her to love her father the way he did. But no one understood what it was like to have a father on death row. It was not exactly dinner party conversation material. Even in Clam Harbor.

Chloe stared down at a pool of blood drying in the sun and darkening to a deep brown. "Death isn't such a horrible thing, you know. Limbo is much worse."

Chloe pulled a bottle of Cristalino from the cabinet in the wheelhouse. She had stowed it for celebrations. Somehow, today, it seemed appropriate.

"He would have been proud of that halibut we caught today," Butch said. "When I missed it with my first harpoon, I thought of him, how he'd never miss. He was so good and so lucky at fishing. Unlucky at everything else."

When Butch's chin trembled, she saw it coming. His face contorted as he resisted the inevitable. She fixed her gaze on the Cristalino, afraid to see his face again.

"Butch, it's all right," she said, reaching out to him.

But she did look and it was worse than she had expected. Tears covered his face. "I shoulda done more. He was the best friend a fella could have. It's all my fault."

"It's not your fault."

"You… don't… know." His words were broken into pieces of great gulps and weeping.

"What are you talking about?" Chloe handed him a glass of the sparkling wine. He refused and put his arms around her. She tensed; his drenched face dampened her collar. With each of his loud sobs, she felt her neck tighten. She patted his back.

Chloe wanted to look at her watch. But she didn't dare do anything to upset Butch further. How much longer could this day go on?

"I just can't do this," Butch said, his voice cracking. "It's not right. There must be something we can do."

In the blurry light of the fog, Butch looked like the young man he once was. In fact, with his face shiny and wet, blotched with red and white, and his nose slick with mucous and swollen at his nostrils, he might have been a young child in need of comforting. He sat with both hands cradling the wine, and his face trembling with the emotion. Despite the helplessness in his face, he looked so free—free to get slobbering drunk whenever he felt like it, free to tell silly groaner jokes to fisherman, free to cry when his best friend died.

Chloe pulled Butch's handkerchief form his chest pocket. "Use this."

"You don't have to act tough with me," he said, taking the handkerchief.

"I'm not acting. It's just the way of nature, no different from that halibut up there. One day you're swimming around the ocean eating your fill of fish smaller than you, and the next day, you're dead."

"We ain't like fish."

"We are exactly like fish except we got legs. All those people out there who want to be famous, they want to be somebody. They think they are going to be different, like they're gonna be the ones to beat it.

"Beat what?"

"Death," she said. "They think they're going be the one person who beats it. But no one does."

The afternoon fog surrounded her now. Foghorns of other charters blew into the mist. Chloe pulled her wrist up to her face to see the time—a few minutes until four—six o'clock Texas time.

"Daddy, here's to you, and here's to what could have been." Chloe lifted her glass. "And hey to Davy Jones."

She gulped the champagne and hurled the glass into the very blue mouth of the Pacific. "Rest in peace."

The day had turned gray. The sun, now just a fuzzy blur obscured by the fine veil of fog blowing in from the West, shed barely enough light to see the splintered wood in the wheelhouse, the rusted hinges on the door to the head, the mold on the cushions.

She fumbled her way to the stern and plopped next to the bell, her father's bell. She rang it. Amidst the blasts of foghorns, the bell sounded with a deep clang.

"Where's the fish?" Brian asked from somewhere in the fog. "Why are you ringing the bell?"

She didn't acknowledge him. Butch slid beside her on the bench, touched her bell-ringing hand, "How many?"

"Fifty-five. Once for every year." Chloe placed the rope in Butch's hand. "I've done thirty-five so far."

"I'll do ten." Butch tugged the ringer chewing on the corner of his lip as the tone pealed into the lonely fog. "Sorry ol' buddy. I wish I'd…."

"What?"

"Nothing, it was nothing." The bell buried his voice with a chime. Sorrow and pain had crept into every wrinkle on his face.

He pulled the rope another ten times and handed it to Chloe. She rang the bell again and again until they reached fifty-five times in all. The last of the peal lingered in the air until a gull perched on their mast and started squawking for dinner.

Chapter Three

The next morning, I read Calvery's obituary in the prison newspaper, The Echo:

Calvery Thomas, death row inmate for twenty years, was executed last night. He was fifty-five years old. Thomas was convicted of murdering a Galveston man, Carlo Rossi, and spent most of his years incarcerated in the Ellis Unit. For his last meal, he requested fried shrimp and steak, baked potato, spinach soufflé and apple pie. No family was present at the execution. His final words were, "See you in the thin places."

Just as I finished Calvery's obit, Spud appeared at my cell. I looked at the obit again, and then looked at Spud. "What do you suppose that means?"

"What what means?" Spud held a brightly labeled cardboard box with the regal yellow-and-red Del Monte label on the side.

I pointed to the obit. He read it, shook his head. "Just crazy talk. Maybe you'll go crazy, too. Here's all Calvery's stuff. He wanted you to have it."

"Why me?"

"I suppose he had his reasons." He stood there shifting his weight from one hip to the other.

"I'm just curious," I said. "He ever talk to you about the thin places."

"People on death row say a lot of strange things. The

only way to survive working there is to keep your distance. But Calvery never gave me any trouble, I'll say that. It was like he'd already left." Spud twisted the Masonic ring on his left hand.

"So all that time, he never said nothing?"

"That's what I said. Nothing is more than you ever want to know about a guy like that."

"I thought you said you liked him," I said, wondering why Spud was so dead set against offering any information.

"I said he never gave me any trouble," Spud said, pressing his finger against his hearing aid. "That's the most you can hope for in a place like this."

Spud worked as a rancher on the side and was a bull of a man with a heaping helping of dough around the middle. Under his deceptive layer of brisket and beans were thick muscles primed from years of loading hay bales and throwing fifty-pound feedbags over his shoulder.

Early on at The Unit, I had decided to play nice with the hacks. Spud took a liking to me. He had no patience for attitude. Because I'd dropped mine at the door, we got along all right.

Tiny purple veins covered his nose, more crowded than a map of Texas farm-to-market roads. He had the nose of a serious drinker, the first-thing-you-see-on-his-face schnoz. Perhaps that was another reason why we got on. Addicts attract addicts. Bottles or needles. No difference. He leaned closer to me and blew coffee, peppermint, and tobacco breath across my face. I smelled alcohol too, but he had done a good job of covering it up.

"Let's see what's in it, shall we?" I started digging into the box. "Look here a calendar of Oregon." Spud had already disappeared down the hall.

Most people have more to show for a life than a cardboard box with a picture of canned pineapple on its sides. But Calvery's life fit into a box that had once held canned fruit. On top, I found a calendar of the Oregon Coast opened to August. He had circled the day of his execution, August 27th, and written "St. Monica's Day" in the square. Flipping through the rest of the calendar, I found the only other month with writing on it. Underneath the March photo, an aerial view of a place called Devil's Churn, Calvery had written "Cape Perpetua."

Seeing that picture—a massive fist of a mountain covered in fir trees jutting out into the very blue Pacific—a memory of Calvery flashed through my mind. I heard Calvery's talk-show-host voice telling me about the soul of a prisoner, "The soul of an old man either gets trapped in his body, buried deep inside his lonely, silent, dark, toothless world, or he releases his soul before he dies — long before he loses his ability to set himself free—because the old man was smart enough to know about the thin places. In prison, if you know how to get there, you can travel to those thin places."

Mother always had me visiting nursing homes with her, so I understood what Calvery was saying to me. You don't have to be behind bars to be in prison.

As I stared at the picture of Cape Perpetua, imagining being there, I heard Calvery's voice again, "You'll get there one day."

Beneath the calendar, I pulled out a Bible and a couple books. Inside one of them, I found Calvery's treasure map and grinned. He had written a poem with all the usual Irish nonsense—faeries' rings, a treasure, a pot of gold and those words again—thin place. I stowed it in the Bible and searched the rest of the box.

While stowing the poem in the Bible, I found the picture of a little girl about the age of Lacy. I compared it to the photo of Lacy I had next to my bunk. The girls looked about the same age except the girl in Calvery's photo looked solid, like a Russian gymnast. The back of Calvery's photo was blank. Of course, it had to be Chloe. She had reddish-brown hair, dark like Calvery's but with a red cast instead of black. It curled down past her shoulders and rested on the pockets of her starched white blouse. Her smile revealed two missing teeth and a big dimple on her chin, just like Calvery.

As I held the picture, thinking about the sweet little girl without a father all these years, I wanted to see Lacy so bad it was hard to keep a stiff upper lip. I felt some survivor guilt as well. I still had a shot at making it up to Lacy. For Calvery, it was too late.

A scratching inside the box startled me. I peeked inside. Beneath a layer of various shapes and sizes of origami boats, I found a layer of alfalfa and Augustine. The grass shifted. I jumped back. Gawd, I hoped it wasn't a cockroach. I reached for a pen and poked at the dense pile of grass. The tip of the pen tapped on a hollow-sounding rock. I don't know what I thought would jump out at me from a shoebox, but prison does that to people. The scratching stopped. Summoning all my courage, I reached in and picked it up, the rock, quickly realizing my inheritance had descended from prehistoric roots, and the "rock" was the domed shell of a three-toed Texas box turtle.

"Well, I'll be damned. You the treasure, buddy?" I said, pulling off the piece of paper taped to his shell. "Sport, is that your name?"

Also, in black ink someone had written the initials "DCC" on Sport's shell. It looked to be freshly marked, and I vaguely remembered that turtles lose their scutes every year. This mark couldn't have been something the turtle had on him when Calvery found him.

After a moment, Sport's head emerged. I lifted him and placed him on the palm of my hand. He barely fit.

"You miss Calvery?" I said, talking to the turtle in baby jive and grateful Cellie was not around to hear it. "Don't you worry. I'll take care of you. I'll take real good care of you."

Sport—the name belonged to a fluffy rabbit or even a rat, not a reptile, and not a cold-blooded, hard-shelled turtle with leathery skin. From my biology days at Baylor, I knew the limits of the reptilian brain, but Sport sure seemed to be looking for something. Maybe he wanted dinner. I liked to think he missed Calvery.

I gave Sport a pat on the head, promised him a nice head of lettuce and placed him back in his shoebox terrarium. I felt good. Things at The Unit had just improved. After all, I had Sport.

The next morning, after running a couple laps around the yard, I returned to my cell to find Jules, the captain of the prison biker gang, inspecting my room. I knew they called him Jules because of his glass eye. His face was scarred where the reaction exploded in his meth lab. He must of got a pretty good look at it, cause it tore his right eye clean out. He had one hand in Calvery's box, the other holding a cigarette. When he saw me, he turned calmly, pulled his hand from Calvery's belongings, brushed off my desk, and blew a throat-burning puff of smoke into my face.

"You lose something?"

"No, no." He didn't really make eye contact as he pulled on his cigarette. "Just paying a social call."

It didn't seem a bit like idle curiosity. But at the time, I didn't figure I had anything to hide.

In the joint, the cell was a man's castle. Everyone had their stuff organized just so. I liked to go in to other guy's cells and mess things up just for the hell of it. I got away with it because I was known as bit of a prankster. It also didn't hurt that word had gotten out about how I was Golden Glove and all that. The bit about Golden Glove was a slight exaggeration, well, not slight, let me just confess, it was a bold-faced lie. However, I did know how to box. My father had taught me. In prison, some things were necessary to survive. My little white lie was one of those things.

Back to Jules, given his rank, he could rifle around wherever he wanted to. But I didn't like him in my house, not one bit. He sat on my bunk, still silent, and unfolded a towel onto my blanket. In general, the folks in prison are on the low end of the looks department, but Jules won the ugly prize. Judging from his impressive collection of scars, I doubted he was born that way.

"Sit down, boy, I brought you and your turtle some dinner." He pointed to two sandwiches and tossed a head of lettuce on the bed.

The crisp golden edge of a fried egg poked out from between the slices of Texas toast. In prison, chicken, cheese and eggs were rare as punk rockers in a honky tonk. Plus he had two Cokes with a long bag of ice. I hadn't seen ice in months.

"You got some cups?" he asked.

About the time I got the Cokes poured, his gofer ran in with a big bowl of Frito pie.

"Do you eat like this every day?" Mother always taught me to compliment the chef's cooking.

"I've been here a long time," he said, smiling as if a CEO bragging on his track record. "I have connections. You need anything, let me know."

"Got any of that parole I keep hearing about?"

"One of the few things I can't do." He laughed and in doing so revealing a full set of pearly whites. This impressed me. "You seem like a good guy," he said. "I don't want you to be out here all on your own."

When I took a bite of the sandwich, the yolk squirted onto my lip. Jules tossed me a paper towel. I nodded in appreciation while I chewed my sandwich.

"Sure is good. I haven't eaten like this in three years."

"Like I said, whatever I can do."

He watched me as I ate, seemed pleased I was enjoying myself, so I added extra noises—um, this sure is good, just like mama used to make, a bit of lip smacking—just to be sure I appeared grateful and remembering another one of mother's rules: Keep your friends close and your enemies closer.

"Funny you would come by today," I said.

"I apologize I haven't been by sooner."

He talked with the overly polite voice of a con trying to smooth over a delicate situation. I tried not to let on I was suspicious, gave him a tight smile full of egg yolk and mayonnaise. It wasn't hard to pull off. After all, I owed him for one hell of a fried egg sandwich.

When Jules left abruptly, his food untouched, I tore off a couple lettuce leaves for Sport. He moseyed toward them with his little turtle eyes gleaming. From the little I knew about turtles, I figured a pile of greens might last the little fella at least a couple days. I made a mental note to check the prison library for books about turtles.

I sucked my teeth and watched Sport tug at his lettuce. The brief taste of good food brought with it the same sated feeling of contentment I always felt after one of mother's home cooked meals. For a moment, I was sitting in the deep violet shade of our backyard, watching kids hiding under the porch, skidding into tag the trunk of our oak, or clapping their hands around blinking fireflies.

I thought of Brooke in a pile of rumpled sheets, her blonde hair fanned over the pillow, the smell of face cream and her sweet shampoo, the hot humid air of summer slick and shiny on her tanned skin. Then, I started to counting up the days since Brooke's last visit. How long had it been, six weeks, eight weeks?

Sport examined me, his tiny head tilted as if wondering why the lettuce didn't thrill me as much as it did him. Jules' visit puzzled me. After three years, why now? The last thing I needed was the biker gang nosing around, though I sure enjoyed that sandwich. In the unit, inmates shouted back and forth, metal doors slammed, keys jingled, and I felt like a toothless carny had just strapped me in for the last ride of the night.

Chapter Four

On the way home from the charter, Chloe stopped to see her mother. Because of Multiple Sclerosis, she had lived in Golden Years Nursing Home for about five years now. Just after Chloe's grandmother died, Chloe was forced to make the hardest decision of her young life. She knew she couldn't care for her mother by herself. But every time Chloe left Golden Years, she vowed to move her mother out of there someday. She wouldn't let both her parents die in prison.

Chloe chose the long route home. All she wanted was to clear her head. The champagne had been a mistake. Now, she was dull and tired, so tired she couldn't think. The scenic by-way looped around Clam Harbor through a tunnel of firs and an undergrowth of rhododendrons until the road crested the hill overlooking the bay. Most boats had cleared the harbor leaving the still ocean the color of faded jeans. A lone sail gleamed in a shaft of sunlight and tilted at a thrilling angle as it sliced through the water.

Chloe's pickup stuttered at the top of the hill before she downshifted; she took in the view of Clam Harbor. It rose from the waters on densely covered hills with its ocean view homes wrapped snuggly in shore pines and fir as if their boughs were winter coats. She found herself wishing—selfishly, unrealistically—that this were a town unknown to her and a place where she could get a fresh start.

Chloe lived on the south side with the forest view. Her mother and father had purchased the house for a good price in the seventies and lived in it for fifteen years before her father went away. When she pulled into her driveway, Jazz jumped out of the truck and up onto the front porch. Flower bouquets and wreaths covered the steps. Each time he sniffed a bouquet, he looked to see if Chloe was watching him.

"It's okay, boy." Chloe unlocked the door and entered the house.

She proceeded straight to the answering machine, though she wanted nothing more than to fall into bed with *Frenchman's Creek*. She'd been on a Daphne duMaurier binge for a couple months.

Chloe pressed the button on the answering machine. Twelve new messages: The Oregonian calling. We wondered if you wanted to make a statement. Our number is… Sarah, here. Wanted to let you know we'll be down at Brewers. Come by. Call me back. I know how you are…. Ms. Gallagher, this is Captain Olson from the Texas Department of Criminal Justice. Please call me whenever you get this message, no matter how late. The number is….

Chloe stopped the machine, replayed the message. She yanked open the junk drawer and pulled it all the way out of the counter. Tossing batteries, rubber bands, packages of gum and books of matches aside, she looked for a pencil. Locating a pen, without a cap, she tore off the corner of a paper bag and scribbled on it, trying to get the ink to flow. "Shit." She found a pencil with a broken lead. "Dammit." Finally, Chloe's search produced a broken crayon, no telling how long it had been there.

She picked up the phone and dialed. Spud Olson answered with his name. He had a low, gravelly voice with a heavy drawl.

"This is Chloe Gallagher. I didn't expect you to answer. It's so late. You called me today; I guess it was about my dad."

"Ms. Gallagher, yes, I'm glad you called," Mr. Olson said. "You doing all right?"

She thought it over. How was she doing? As well as can be expected. I'm holding up. All right for the shape I'm in. "It's been a long day," she finally said.

"I don't usually call the families. But I've guarded death row for twenty years. I got to know your father pretty well." Mr. Olson coughed, and then spoke, "They wanted to know if you want him cremated, if you can afford it. Or would you like us to put him in the cemetery here?"

The question hung in the air. It was not the kind of thing someone should ask a girl who never knew her father.

"I just found your address in his paperwork."

"We weren't in touch because…," she said, her voice drifted off as she tried to think of an explanation.

"I understand. A lot of families aren't involved," he said. He had a thick twang in his voice that made him sound kind and understanding. "I just wanted to be sure about the arrangements."

A second of silence. This would be the perfect time for a cigarette, but nobody smoked anymore. And what had they—the people in charge of health initiatives—left her to replace it, dark chocolate covered almonds, flaxseed tortilla chips, Kashi bars?

Every bit of light had finally drained from the sky. She was standing in the dark kitchen, talking on the phone to someone who had known her father, maybe even killed him. She flipped on the kitchen light then stared at the receiver. "Did you do it? I just wondered who did it."

Mr. Olson answered. Had he been talking all this time? "No, ma'am. It wasn't me."

"Who was it?"

"That's confidential." Long pause. "For security reasons."

Oddly, she felt sorry for whoever it was. What kind of a person executed people? She imagined him (or her) coming home for dinner. How was your day, dear? Everything go okay with—the spouse glances at the children—with work today? They exchange meaningful glances. The wife (she had now decided the executioner had to be male) kisses him on the forehead, tasting the execution room sweat.

"I didn't have anything to do with him," she said finally. "I only just learned about this a few years ago."

"No worries," Captain Olson said. "All the same, if you want his remains—"

"I do." She blurted out the words half surprised at her reaction.

Of course she wanted his remains, it was her father, she had his boat, he deserved this one thing—to rest outside with the fir guarding him at night, the mist falling on him faithfully each dusk and dawn, close to the sea but not chilled by it. "What about his belongings?"

"He asked me to give his belongings to an inmate."

"Seriously?"

"Your father took a liking to this porter," Mr. Olson said. "He mopped the floors of death row." His voice was low, calm, and sweet. "It was just a few books is all, fit into a cardboard box."

Her father had no reason to believe Chloe would want them. "I guess he didn't know anything about me."

"He went peaceful," he said, his words faded into a period of silence. "He'd want you to know that. No problems."

"Geez," she said. A sick feeling hit her stomach. "This sucks."

"Yes, ma'am," he said. "It's enough to make you lose your religion."

She smiled into the receiver. Chloe's religion was the sea, the tide, the fishing. Nothing ever seemed to interfere with that.

"The thing is, they weren't my troubles, I mean, not until a few years ago. I thought he was already dead, now I've got to go through it again." She picked up a wineglass left over from last night's binge and tightened her fingers around it until they squeaked. "I suppose if I didn't take his remains, they'd bury him in Joe Byrd without a marker." To Mr. Olson, her voice might have sounded business-like, but anyone who knew her would have recognized the sharpness in her speech, the deliberate and exact pronunciation of each syllable.

"That's right, we can take care of this for you," he said. "You don't need to do anything at all."

She rubbed her right thumb across her glass pressing into it, daring it to bend to her strength. "Easy for you to say."

"I ain't aiming to cause you any more grief."

"I want the body," she said into the phone. "I mean the ashes."

"There's a service here that will do it for a thousand dollars. Then, I'll assure they mail the ashes to you. You got a thousand dollars?"

She pictured her wallet and counted the bills inside—three twenties, a ten, two fives, five ones. There was the money for the charter today; it should be in the bank by now. Another five hundred dollars would wipe her out. "Of course I have a thousand dollars."

Mr. Olson gave her the name of the service. She trusted him, for some reason. Maybe it was the name. Or maybe it was because he had said her father was a good man.

Chapter Five

The mailroom opened at ten and I had a pass, a notification of a package or magazine. Lois, a sixty-something woman with Texas-sized hooters, had managed the mailroom for forty years. Mom was always sending me books, so I came by often.

Lois acknowledged me with a raised chin. With her head inclined to the side and the red ball of her earring dangling above her shoulder, I pictured the girlhood she once enjoyed. In her case, I imagined the years had piled on quickly after thousands of packs of Salem's, working in a prison, living in Huntsville and two failed marriages. For Calvery, it was just prison. For me, my mother would say, there was still time.

Lois yelled from her window. "Tully, show me that mail notice you got."

I unfolded the notice and slid it across the counter. In a few minutes, Lois came back with a certified letter. She handed it to me, patted my fingers as she pushed it through the slot. She also gave me a letter from my mother. The return address of the certified letter said Joseph P. Barnes, Atty. Worse yet, the letter was from a Dallas attorney I had never heard of.

Dear Mr. Tully:

I represent Brooke Tully in her action against you for divorce. Enclosed please find the Original Petition for Divorce, in which Mrs. Tully will be seeking custody of the minor child, Lacy Tully, due to your incarceration. If you are willing to waive citation in this matter, please sign and notarize the enclosed Waiver of Service.

If you have an attorney who will represent you in this matter, please have him or her contact me as soon as possible. In addition, this letter is to advise you to have no communication with Mrs. Tully about this matter. All correspondence or communications must be directed to me.

Thank you for your attention to this matter.

Very truly yours,

Joseph P. Barnes, Esq.

Divorce? Could she divorce me now? If she's thinking she's going to take Lacy from me, she needs to think again.

Mr. Barnes letterhead was printed on a fine paper with a watermark shaped like the state of Texas. "Pretentious bastard." I wadded up the letter and, with a perfect free-throw arc, planted it in a wastebasket in the hall.

"Bad news?" The big red bead at the end of Lois's earring swung out from her neck as she tilted her head.

I retrieved the letter, smoothed out the paper until the state of Texas was visible again, and slid it across the counter. "Good riddance to bad rubbish."

"What is it?" she said.

"The bitch wants a divorce."

She shook her head. "I must have seen thousands of those letters over the years." She tried to hand the letter back to me.

I waved her away. "Who needs her anyway?"

"You don't mean that."

"No, I don't." I muttered the words, but she knew what I had said.

"You better keep this." Lois stuffed the paper in my shirt pocket, neatly positioning it as if it were a handkerchief.

"Lois." I opened my arms as if she would actually run out from behind the mail window and walk out of the prison with me. "I'm all yours. You're looking at a free man."

That bitch. But I knew I had it coming. I knew it was over that day I was in segregation when Brooke came to visit. The hacks escorted her back to the room where all the prisoners in seg got their visits. She told me she had to walk past all the other families—the ones who were in the big visiting room—and into the back room. Filth covered the vinyl floor, and piles of dirt and dead ants formed tiny permanent pyramids in the corners. I remember the look on her face when she saw me shuffle in with my feet and hands shackled.

I offered her my most angelic smile.

She shook her head. "You'll never learn will you?" She said, speaking into the telephone, the glass separating us.

I put my hand to the glass. Brooke just looked at it.

"It wasn't my fault," I said. "I had to do it."

"I've heard that before," she said, her blue eyes cold and narrow, her mouth pinched.

I wish she had cried, anything would have been better than her glaring at me with that stony look of hate.

"He was a preacher and a child molester," I said, pleading with my eyes. "If I hadn't done it, someone else would have."

"It's not up to you. Did you ever stop to think what would happen?"

"Society counts on us to take care of things like this."

"Are you shitting me? Did you actually say that?"

"What if it was Lacy who had been molested? Wouldn't you want the sonuvabitch to pay in prison?"

"Oh my God, do you hear yourself? Your job was to take care of us," she said with emphasis on was.

"I'm sorry."

"Look what you've done to your child," she said. "Another year without you?"

I nodded. "I don't guess I'll make parole. I'll have to do it all," I said. Then, in the softest most earnest voice I could muster, I added, "I'll make it up to you. Things will be different."

She stayed the whole hour, even though we didn't talk much more after that. It was mostly chitchat about mother and Lacy. I knew she had checked out. But I didn't want to believe it.

"Tully," Lois said. Her voice reminded me that I was in the mailroom. "Don't take it too hard."

"Naw, I won't," I said. "Who needs her?"

I headed out to the yard to blow off some steam. Heat waves already blurred the super- heated track. One of my buddies was waiting for his set on the bench press.

"I've had a bad day. Pick one out." I nodded to the yard. In prison, there were two kinds of fight—boxing just for fun, to get the anger out, and brawling for revenge. This fight was the former type.

My buddy pointed to the biggest guy out there, an African-American named Big Woo who was shooting hoops on the basketball court.

"Yo, Woo, look out, let's get some recreation." I sauntered onto the court and snagged the ball from Woo.

"What, you wanna play?"

"No. I want to check out your boxing game, catch the square." I threw the ball off the court.

Woo shrugged. "Crazy ass white boy, come on." He had a wide gold-grilled grin on his face.

We fired off at each other but in a fraction of a second, I took a hard right and fell. He let me get to my feet, as per the code, and I faked a left jab to make him juke to his left. My punch landed on his jaw. He just shook it off.

He had at least fifty pounds on me. I didn't care. I

was having a party. Once I started hitting, I felt like a saved man. I liked the feel of the blood dripping over my fingers, the sound of my fist slapping his skin. With each slug, I got higher. It was like sex, the frenzy, the passion, the mess. The salty taste of blood filled my mouth. My cheek trembled, and I could feel my eye swelling. Woo just looked at me. My punches hadn't made a dent on him.

That's when I caught him with a heavy right hook that rocked him just long enough to land a straight left. My next right skinned off the top of his head causing me to lose my balance and fall in to him in an odd embrace. We parted and looked at each other uncertainly.

"You good, white boy?"

Breathless, I said. "Yea, I'm good.

I was good. I was relieved. I needed that.

We knocked fists, and it was over. It took only seconds, but most fights do. He got the best of me, but I went hard. The great thing about fighting as the underdog was that you always look good. If you lose, well, you were expected to; as long as you show heart, you look good. And if you win, you shine. Inmates always covered the rec yard so we had some spectators. No one said anything.

When it was over, I said, "Thanks for the fight man."

"Any time."

The guys just went back to their business. I took to the track for a jog. My woman was gone, but, on some level, I had expected it.

The fight happened so fast the hacks didn't even notice. Then, I ran with all I had and kept running for twelve laps until the sweat ran from me like a hot shower, and my head was dizzy with heat.

When I made it to my bunk, I fell out and slept a couple of hours. Around six o'clock I finally got around to opening mother's letter. It was bound to be full of good news from Bayport—who was marrying, who was divorcing, and who was having babies.

Mother wrote: "Dear Finn, I hope you don't take this

news too hard. My cancer has returned. I'm sorry I won't be up to see you this month. The doctor says I can take the chemo and radiation and maybe get another year. But why would I do that? Our lives are just a speck in time. So my life is a speck shorter."

I threw my pillow at Cellie's Saint of the Month, St. Perpetua, grabbed a shoe from under the bed and slammed it against the tiny window. "Christ Almighty." I said it repeatedly. "A lot of good these saints are doing. And who's ever heard of St. Perpetua?"

Sport stretched his neck out of his shell as if to answer me. I took him over to the window, leaned my chest against the sill to protect him from falling. The sharpened edges of a new moon pierced the southern sky. Maybe another year. I looked at the date on the letter—August tenth. Today was September first. Mother was already twenty-one days into her last year.

I felt weak in the knees and realized I'd never understood the true meaning of the expression. It meant the one thing holding you up had just played out.

"Well, that's another shitty day," I said to Sport, who poked along on the window ledge. "Maybe just the world's worst day ever."

Chapter Six

On Monday, after a busy weekend of charters, Chloe was grateful for a day off. She settled onto the couch and flipped through the channels until she found Live with Emeril. He was blackening tilapia in one skillet, and bamming meat and rice with cayenne in the other. Next to her, on the old crab pot she used as an end table, Chloe reached for her Joy of Cooking cookbook and opened it to the seafood section. In the background, Emeril's band played IKO, IKO. Chloe tapped her toes, and when Jazz came over to give them a suspicious sniff, she scratched him with a coordinated maneuver of her right foot that ended up causing a cramp in her instep.

When the phone rang, she hopped over to it wondering why the phone was always somewhere she wasn't. It was Brian, and he wanted to see her for lunch. He had a business proposition, he said. A man she needed to meet. At first Chloe hesitated, reluctant to interrupt her lazy day. But she couldn't lose Perpetuity, and she couldn't watch her mother waste away in Golden Years. Maybe this business deal was just what she needed.

Chloe pulled a pair of black leggings, a gathered skirt and an embroidered peasant blouse from her closet. It was not particularly professional, she decided, though the outfit conveyed a certain sense of style and confidence. She wished Sarah were here to weigh in, but there wasn't time.

She drove around the mountain to Clam Harbor, listening to White Stripes—Icky Thump. They had agreed to eat lunch at Mo's, a local favorite and tourist haven famous for fresh fish and homemade chowder. As usual, diners filled the tables. Chloe found a booth in the back, just beneath the sign: Fishermen Know All the Right Lines.

Not long after she had settled, Scooter stepped in. Chloe buried her head under a menu and started sliding out of the booth. Scooter strode over to the bar. His uniform was Clorox-white, and the navy stripe on his trousers reminded her of his orderly bedroom. Even as a teenager, Scooter was all spit and polish.

With his back turned from Chloe, she headed toward the front door. This town was entirely too small. When she pulled the door open to leave, the bell over the doorjamb sounded. She felt all eyes turn towards her but didn't look back. Quickly, she headed to the street corner.

She pulled out her cell phone and dialed Brian. "Where are you?" she said when he answered.

"We had to park way the hell out, up on the hill."

"I'll be a little late," she said. When she looked up, she saw Scooter. He looked straight out of An Officer and a Gentleman. If she were smart, she would let him sweep her off her feet and carry her away, just like Richard Gere did with Debra Winger. "Gotta, go." Chloe hung up on Brian.

"Hey you," Scooter said, giving her a hug. The familiar smell of his pine-scented cologne reminded her of all those dates making out in the back of his Chevy Malibu. "Why haven't you returned my calls?"

"It's been…I've had so much to do."

"Anything I can do?"

"I'm all right, really. Gosh, you're sweet. But it's fine really. Really it's fine."

"You said that," he said, reaching for her hand. "I'm not trying to pressure you. I know it's over between us."

She gulped. Hearing him say he knew it was over

made her just a little uncomfortable. She looked down at their joined hands.

Scooter squeezed her hand and released it, saying, "I just want you to know, I'm sorry. I wish they'd stopped it. Dad said your father was a good man."

"Thanks," she said, looking away. "I need to go. I'm meeting someone."

Scooter nodded. Behind him, Chloe saw Brian decked out in golfing clothes—a shirt bright as a spring daffodil and knee-length plaid shorts—an outfit so garish even the tourists turned to stare as he strolled by. Though Scooter would be too polite to comment, she could just imagine what he would think if he saw her with Brian. They always used to make fun of the out-of-towners.

"A beer maybe?" Scooter asked as she hurried away.

"Sure. Next week. I'll call you," she said, knowing she wouldn't.

She rushed back into Mo's and joined Brian at a booth in the back. With his bright clothes and pale skin, she couldn't help thinking he looked badly in need of a spray tan.

Chloe gave Brian a friendly hug. "Nice shirt."

"A little bright?"

Chloe reached into her straw bag and pulled out a pair of sunglasses, "No, not at all."

"Give me a break," he said, pulling the glasses from her. "It's better than all the black shit these kids around here wear."

"You got me there," she said.

Actually, she agreed with him. With the town of Forks, home of the Twilight series books, so close by, this vampire thing had gotten totally out of hand.

After Chloe and Brian ordered waters, Brian told her that he had found the perfect solution to her problems. This man was an entrepreneur with plenty of money. He told Brian, he needed a boat and a Captain. Immediately, Brian had thought of her.

"That's him," Brian said, nodding toward the door. He rose and waved to the man. The man wore heavily starched khakis and cowboy boots and a light gray Stetson. As he approached, his pants rustled.

"This is my friend Duke Summers. He's from Texas."

Duke wore a pinkie ring, and when he smirked with a sideways smile, she caught the glint of a gold filling in one of his molars. Though he stood about five six at most, his posture and attitude commanded attention. He slicked his long hair back with gel, leaving a clear view of his face, which was hard with eyes that looked like they held a secret.

Chloe looked at his hat, his boots. "I might have guessed Calgary except for your belt buckle."

"You like that?" He grabbed hold of his buckle—a brass Texas flag the size of postcard anchored onto his leather belt. "It's not too much?"

"Naw, we were just talking about that. It's a nice change from vampire teeth."

"That's right. I just passed through Forks. The darkest place in the nation."

"The place where the sun don't shine," Chloe said.

"Funny, I thought that was someplace else entirely."

Chloe laughed. "What brings you so far from home?"

"Opportunity," Duke said.

"No opportunity in Texas?"

"Not the kind I'm looking for."

"You haven't lived until you've had Mo's clam chowder." Brian patted Duke on the shoulder.

They settled into the booth, Duke on one side, Brian and Chloe on the other. Duke removed his hat. What was left of his hair circled the lower half of his skull leaving the top of his head smooth and shiny. With his hat on, he looked ten years younger. The hat's absence, endeared him to her. She had never cared for vain men. He gave off an odor of cloves; this smell put her immediately at ease. It was hard to think ill of someone who smelled like pumpkin pie.

Chloe pulled the thread from a saltine wrapper and took a bite of the cracker. "How was your halibut?"

"We had a big fish fry, lots of beer and girls." He shot a grin over to his friend.

"I never met a girl who captained a boat. Tough business, I imagine." Duke gulped his Anchor Steam.

"I get by." She wasn't about to play the distressed damsel around these two guys.

The waitress brought the chowders. Duke looked her up and down and said, "Thanks, darling. Look's good enough to eat."

"Seriously?" Chloe cringed. She exchanged glances with Brian.

"I don't want you to get the wrong idea, darling," Duke said, his expression now apologetic. "In Texas, that's just the way we talk."

"In Washington, if the men talk like that, they get slapped." She made her point with a good-natured tone. The last thing she wanted to do was alienate someone who might be able to help her. Maybe he was right, maybe they did talk differently in Texas.

"Well then, thanks for not slapping me."

"I'm on my best behavior."

"I'd hate to see you misbehaving," Duke said. The muscle of Duke's upper arm twitched when he reached for the salt and pepper. He had the build of a small man who worked out to make up for his height. "I hear you have a nice charter. You ever have any accidents?"

"Why would I?"

Someone had played "All My Exes is from Texas" on the jukebox, and Duke started singing along with a big smile across his face. It occurred to her that Brian knew a lot of men like Duke—moneyed, jovial, always telling stories and jokes.

"Now sweetheart, I'm just trying to find out if you're a good risk." He shifted in his seat. "For my business."

"What business is that?"

"The importing business," Duke said, the words thick with his Texas drawl.

Brian said, "I'd hate for you to get in trouble with a loan and not be able to pay it back. This might be the perfect solution. Very lucrative."

"Y'all go out on the boat most days?" He smashed a bag of crackers in his fist and poured them over the chunks of clams, potatoes and carrots in his chowder. "They got Tabasco here?"

Brian hailed a busboy. He definitely wanted to please this man, Chloe thought.

Duke shook the Tabasco into his chowder until the stew took on an orange glow. "How far is it to Canada, anyway?"

"It depends on where you're going," Chloe said. She had the feeling she was being interviewed for a job she didn't want.

"Vancouver Island," Duke said, with an eerie clandestine tone to his voice, eyes zeroed in on hers.

The way he had said Vancouver Island set off her internal warning alerts. If they went to Victoria, the harbor was crowded and a hassle to get in and out of. The rest of the island was mostly deserted. "It's not far at all," Chloe said. "An hour at the most."

"Just you and this fella that works for you? What's his name?"

His eyes were experienced and intense, and she had the sense he came from a place where his convictions were firm, whether they made any sense or not.

Brian answered. "Butch."

Duke nodded. "He reliable?"

Chloe lifted a spoon of potato and clams to her mouth. She looked Duke directly in the eyes and said, "I trust him." Then, she swallowed her chowder.

"Brian says I can trust you. That you're the kind of girl who can keep quiet about things."

"Brian's right about that," she said. "But it's not because I have anything to hide."

"Now I like that." Duke lowered his voice. "He says you're interested in making some money."

"He's right about that, too," Chloe said.

"I don't do business with just anybody," Duke said. "And, I don't do business with women."

Chloe pulled back. “Really?” She said. “I guess that counts me out.”

“What about Butch?”

“It’s my boat. I’m the one who needs the money,” Chloe said, her voice firm. “But if you don’t do business with women, I understand. I guess Brian forgot to tell you I was female.”

“No, he told me,” Duke said. He was smiling now and clearly trying to make amends. “He’s trying to convince me you’re not just any girl.”

“I don’t know whether to be offended—”

“Honored,” Duke said. “Definitely honored. For this job, I need someone I can trust.”

“My experience, it’s not easy to find someone to trust.”

“You don’t mince words.” Duke picked up a saltshaker and examined it. “I like that. You say what you think.”

“So, you’ll overlook your all male rule?”

“In your case, darlin’, I’m considering it.”

“If we’re both going to consider this, let’s get one thing straight,” Chloe said. She had the edge on this guy. If it came to it, she could walk away from this whole thing. “I’m not your darling.”

“It’ll be a hard habit to break,” Duke said, lowering his head to her in respect.

“What is it you want me to do, exactly?”

“Canada is known for its high tax on alcohol. We’re doing the Canadians a favor. We buy tax-free liquor from the Indian reservations in Washington,” Duke said, “and sell it to the Indians on Vancouver Island. Everybody’s happy.”

“What the fuck?” Chloe said. “You’ve got the wrong girl.”

Duke didn’t blink. “The beauty of it is, nobody thinks about smuggling alcohol. The Coast Guard is looking for pot. Marijuana smells. They got dogs to pick up the scent. No one’s looking for liquor.”

“It is illegal.” Chloe fumed. She looked at Brian.

"Did you know about this?"

He nodded. "I told him you were a great Captain, steady, not the kind of girl to make a fuss about things."

"A fuss. You thought I'd do this because I don't make a fuss about things."

"I thought you'd do it because you're broke," Brian said. "You've been broke for the last three years. Every time we go out on the boat, I wonder if this is the last time."

Chloe's stomach turned into one heavy block. "And, how is it that you know Duke?"

"I've been helping him invest his money,"Brian said. "We play golf together."

She'd known Brian for at least five years now. He had always hinted at wanting more from their relationship, and when she rebuffed him, they had become friends.

"And I suppose you make a little as well," Chloe said.

He shrugged. "A guy's got to make a living."

Chloe took a sip of her coffee. With the mug to her lips, she heard the bell over Mo's door sound and watched Butch burst in. Chloe jerked and spilled coffee across the table.

Duke scooted aside, "You all right?"

Chloe sent mental messages to Butch: Please don't come over here. Turn back. She focused her eyes on him as he sidled through the tables patting everyone on the back. Of course, he headed right toward her. There was only one thing to do.

"Butch is headed this way." Chloe elbowed Brian. She made eye contact with Duke. "Let's just keep Butch out of this."

Duke shrugged and offered a smile indicating he understood. Butch scooted into the booth next to Brian. Either Butch still smelled of last night, or he had managed to down a wake-up beer for breakfast.

"That was some halibut we caught the other day. Just like the good old days. Say, I don't know you, my name's

Butch. I guess I've been fishing here in Clam Harbor as long as anyone." He puffed out his chest just enough for Chloe to notice. "Twenty years on Perpetuity. She's a good boat, she is." Butch offered his hand to Duke.

"Call me Duke." Duke shook Butch's hand vigorously.

"Say, you're not from around here," Butch said plopping down next to Chloe "Wait, don't tell me. You've got an accent. Say something else."

Duke laughed as he stirred Tabasco into his chowder again. "It sure is pretty country up here."

"What brings you to Clam Harbor? Fishing?" Butch asked.

Duke hesitated and chewed on his lower lip. "That's right," he said at last, making right into a two-syllable word.

"We're the very best charter in town." Butch checked out the table. "That was a mighty fine fish the other day, hey, Brian? How about a round of drinks to celebrate?"

Chloe nudged Butch. "We were just leaving."

"That's all right, darling. I could drink another beer." Duke waved for the waitress.

"This is my day off; I've got all the time in the world." Butch settled back into his chair as if avoiding eye contact with Chloe.

The server delivered four mugs of Anchor Steam. Duke raised his glass and said, "To my new friends in Clam Harbor." Then Duke turned to Butch. "You've been fishing here a long time?"

"That's right, since I was knee high to a buoy."

Chloe stared intently at Butch trying to telegraph her thoughts. Don't say anything about my father. Butch loved to blather on. After a couple of beers, Butch would tell Duke his whole life story.

"So you were born here?" Duke leaned forward on his elbows.

"Yes, went into a business with my best friend."

"That right? That's nice. Your friend still around?"

Butch shook his head and kept his eyes focused on

the near empty beer in front of him. Duke waved for the waitress.

"What about you, Duke?" Chloe blurted it out perhaps a little too quickly. Realizing she sounded too eager, she paused, rearranged her napkin, and then added, "Were you born in Texas?"

"I knew it, I knew it all along. I knew you was from Texas." Butch slapped the table with the palm of his right hand.

"A place just outside of Houston, Seabrook." He shifted towards Chloe. "And you missy, how does a girl become a charter boat captain?"

Several responses ran through Chloe's head. Her pat answer was always, It's a family business. This response required an additional quip to maneuver the conversation to another subject. Today she lacked the energy necessary to steer a conversation far away from her father and safely into unemotional territory.

Finally, she said, "I'm going to let that go, knowing that men from Texas talk different, I figure they might think differently as well. Up here, women do whatever it takes to survive."

"Darlin'," Duke said, as if seeing Chloe in a whole new light. "Give me some time, you just might be able to teach me a few things." Duke nodded to her as the corners of his mouth turned into a slight smile.

Chapter Seven

On the day of my release, good ol' Spud pounded on my cell door and said, "Tully, gather your stuff and get the hell out of my prison."

The night before I had carefully packed Calvery's box. Everything I owned fit into a paper bag.

I looked at Spud, then at Cellie. "I guess this is it."

"I'll keep your bed for when you come back, Holmes," Cellie said, lowering his eyes.

"Naw, bro, I'm done with all this. You'll have to hold it down for me. I'll drop you a postcard. " I said, knowing he was sad to see me go. "I'll miss you and your saints of the month."

For September, Cellie had departed from his usual female saints and drawn Maximillian Kolbe, a Catholic priest who gave his life at Auschwitz to free another prisoner. The deliberate anti-Aryan selection was not lost on me.

Cellie shook my hand, then hugged my neck. "Be cool, Holmes."

Spud took my box and said, "No long goodbyes. You'll be back. I'll keep a light on for you."

We started down the tier. "I'm a changed man, sir. No shit in your shovel. But maybe our paths will cross in a better place."

He escorted me to the van that drove the inmates to

downtown Huntsville for processing. “Good luck, Tully. Don’t kill that turtle.”

I started onto the van, turned and said, “Thanks.”

“You ain’t gonna get all emotional on me, are’ ya?”

“I guess not. You’ll find someone else. There’s someone for everyone, Boss.”

“Fuck you, Finn. You come back, I’ll throw you to the dogs.”

Sport scratched at his box and I lifted it slightly, motioned to Spud. “Anyway, I think I know how to take care of a turtle.”

Spud settled his hands on his stomach and twirled his thumbs. “Maybe so.”

***

Mother wanted to pick me up in Huntsville, but I insisted on taking a bus to Bayport. She was sick, after all. Anyway, I supposed riding the Greyhound was a fitting way to end my time.

When I reached Mother’s house, I ran up the back steps into the kitchen, the most likely place to find her. Sure enough, there she was, standing at the kitchen sink, her hands immersed in dishwater.

“Here I am, the prodigal son returns, kill the fatted calf. Or, was it a pig?”

She pulled her dishwashing gloves off her hands, her face lit up. Her hair was gray now, still long and pulled back into a ponytail secured with a silver barrette.

“They were Jewish, remember. They didn’t eat pigs.” She hugged me and kissed my cheek. “You look a little pale.”

“You look a little thin. You feel thin.” I rubbed my hand down her bony back.

“You can never be too rich or too thin. Look at Mick Jagger.” Pots, pans, and dishes covered the dinette and The Stones rocked from a portable CD player on the kitchen table.

“I’ve got a present for you.” I put my shoebox

containing Sport on the table. "Open it."

"What is it?"

I nodded to the box. "You'll have to see for yourself."

Sport took advantage of the moment by scratching against cardboard.

Mother jumped away from the table, gripped her hands and held them across her chest.

Sport nudged at the box lid and tipped the lid over. I think he was surprised to find himself on a waxed wooden table.

"Mother, I'd like you to meet Sport. Sport, my Mother—the love of my life." I picked him up. He immediately retreated into his shell. "Now is that polite?"

Mother laughed, sidestepped to the refrigerator and said, "What do you and your turtle want to eat?" When she bent over and scanned the shelves, I noticed she'd lost a good bit of cushion from behind. Mother had never been fat, always healthy and muscular. Now she didn't weigh much more than a goat. "I made you some pot roast—"

"Now that's what I like to hear." I lifted her and spun her around. She was as light as a push broom. "You hear that Sport, Mother's pot roast. You're in for a treat."

Mother took to Sport right away and found him a big plastic wading pool. She pulled it in from the storage room and set Sport in it with a half a head of lettuce. Shortly after, I settled in to a big plate of pot roast with mashed potatoes and carrots. Food for kings. Chunks of beef surrounded by burgundy gravy steamed before me. I pushed a bay leaf aside and stabbed at a piece of meat. It fell apart in my mouth before I could gnash it with my molars. Memories lived in that pot roast, all the Sundays after church when she made it just for the two of us, then the Sundays when Brooke and Lacy were with us.

"Do you have any plans?" She spooned more mashed potatoes on my plate.

"I want to see Lacy."

"You'll need a job."

"I thought I'd just mooch off of you for a while. You don't mind, do you?"

She wadded up a napkin and threw it at me. It bounced off my chest, landed into a pool of gravy and splashed onto my "clown suit." "Look what you've done to my nice clean shirt. Prison issue. You could get arrested for destroying government property."

"Seriously, what are you planning to do?"

"Could I work with you in the shop?" Mother had a shop downtown—The Rake and Hoe—where she sold plants, seeds, fertilizers, pots.

"I'm letting the shop go. I figured it was time for me to take it easy and enjoy life. I sold it to a nice young lady from Houston. Maybe you'd like to meet her. She's single."

This piece of information shocked me so much that I choked on my half-chewed carrot and it flew from my mouth onto the table. I grabbed the soggy thing with my napkin and said, "You've got to be kidding."

"Things change."

I scanned the room. On the refrigerator, I noted an appointment card. I took it off, tossed it onto the table. "I want you to tell me the truth. How bad is it?"

"I can still buy green bananas," Mother said. "For the time being, at least."

I pushed my plate away and dropped my head into my hands. "Surely there's a treatment they can do. We'll go wherever we need to go. I'll take care of you."

"Houston has some of the best doctors in the world," she said, her face serene and reassuring.

"Maybe you need to try some holistic medicine," I said. "Go to a spa and get one of those cleansings. I read about it in prison. How about it?"

"Eat your lunch."

"I heard about this guy who cured himself of cancer by eating flax seed oil and lots of broccoli." I jumped out of my chair and ran to the fridge. "Look what you have in here. Except for the pot roast, there's not enough to keep

Sport alive. From now on, you're eating nothing but broccoli. Broccoli morning, noon and night."

"Can we throw in some brown rice now and then?" She sat calmly at the table.

"You're absolutely right," I said. "Brown rice would be good for you. We'll go to the Health Foods store just as soon as I get back from seeing Lacy. And no more red meat. It's full of carcinogens." I searched the vegetable bin.

I returned to her side and hugged her neck.

"It would mean a lot to me if I could see you settled in before I go," she said, her tone serious now.

"You're not going anywhere except down to the Whole Foods store with me. What did he say? Supposing I believe this doctor, just for the sake of argument, just how green can you buy your bananas?"

"You never know about these things."

"Seriously, how long?"

"Like I said in my letter, a year. Enough to see you turn into the man I know you can be."

I wondered what kind of man that would be. That night I wrecked the car with Lacy in it would not leave me. Instead, it was a recurring nightmare. In the dream, the truck blazed, and the fire surrounded Lacy. I tried to reach her, but I was too high to move, and she kept crying for him, reaching her arms out to me.

Then, I would wake up and pull her school picture from under my cot, and I would hold it in my hand until the pounding in my chest subsided. That night no one was hurt, the truck didn't burst into flames. I guess the nightmare just kept coming round to remind me, it could have been worse.

"I will. You'll see. I will." Inside of me, I believed it. Outside, I didn't know if I could pull it off. "How about if I borrow your car and go see Lacy. When I get back, we'll go shopping. Put some meat on your bones."

"I don't know if it's a good idea for you to go see Lacy. Brooke doesn't want you to see her. She's trying to start over, give Lacy a stable life." She patted my hand, the way she used to when I was a kid. "Maybe it's for the best if you stay away. For now."

I stared into space longer than I wanted to, trying to keep my insides calm. It took awhile for me to wrap my arms around the situation. My wife had slammed the door to my future—Lacy. Could Brooke take Lacy away from me? I'd burn it all down before I'd let anyone take my little girl from me.

"I'll be damned if I'm going to let that woman take my daughter away from me." I threw my prison check on the table. "Here's my fifty bucks from the prison. Can you spot me another fifty?"

"Leave her be."

"I'll be all right," I said. "I just want to see my Lacy."

"Not on my watch. You've done enough."

"I'm going."

"Not in my car."

I had to see her. "Give me a break."

Brooke had to listen to reason, let me see my girl. One look at me and she would know I was a changed man. She would forgive me. She always had before.

Mother shook her head. "I don't have enough time for you to screw up again. I need you to sit down and make plans."

"I've got to see her," I said. "It's my first day home. Give me the keys."

"No."

I slammed the door and went into the garage to check out my old Harley. I knew Dad had been riding it while I was gone—reason number 999 why I hated him so. He couldn't bother to visit me in prison, but he could keep the Harley running. I cranked it up and headed to Brooke's house. She had moved into a small rental just outside of Bayport.

What if Brooke took one look at me and changed her mind? Maybe she regretted hiring an attorney. Life as a single mom couldn't be easy. We had a chance to start over.

But fantasies are the fuel of dupes, and my daydream

soon ended. When I pulled up into Brooke's driveway, the chrome grill guard of a shiny black Ford 150, greeted me. All right, I knew this was coming. Probably some douche bag.

Brooke's screen door banged back and forth in its jamb, a wind chime jingled on the porch, and a plastic bag tumbled across the yard. When I reached the porch, three sets of eyes looked out the front window—Lacy's, Brooke's and—the sight no man ever wants to see—the eyes of another man. I clinched my jaw, bounded up the steps. Just as I was about to pound on the door, Brooke stepped out. She closed the door quickly and moved away from it.

"You shouldn't be here," she said.

"Nice to see you, too. You'll have to excuse me, but I've never been divorced before, I don't know all the rules," I said. "I never figured you for someone who would kick a man when he's down."

"I had to think about what was best for Lacy," Brooke said. "She deserves better. She needs a normal life. I deserve better, too. There's no reason we all have to suffer because of you."

Boy, she looked good. She was always built, and the baby had put a little something on the rear that was appealing. She looked so soft and sweet. Her hair was streaked with blonde and fell around her face in loose waves, and her legs were the color of summer on Galveston beach.

"I'm just trying to get back to where I left off." I moved a step toward her, clutched my prison issue slacks to prevent myself from reaching out.

She moved back. Her flip-flop caught on the rough edge of a plank. When she stumbled, instinct told me to grab her. Instead, I gripped my pants.

"I've heard it all before." She turned away, looked beyond me out towards the street. "It's not easy for me. I loved you. Once. I just can't do it anymore."

"Who's the guy?"

She shook her head. "Don't go there. You don't have

any right."

"I was your husband, remember? You remember, till death do us part."

"We never said that. You didn't want it in the vows, remember?"

I did remember. I never expected it to backfire on me. "But you did."

"Look, we did our best. Maybe Lacy can have a dad that's around, that's sober. Do you want to take that from her?"

"I can be sober. I've been sober."

"It's too late. We can't go back." She paced to the edge of the porch and back. "I wish we could. But we can't."

I heard a child's voice. "Who's Mommy talking to?" I wanted to believe Lacy asked the question because she couldn't see me, but she was looking straight at me, through the window. She was only seven, and I'd been away three years. She saw me all right. Too bad, I was a stranger.

A deep voice said, "Lacy, stay here." The screen door slammed and a man strolled out, ducking as he stepped through the door. "Everything all right?"

I offered my hand, and he returned the gesture with an overly firm shake.

"I'm just trying to figure out where I stand here," I said.

Brooke said, "We're all right here. I can handle it."

He put his hand on her shoulder. "Why don't you go back inside?"

She nodded, obliging him in a way I'd never experienced in all our married days, and left me alone with the man who had stolen my wife. I was ill-prepared for the moment. Somehow, despite three years of prison daydreams, I'd never played this one out.

I sized him up. He wasn't overly handsome, and with all the working out I'd done in prison, though we were the same height, I had him beat in the muscle department. Silently, I celebrated his regular guy looks. Brooke's new man wore a pair of exercise pants with a stripe down the side and a matching tee shirt, but he looked more like the kind of guy that wore an exercise suit than the kind of guy who used one. This I also counted as a small victory.

"I don't have anything against you. Not one thing." Brooke's boyfriend shifted from one running shoe to the other. "Brooke has a right to want a normal life."
Normal life?

"I want to see my daughter, that's all."

"I don't want any trouble," he said. "The way I figure it, you and I have one thing in common, we both love her."

His words cut so deep I felt like I was bleeding inside. My eyes shifted to the window where Lacy's face peeked out from the edges of curtain sheers. Her hair, gilded with a sheen from the sun, sprung from her head in loops, and the gauzy curtain blew gently around her like a pair of wings. If it weren't for the fear in her face, she would have looked like an angel.

"It was nice meeting you. I'm hoping we can work this out, after awhile." Mr. Tall Nice Guy said.

"Just the same, I need to see my daughter." I stepped up closer to him and straightened up so that I showed every inch of my height. "If you don't mind."

"Brooke would prefer you don't see her," he said, his voice not quite as firm and convincing as before.

"I don't know buddy, what if it's not?"

"Look, Finn, we don't need any problems here, I mean c'mon, you just got out of prison, aren't you on parole?"

"Naw, I discharged my sentence, not a day early for good behavior."

He was intimidated and I was playing on it. He was handsome, a good guy for Brooke, but I had to set the tone, I mean after all, he was in my little girl's life.

"Like I said, we don't want any trouble here," Mr. Tall Nice Guy said.

"Don't back paddle now, bro, you stepped out of that house real confident. How did you think this would play out?"

"I'm sure you understand."

I knew how to size someone up. Mr. Tall Nice Guy was caving. He had sense, I had to give him that. After all, not to brag, but after three years of bench-pressing with the big boys, I was more than buff.

With my eyes steady on his, I kept cool, my expression neutral. He blinked no less than twenty times in the brief minute I held my gaze on him.

Finally, when I knew I'd successfully intimidated him, I said, "You're sure I understand? I'm a bright guy and all that. But I have to say, I don't understand. I don't understand why my daughter is in there, and I'm out here. I don't understand why my wife left me, and why she chose you. I don't understand why you're sleeping in my bed, and I am sleeping at my mother's house. So, I don't understand. Do you understand?"

He nodded, his lips clamped shut, his eyes still blinking. "I don't want any trouble."

"So you do understand," I said. "Let's just make this simple. Bring Lacy out to see me and then maybe I'll leave you be. You got that?"

He nodded to Brooke. "Let him see Lacy."

Once again, Brooke obliged him. If it hadn't meant I was going to see Lacy, I wish she would have protested. The screen door slammed behind her when she stepped out of the door with Lacy clutching her hand.

I crouched down and opened my arms to Lacy. "Come give your dad a hug."

She shook her head and turned away. Her pretty little face was in her mother's shorts.

"Brooke, tell her."

"You don't care about her," Brooke said, her voice filled with anger. "You don't care who you hurt along the way as long as you get what you want. You can't bully her into loving you."

So on point was this that it felt like Woo had blasted me in the gut. There's nothing worse than the truth to knock the wind out of you.

With Lacy still cowering in fear next to Brooke, I backed off the porch.

This high-pitched voice said, "Is he gone now?"

"It's all right now," Brooke said.

"Things always work out," Mr. Tall Nice guy said in a loud encouraging voice.

Maybe the words were for my benefit, maybe not. He seemed just the kind of guy to talk so rosy and hopeful. I wanted to dislike him for it. Instead, I envied him his attitude. I really wished I hadn't seen that expression. I really wished she hadn't seen me.

It would have been so much better if old-what's-his-name, Brooke's friend, was a first-class jerk. If only I had been so lucky.

I didn't feel like going back to Mother's, not on my first day at home. Instead, I drove to the liquor store, bought a bottle of Maker's Mark bourbon, and headed toward Dad's house. He lived in this condominium on the south side of Bayport. If his car, a Corvette most likely—he always drove a Corvette—was parked out front, I would either drive by, key it, smash into it or stop and give him a piece of my mind.

Sure enough, a black Corvette was parked out front. I drove past, down to the end of the road where it dead-ended into a levee, and then whipped the Harley so fast its rear wheel skidded in the anemic dirt. I sucked in a whiff of humid air and smelled both dust and the super-heated smog blown in all the way from Houston, a good thirty miles. One thing Dad and I had in common, we liked the heat.

The last thing I wanted to do was surprise Dad and one of his lady friends. I put my ear to the door, listened for panting, moaning or exultant cries of passion. Hearing none, I pounded on the door. When after ten seconds he didn't answer, I pounded again.

Just as I was hammering the door with my fist, Dad opened it, catching me mid-knock. He looked ready to go out on the town—starched jeans, a button down silk shirt—his hair slicked back, still wet from a shower. I noticed more gray at his temples, just enough to make you think he didn't dye his hair, but I knew he did. He wasn't the kind to give in to aging willingly.

"I'm here," he said. "C'mon in, son. It's good to see you."

"That right?"

"If I'd known when you were getting out, I'd have been there to pick you up. How'd you get home?"

"The bus."

"Well, I guess that's the way to end it. A drought usually ends with a flood." He glanced over to the end table where he had a Lone Star longneck, a Sports Illustrated, and the remote control.

"I wouldn't have minded a lift, but I'm not complaining."

I felt that same helpless sense as I had when I was ten, looking out at the bleachers to see if Dad showed up for the baseball game. Mother was always up there alone. I had that feeling like What's the Point? No one cares. That same day, I struck out, three times. I was glad he wasn't there to see it.

"That's fine. That's fine, son. You got through it, that's the main thing." He put his arm on my shoulder and it felt like it weighed ten pounds. "They didn't give you any trouble, did they?"

I turned on my heel and looked him in the eye. "No, Dad. I didn't turn queer, if that's what you're suggesting."

"It's just that, I know how these things can be," he said.

"You know? That so? Well, I wonder why you didn't just up and write me a letter or two and give me some advice."

My father took a moment. "I guess I deserve whatever you want to dish out," he said, his voice turned sullen. "I never pretended to be much of a father."

I took a pull of the whiskey. "Let me tell you about my day. I come home, find my mother has shriveled to half her former self and has sold her store."

Dad marched to the window and checked the view. I don't know what he expected to see. Shaking his head, he said, "She's a good woman."

"But there's more," I said. "Turns out my wife took up with another man, and I can't see my daughter."

Dad went on to say, "I'll work it out with Brooke to bring Lacy over here, then you can see her. We can take her to Galveston. She's a doll. You should have seen her when I taught her to ride a bike—"

"Brooke lets you see Lacy?"

"I suppose you have every right to hold a grudge against me," he said.

A grudge? He talked liked someone who had committed some minor offense like missing Sunday dinner once or twice, not like someone who had always missed everything.

He softened the tone of his voice and said, "I'm trying to make it up to you through Lacy."

I squared up to him and grabbed his shirt.

"You can spare us your half-assed attempts."

"Son—"

"Naw, man, don't call me that."

"It's all right." He just looked me in the eye calmly. "Get it off your chest."

"You're a sorry excuse for a father. You deserved a good ole fashioned jail house ass whippin'."

"You've had some bad breaks, I won't deny it." He ran his fingers through his thinning hair. "I was trying to get a business set up, so you'd have some money when you got out."

"And you and I will go off to the islands and lie in hammocks all day long." It was another one of his dreams. Over the years, I'd heard plenty of them. "It's just typical of you. When have you ever once been around when I needed you?"

"You're under a lot of stress," Dad said. "I'm here now."

"No, I'm here, and I'm just here to tell you what I think of you. I mean, not one letter in three years to your son in prison."

"C'mon, son."

"I don't see any other way. I think I have to whip your ass. Step outside."

Dad was the one who had taught me to box. He looked in good shape. I didn't care. This had been a long time comin'. Once for every summer he had abandoned me. Once for every year I was in prison. Once for every promise he had broken. Then, I'd move on. Pain begets pain.

My anger had topped out, and when we stepped off the porch I wasted no time. My old man was fast, but his heart wasn't in it. When I caught him in the jaw, he had stopped defending himself. The blow twisted his face to the side and then he looked back at me. This time staring at me square in the eyes. If my punch hurt him at all, he didn't let on.

Looking at Dad, I remembered the fear in Lacy's eyes and a memory shot through me. It hit my head like a double-double espresso, and that feeling traveled down my neck and through my arms all the way to my clenched fists.

Along with it came a moment of clarity, and it was Calvery in my head. The two of us shooting the breeze, exchanging sugar for wine. I had complained to him about my father.

"You remember any good times with him?" Calvery asked.

"When I was about twelve, he took me to Louisiana, and we hunted alligators. It was great, you should have seen the boatload of alligators we shot."

"So you remember that," he said. "Nothing else matters. Time is too expensive to be spent in anger."

Standing there with Dad, I had a moment with Calvery, clear as a movie on Blue Ray, and others might call it nothing—my guilty conscience, my messed-up head—it felt different: a visit from the other side, if you believe in that sort of thing. Dad stared at me, his eyebrows pulled close together; his dark eyes regarding me like a father. I backed away from it. Time may be too expensive to spend in anger, but I had nothing else left.

Chapter Eight

Chloe sat at her desk with a cup of tea. At her feet, Jazz circled the rag rug three or four times before settling onto it with a throaty sigh.

"I know how you feel," she said and reached out to her Airedale. He moaned again. "What would you do? Take the booze-smuggler's money and risk your father's boat? Or don't take the money and lose your father's boat?"

Jazz stood, his tail wagging vigorously. Actually, his entire backside danced a complicated salsa. It was their usual time for a walk.

"Not now, I'm busy choosing between poverty and jail," Chloe said, looking at Jazz with sincere apologies. "In your case, imagine deciding whether to take a bath or swallow your heartworm pill."

With that explanation, Jazz settled on the rug again. Chloe had never imagined her father's death. Rather, she pictured him arriving home one day a free man. It was her most frequent daydream. She would be out on the dock hosing down the boat when he appeared dressed to go fishing, wearing boots and a yellow slicker.

Since that day—the way she now referred to her father's execution—her daydreams had stopped. Abruptly.

She pulled up her online bank account, stared at the balance—three hundred dollars—and cringed at the stack of bills lying on her desk. "Eenie, meenie, miney, mo, which of these bills has got to go?"

Closing the screen, she pushed away from her desk. "Jazz, come." His head comfortably positioned on an elevated portion of his bed, he opened his eyes sleepily and stared at her. "I said, come!" Jazz turned away, then unfolded his furry legs and pulled himself to standing, his tail tucked between his legs. "That's a good boy. You're all I've got. It's just you and me." She scratched at the scruff under his leg. His tail wagged. "You'll never leave me, will you boy?" With that comment, the wagging increased. She knew he was just a dumb dog. But he loved her. He didn't cost much. And a wagging tail never failed to bring a smile to her face.

She returned to her books, one hand on Jazz. Even the day's charter wouldn't get her anywhere close to coming up with five hundred extra dollars to cremate her father let alone rescue her mother from the rest home. What now? Risk defeat at the hands of a Coast Guard cutter, or die a slow, agonizing financial death? Why drag out the agony? Go for broke, all or nothing.

She punched in Brian's number. "Tell Duke I'll do it," she said when he answered.

"He's right here. Tell him yourself."

Brian put Duke on the phone.

"I'd like to see you," she said. "About—"

"I'd like to see you, too. I always love to see a pretty girl."

"I mean—"

"I know what you mean. Maybe I can take you to dinner?"

"But…" She finally understood that the phone wasn't the place to have a conversation about committing a crime. "Meet me at my boat."

Chloe rushed down to the wharf. As she hustled to her boat, she passed some of the townsfolk. First Sam Tarbox, the owner of the tuna packing plant, glanced her way, then ducked into Taffy Works. Chloe watched him inside the store, wondered if he really wanted to buy any taffy. Next, Veronica Millbank disappeared into the wax museum. No way would Veronica want to go to the wax museum. Towners never set foot in the place unless they worked there—Veronica didn't—or knew someone who did.

What did it matter? Besides, Chloe understood. What would they say to each other? Sorry to hear about your father? Hey, Chloe, I heard your father was executed the other day. Tough break. If Chloe were in their position, she would ignore them as well.

"People are avoiding me," she said to Butch when she reached the boat. Butch waved his hand in a gesture of don't worry about them. "Glad it's so easy for you to brush off," she said. "It's weird, like I no longer exist in this town."

Butch sat on the deck drinking his rum and Dew. "It'll blow over, you'll see. That's the way these things are."

"These things? How many times have you had this happen?" She said, noticing he'd finished a bottle of rum. "What're you doing here, anyway?"

"I just wanted to be alone," he said, looking out onto the bay. "I like it here at night when the lights come on. Reminds me of the old days. We used to sit out here—"

"Stop," she said, raising a hand. "Let's not go there."

He shrugged and stared blankly into his glass. "I feel lonely, that's all."

"It's just that I've got this thing," she said, looking at her watch. "I didn't expect you to be here."

"You want me to leave?" He said with a whine in his voice that sounded like a teenager placed on detention. Then he added, "What are you doing here, anyway?"

Chloe pressed the tips of her fingers together and touched them to her lips. This was a stupid idea. She had agreed to this plan without considering ever-present Butch and wondered how she would keep this secret from him.

They sat there, Butch unusually quiet. Water slapped against Perpetuity shifting the boat to port. After vacating another boat, a flock of gulls zoomed toward Chloe and circled overhead while laughing with high-pitched squeals. Then there was a downpour of gull droppings. Butch covered his glass.

"Geez," she said, wiping a white clump of bird shit from her sleeve. "They're like flying rats."

"Since when don't you like seagulls?" Butch looked at her with his jaw hanging.

It was a fair question. She had turned into a complete bitch because of all this. "Sorry." She glanced at her watch. "I don't know what's gotten into me. But I've got someone coming by. I didn't think you'd be here."

"You trying to sell the boat?" Butch had a look of shock and fear on his face.

"Oh, God, no," she said. "I would never do that." Chloe reached for Butch's hand and squeezed it. "I would never do that," she repeated, then added, "It's just that I need to talk to someone about a business deal and I don't…." She paused uncertain how to finish the sentence.

Butch grabbed his bottle and stood up. "That's some way to thank someone who has been beside you all your born days. Some way. That's all I can say."

Chloe stood, grabbed his sleeve, "I didn't mean—"

"You didn't mean to, but you did it." The boards of the dock shook as Butch stomped off.

She felt bad about chasing him off. But the last thing she needed was Butch involved. Chloe lifted her watch face and read seven o'clock.

She searched the dock for Duke. It was one of those eerie, last-day-on-earth kind of dusks, purple and quiet with the usual sights and sounds. The smell of wet wood rose from the docks as the Pacific lapped up against them, and the lampposts, wrapped in tiny white lights, blinked on just as the last bit of sun left the sky. No one would suspect the aliens were about to land and change everything.

There he is, she thought, the same quick gait. For an old guy, about fifty she supposed, he had a certain confidence in the way he moved, not like Butch who wobbled on the docks, even when he wasn't drinking. Duke's cowboy boots landed with a hard thud on the dock.

"Evening, little lady."

"Where's Brian?" Why had he left her alone with this man?

"He decided it's best to keep a low profile."

"All of a sudden he has a profile?"

Duke shrugged. "Okay with me. This is the kind of thing where you don't need or want a lot of people involved. That's the beauty of it."

There's no beauty in this! She wanted to scream. Do you think I would be here talking to you if there was any other choice?

"Well, this is it," Chloe said, waving her hand toward the bow.

He stopped at the bait box and lifted the cover. "Nice size. You can get a few cases in here." Duke shook his head. "How many gallons of gas does it take to get to Canada from here?"

"Diesel," she said. "We run on diesel."

"You're kind of a sassy one aren't you? Diesel, then."

"Sorry," she said. "I'm a little edgy."

"C'mon now, honey, no need to worry about a thing." He started to reach toward her then appeared to think better of it. "How'd you get this boat anyway?"

"Inherited it."

"How old did you say this was?" Duke sat and patted the seat next to him.

"1984," she said. "It's seventeen years old. Not that old for a boat."

"No offense. I was expecting a boat a little larger and a tad slicker. But I suppose even a tugboat can push a big barge, isn't that right, darlin'?"

She scowled at him, then remembered her mission and forced her lips into a smile. "This isn't a tugboat."

"I was making a comparison. I do know a tugboat

when I see one." He shook his head. "Anyway, looks like you could handle fifty cases at a time. But with the alcohol in bottles, there's always a chance you'll get caught. It would be safer for you…" He patted her leg. "We don't want any harm to come to you now, do we?"

She tensed even though it was a harmless pat, not the kind of gesture that implied anything more. "What would be safer?"

"We could put it in inflatable tanks, store them in the bilge. You can fill up two one hundred-gallon bags, that's ten thousand dollars worth of liquor in Canada. Your take is one thousand dollars a trip. You can bring in five thousand dollars a week."

And I'm taking all the risk, she thought. But she would never have come up with this on her own. He was the brains; he knew how to do it. The five thousand a week sounded too good to be true, but she was too broke to care.

Out on the bay, the moon laid a shiny highway, a highway that would make her rich, or at least not in debt. It was an easy two-hour trip to reach Vancouver Island. She could take fisherman over for the day, bring them back at night and no one would be the wiser.

Duke pulled out a roll of bills. "Here's a little advance for you and some advice to go with it."

She thought about what the money could buy. It was a cigar-sized roll tightly bound with a rubber band. A hundred on the outside. Should she take it and count it or stuff it nonchalantly into her pocket?

"It's a thousand dollars a trip," he said, craning his head to examine the boats surrounding Perpetuity. "Most people get greedy. You got to think small. It's not how much you can haul each time, it's how long you can keep this up. One guy I work with made two hundred grand last year, just by lying low, one little trip after another. You're life is about to change, little lady."

She looked at the money. Remembered her bank account. It was a lot of money for alcohol. She knew of people who smuggled marijuana in fishing boats; the

Coast Guard wouldn't look for alcohol.

"Anyone get arrested doing this?"

"Back east, they drive it over the border in trucks. Just the other day a truck broke down in the middle of a farmer's field. It had fifty thousand dollars worth of liquor in it. But we've got a new angle. No one's been taking it over in inflatable gas tanks. Or if they have been, they haven't gotten caught. You've got to keep this quiet. You can't tell anyone." Duke leaned back on the rail and looked out over the sunset. "Yes, sir. It's a great little scheme." He grinned flashing a row of movie star teeth that gleamed with a professional polish. "That money there is just a little taste of what's to come."

"And what happens if I get caught?"

"I'm sure that won't happen." He lowered his voice. "The secret is to act normal. You can't think about it. Look at me, do I look worried?"

"You're not piloting the boat."

He exhaled through his nostrils with a muffled chuckle, then snapped his fingers and pointed at her. "I like you. You're all right. I'm telling you, it's a cinch." He shrugged his shoulders. "But if you're not interested…" He reached his hand out to Chloe indicating he would take the money back.

The thought of parting with the money scared her more than going through with it. "I'll do it."

"That's my girl. After all, isn't it your turn for some good luck?"

What did he know about her turn? "I can take care of myself."

"I believe you can."

Chloe stuffed the roll into her backpack and thought of her father. Was this how he started?

Duke meandered over to the bed and lifted the mattress to the berth. "A lot of space under here, too. Girl, you're sitting on a gold mine. A girl like you. No one will ever suspect. I'll have this filled up for you tonight."

Butch was no doubt angry with her for chasing him

away, and she was sure he was up at the bar drowning his sorrows. She wished there was a way to do this without him. If anyone could blow this for her, it would be Butch.

"You check the weather, or whatever it is you do. I'll fill your boat tonight. You'll leave tomorrow." Duke hopped off the boat and headed back to town.

Chloe plopped onto the bench, stretched her legs out in front of her, rested her back against the cabin and watched as Duke disappeared into the Clam Harbor wharf. She felt like a complete idiot. Any minute Scooter was bound to appear waving a pair of handcuffs and shaking his head in disgust. It was too absurd. Minutes ago, she was broke, now she had a wad of cash in her pocket. Maybe it was all because nothing seemed to make sense any more, even fishing.

Chapter Nine

After my fight with Dad, instead of the relief I had hoped for, a depression settled in on me. I felt petty and selfish about hitting my own father, and even worse about hitting him when he didn't hit back. When I reached the Harley, I took a pull on the whiskey and stared at the street thinking about what to do next. It was only three o'clock. I'd run through my family so quickly that an entire evening lay ahead of me. I had one good friend, Jacob. He seemed my last option, so I decided to drive over to Galveston, only thirty miles, and find him.

Galveston was a great place to get slobbering drunk, and I was well on my way. By the time I reached Broadway and The Texas Heroes Monument, the giant memorial for Texas Independence from Mexico, my drunk turned bad on me. I had entered a bluesy realm of loneliness and regret where only one thing could help me—heroin.

I drove down Post Office Street to a bar called The Dive, stucco front, barred windows. Not far from the wharf, it had a dependable clientele of merchant marines, shrimpers and dockworkers. I staggered past a worn-out bouncer, and greasy walls covered with sweat, blood and band stickers. Once my eyes adjusted to the lighting, I scoped the bar out. As I glanced around the room, a couple of barflies whistled at me. They were older than mother, or looked it, and probably had spent most of their lives sitting there drinking. Jakes, the same bartender who'd worked there six years ago when I started using, looked up from drying a glass and nodded at me.

A black vinyl rail padded the edge of the bar. I leaned over it and offered my hand.

"Been a while, kid."

"Four-and-a-half years."

He scanned me as if looking for war wounds.

"Pour me a tall whiskey," I said.

He pulled out a bottle of Canadian Club. It wasn't the kind of place to sell expensive brands. Jakes pushed the glass across the bar. "On the house."

I scanned the bar. Two merchant marines were talking to the barflies. In the back, a merchant sailor's head dipped, then jerked back awake. He was someone who would know where to find some horse.

Jakes called after me, "Why don't you leave it be?"

I waved him off. What did he know about it? I kept thinking of Lacy's eyes looking at me through the window. Only one thing could make that image disappear.

From the center of the table, a red votive flamed. Round, smooth cysts covered the thick red glass, and inside each bubble, a miniature flame glowed gold and white. I slid into a chair. The guy looked about fifty, I guessed, eyes pinprick, half-mast, and he had a tattoo with a naked-breasted woman in a hula skirt on one forearm and a large-lipped catfish on the other. Scratches, scabs and patches of dried blood covered both arms. Other than that, he looked like someone to have on your side in a fight. His forearms bulged and a tight shirt outlined his chest and arm muscles.

I pointed to the scratches and said, "Long time between ports."

The sailor lifted his eyelids, barely able to reveal half his iris.

"I knew a guy in prison with a catfish tattoo," I said.

He mumbled then half looked at the arm as if he had

forgotten about it.

I leaned in toward him and asked him what he said.

"Fifty bucks."

I pictured Lacy's fearful eyes staring at me. I reached in my jeans, felt the fifty bucks in my pocket. In front of me, the sailor's head wobbled until his chin landed on his chest, and his face turned into an older version of my own. It wasn't pretty.

I jerked my hand from my pocket and shook it. "Never mind, man, I'm broke."

Out of the corner of my eye, I noticed Jakes grinning at me like the proud father. I waved at him and marched out the door.

It was about five o'clock. About time for Jacob to dock his dolphin-watching boat at the wharf. Out on Post Office Street, I squinted at the bright sun and donned my sunglasses. One of those World War II amphibious vehicles passed by filled with tourists. They waved and laughed at me. I guessed the tour guide had made some wisecrack about The Dive.

Post Office Street smelled of diesel and fried fish. Maybe Jacob and I could grab some fried shrimp. I was all the way to the dock before I remembered I had left the Harley at The Dive. Just as well, I decided.

When I arrived, Jacob held a hose in one hand, a brush in the other. Soapsuds covered his boots and the deck of the Dolphin Chaser, a sixty-foot Cat tour boat with indoor and outdoor seating. He waved and tossed me a beer, as if I'd just returned from an errand. I fisted the beer—Samuel Adams Light—and gave Jacob the thumbs up.

I examined the bottle. "Since when you start drinking sissy beer?"

He patted his stomach, set the hose down and gave me a man hug. Jacob had written me five or six times while I'd been in prison. It was fine to have someone other than my mother actually glad to see me. Behind him, a tugboat guided a Dole pineapple ship into port.

"Geez, you smell like one of those merchant marines

on The Strand," Jacob said.

"I just got out. Went over to see Brooke."

"Sorry about that." Jacob took a long good look at me. "You all right?"

I shrugged and took a swig of beer. "For the shape I'm in. So you heard about the divorce."

"Tough break."

"Who's she's with?"

"Leave it be, Finn," Jacob said, rolling the hose into a neat pile.

"Easy for you to say. Not your wife."

"You got to admit," Jacob said, "you were out of control."

"Thanks for your support," I said, the sting of his remark hit me straight in the heart, but I didn't let on.

"I'm just saying."

"Who is he?" I squared off in front of Jacob, unconscious of the intensity of my body language.

"You gonna beat me up?" He was holding a scrub brush in one hand and a hose in the other. "Look at you, you've screwed over everyone who ever loved you."

I put a finger to his chest. "You putting yourself in that category?"

He looked at me as if I didn't have a clue. Maybe I didn't. I dusted his left shoulder and slumped onto the bench. The bumpers on the Dolphin Chaser squeaked against the dock. Seagulls screeched above me. "I'm sorry man, I just…."

We sat there looking out over the ship channel. So it had come to this, Jacob and me again. Where do I go from here?

"Forget it." Jacob jumped to his feet. "Let's go fishing. Better yet, giggin'. That'll cheer you up."

It was our ritual. Back in the day, after we tired of chasing girls, Jacob and I either surfed, fished, or grabbed a couple six-packs, our gigging gear, and spent the evening shuffling along in the gulf stabbing for flounder.

Galveston brought on mostly good memories for me—a beach filled with girls in bikinis, their breasts barely covered with thin strips of cloth, the thrill of seeing the fabric stray sideways revealing hard nipples underneath. I remembered the girls pointing at me surfing and later lying on the hot sand next to one of them and listening to reggae. If I had any money, I took them to Benno's, and we ate shrimp dripping with red sauce. Sometimes I got lucky, before I met Brooke, of course, and coaxed one of them into the back seat of Mother's Impala.

We packed up the beer from the Dolphin Chaser and, after stopping for fried shrimp, drove to the farthest east end of the island to catch the ferry to Crystal Beach, a good place for floundering because the shelf was shallow out five hundred yards. I inhaled a deep breath of the moist Gulf air and smelled the mist coming off the water, the diesel of the ferry. When we landed, we found a scrubby bait shop and parked beneath a flashing red-and-yellow neon sign: Fresh Bait.

Darkness prevailed and except for the flashing of the Fresh Bait sign and the faint stars, the world hid in a pitchy well. We both stepped into thigh-high waders. Jacob handed me my giggin' pole, he decided to hold the lantern and his gig.

The waves coiled toward shore in the fishy-smelling air, and then, as the moonlight hit them, their froth shone white and gleaming like freshly painted walls. A miniscule wave knocked against me, and I lost my balance, that's how unsteady I was.

"You're messed up, Tully. As bad as I've seen you." He stepped out in front of me, his lantern level as a high beam. "I suppose you're entitled. But don't you think it's time to get it together? What's it going to take?"

"I could use a break."

"I never felt sorry for you," Jacob said. "And I never figured you'd feel sorry for yourself."

"Watch yourself, I'm in no mood for a sermon."

"Forget it," he said. "Let's just gig. You should start shuffling your feet here."

"I know. I've been here before, remember? How long

we been doing this, ten years?" And he was my best friend. It felt lousy to be an ass to my best friend. My high was starting to fade, and I was cranky as a two-year-old. The whiskey bottle jiggled in my pocket. I pulled it out for a snort, handed the bottle to Jacob.

"I guess I'll give you some slack today, on account of Brooke and all," he said. "But don't expect any sympathy from me after today. You aren't the only one affected by your behavior."

"Thank you, Dr. Phil."

He was right. I told myself this was it. My last binge. I nodded in agreement. We had played this same game for about ten years now.

Jacob and I shuffled through the gulf toward a shelf where we usually caught a lot of flounder. I kept the Fresh Bait sign in my vision to orient me. By the time we stopped, it had faded into a tiny blur.

We'd landed in the middle of the ocean, or so it seemed. A thin web of clouds hid the stars. Nothing diminishes a man like a staggering expanse of space. Between the whole universe arced above me and the world of water between me and the shore, I felt as insignificant as one of the shells beneath my feet.

Thank God the moon appeared when it did and rescued me from a pointless why-am-I-here rumination. The ocean floor shifted under me and my foot slid into a mushy sand bed. I reached for the air to catch my footing and grabbed Jacob's suspender.

He turned around and put a finger to his mouth. His skin glowed like a jack-o'-lantern, and I grinned at his familiar chubby cheeks. He'd always had a baby face. Jacob looked down, aimed his gig and stabbed it into the calm water. "Dammit."

I inched up behind him. He pointed downward. Three sets of red dots looked up at me.

"You got to get them just right. Go for it." Jacob scanned the water. "You do that one. I'll do this one. All together. One, two, three."

I pointed my gig behind the gleaming red eyes and

pressed it into a flesh the consistency of Polunsky's green Jell-O. "Got it!" I lifted it out of the water. In the light of the lantern, the flounder's blood took on a fluorescent glow.

"You're gonna lose it."

As predicted, my catch took flight and flew from my spear, landing back in the Gulf with a bloody splash.

Fortunately, at the same time I lost my flounder, Jacob landed a bigger one, large enough for the two of us. I was looking forward to stuffing that baby up.

Jacob didn't say anything about me lousing up a perfectly good flounder and for that, I was grateful. After stowing his fine catch, he turned to look out over the water. I searched for the Fresh Bait sign.

"Look at the water." Jacob took his lantern and beamed it directly down into the Gulf where dark jagged threads of blood drifted in the water.

"Poor little dude. He'd have been better off in a frying pan."

"At least we have this beauty." Jacob pointed to the flounder on his stringer. "This thing's dripping blood all over the place, too."

We examined the flounder bed searching for more red eyes then started shuffling back toward the shore. One flounder the size of Jacob's wasn't a bad night's work, but I wanted to redeem myself and take one home. Jacob shed a broad beam across the water. At first, it was a wave approaching with a steady, even pace. Then, the wave turned to a sharp point. Schools of small fish scattered, denting the water as they escaped with a flip of a tail.

I tried to talk, to speak. Words stuck on my tongue. A sudden paralysis struck my arm. How long my muteness and infirmity lasted, I can't say. Long enough for the point to turn to a triangle and for the sound of a shovel plowing through water to reach my ears.

The fin grew larger. Its colors came into view, deep yellow-gray and oily slick. The Gulf parted as the shark sliced the water with its broad flat back skimming the surface. A surge of foaming, bubbling sea preceded him and a split second later, he slapped his tail with biblical force, denting the ocean, and then, because there is always calm before the storm, it was quiet.

One thing worse than seeing a shark, is not seeing it. “Where is it?” I said. “You know they can smell a drop of blood in a twenty thousand gallon tank.” I’d read about sharks in the joint.

“Would you keep quiet?”

“I’m not going to just stand here. Let’s go for it.”

“Stay still,” Jacob said. “We can’t outrun a shark.”

About twenty-five feet away, the dorsal fin headed straight toward me. The biggest shark I’d ever seen in the bay. I did what any red-blooded addict would do. I ran. The water reached up to my knees, not even to the top of my waders, but with one step, I turned into a felled tree and dropped with a loud inviting splash.

Galveston Bay poured into my waders. It felt as if the weight of quickset concrete covered my legs. As I sunk, salt water burned my eyes. Through the blur, I zeroed in on Jacob’s lantern shining over me.

What a great way to end my misery. Just open my mouth and suck in a big swallow of the bay. Not a bad idea. After all, if my homecoming from prison was any indication, my future sucked.

I rubbed my eyes and blinked away the gulf. When I finally cleared them of Galveston Bay, pushed away the ocean floor, the sand, crushed shells and fish eggs with my fluttering eyelids, this strange light hovered over me. It seemed in arms’ reach, but when I offered my hand, the light moved away, as if I were trying to touch a rainbow. In every direction, the night sky was alive with radiance, light particles glittered like slivers of glass and the moon, magnified by the strange illumination, cast a creamy glow over the water.

“Dammit, stay still,” Jacob whispered, but the sound carried well. I didn’t feel like moving anyway, not now.

Meanwhile, the shark swam up within spitting distance. Jacob’s lantern beamed on him. Knowing Jacob, he wanted to steer the shark away from me.

The shark aimed right for me. Sheets of water slid off his greasy fin, so close I watched how his great fin tilted slightly as if to catch the wind.

"What a mother of a shark," I said.

For a split second, I lost sight of my enemy, then he reappeared opening his mouth, like a yawn, not a bite. The smell of rotting fish belched up from his belly. With that, he moved behind me. I heard the rippling of water and a loud splash.

My heart pounded like a drummer on meth. When the shark appeared again he was about six feet away. He dipped his head into the water, partially obscuring his dorsal fin. The fin angled toward Jacob.

"He's got my foot." Jacob winced, clenched his teeth.

I wrapped both my hands around the dorsal tail and squeezed into the coarse flesh. It felt like a metal file scratching against my palms. With a jerk, I pulled a long steady tug, the shark let loose of Jacob's leg and turned his head toward me, pointy-white teeth bared, a smirky grin on his face.

I released my grip just before the great fish opened his mouth and lunged my direction. One row of teeth seemed sufficient, but this guy had at least three. Or so it seemed. The shark dipped his head and then tossed it out of the water with one awful jerk, the jaws surfaced, and he opened his mouth, the stink of foul fish breath filled the air again. My hands trembled as I aimed my pole toward his eyes. I held my breath as I cut through the air with my gig and knocked the thing on its nose. It flipped his head away from my pole, then his whole body swung around.

"Throw him the flounder," I said.

Jacob waved the stringer over the shark and tossed it out into the Gulf. The flounder landed about ten feet away and floated on the surface, its stringer trailing behind.

The tail fin appeared, the most beautiful sight you've

ever seen. It was headed in the right direction, away from us, toward the flounder.

The moon threw a shadow of the dorsal fin across the gulf; the sea serenaded us with its constant rhythm; I felt as if I had traveled somewhere far away, and I wondered if it was one of those thin places Calvery always talked about. Here on the gulf, in the gap between earth and water, I had seen a light like no other.

Jacob and I headed to shore. Behind me, something large slapped against the water. Waves knocked against me. My knees wobbled. Ahead of me, a dozen cabbage-head jellyfish, bobbing like a pack of beheaded aliens, glowed an eerie ivory. I marched right through them.

"How's your foot?" I asked.

"I guess I need a new pair of waders. That sucker had some jaws on him." Jacob offered his hand, and we hugged. "Thanks."

"I don't guess he would have killed you." I stepped away from him.

"I guess he could have." Jacob protested vehemently.

"Okay, okay. He get any skin?"

"It hurt for a minute there. I guess he bit me, but I'm not bleeding as far as I can tell."

"I guess we should have it looked at."

"I'm glad I still have both my legs," Jacob said, patting his thighs.

"You see anything strange about the gulf tonight?"

"You mean other than a shark?"

"It seemed like that phosphorescent plankton was floating on top of the water, all shiny and sparkly," I said, suggesting some explanation other than the one I knew was true. "You didn't see that?"

"All I saw was a mother of a fin. I never want to see one again."

I looked around me, the amazing light had faded. Now the gulf looked a deep gray and the moon offered up the only light—one slender path leading away from me, out of Galveston Bay, and into the Gulf of Mexico.

"Anyway, close call," I said. We bumped fists. I

pulled the bottle of whiskey out of my pocket and held it up to the moon. "You want a drink?"

Jacob shook his head.

"Yeah, me neither," I said and pitched the bottle with a nothing-but-net toss into a rusty trashcan on the beach.

Chapter Ten

I drove Jacob to John Sealy Hospital. A pretty little nurse seemed interested in the shark story, but I detected a little disappointment in her eye when she saw the outcome—a couple puncture wounds, abraded skin, bruises and a swollen leg. Hell, I've hurt myself worse jerking off in the shower.

The nurses and doctors kept talking about the guy who lost his arm or the girl who lost her leg. Honestly, Jacob and I were more than just a little irritated with their attitude. In Galveston, it took an amputated limb to impress the emergency room staff.

While in Galveston, I decided to study up on Calvery's conviction. My inheritance from Calvery had included his court records. I knew that a policeman named Clay Broussard had investigated the case. The phonebook listed three C. Broussards. One lived way out on the west end where they were developing all the new condos and beach houses. Another lived on 31st Street and another on 61st. I decided to try 31st Street first.

On my way to 31st Street, I picked up a fifth of whiskey, to break the ice. That always seemed to work in the movies. I found a small bungalow, its peeling siding the muted green color they used to use in the thirties. A two-seater metal glider sat on the porch and looked out onto the cracked sidewalk.

The unlatched screen door bounced on the jamb as I

knocked. When no one answered, I stepped over to the window. Heavy drapes covered most of it, but I peeked through an opening. Just as I had folded my hands around my eyes into binocular position, the door opened.

"You lose something, boy?" A man in a pair of olive Dickies stepped from the door. His head reached the top of the screen door and he had solid arms and muscular fingers.

I straightened up and offered my hand. "Pardon me, sir. I was just wondering if you were home."

"I am. You go about looking in people's windows, and you could get into trouble."

"Yes, sir. I'm not selling anything."

Broussard slicked his hair straight back, smoothing it close to his head with some kind of hair cream, maybe Vitalis. His smooth forehead rose from a pair of unruly eyebrows that wiggled as he said, "That's one thing in your favor. What do you want?"

"I'm looking for a Clay Broussard who was a detective. Would you know where he lives?"

"Depends on what you want him for."

"I'd rather not go into that until I find him."

"You won't find him until you tell me what you want him for."

I studied his face. He looked like a cop. He acted like a cop. "Are you Clay Broussard, the detective?"

"What you want?"

The sea breeze blew across the porch and pestered the screen door. I zipped up my windbreaker. "I'd like to talk to you about Calvery Thomas. He was a friend of mine."

"He's dead, ain't he?"

I nodded.

"How'd you know him?" Broussard stepped farther out onto the porch and assumed a wide stance.

"I met him in prison. I was a porter when he was on death row."

"You couldn't have been a very close friend." Broussard studied me.

Behind his swollen lids, his eyes were difficult to read. No big loss, my experience with cops, I wasn't likely to read him anyway.

"Why do you say that?"

"Don't play games with me. What you want?"

"You won't believe the truth."

"Try me." His accent was Cajun all the way—soft vowels and lazy sentences—I figured he left high school in Beaumont and decided to settle in Galveston, a little farther away from the armpit of Texas.

"I promised Calvery I would find his daughter and tell her he was innocent."

"That don't sound like much of your business."

"It never set right with me, what they say he did."

"No, it don't set right with me neither."

I nodded. "Besides, what else I got to do?"

"Well, I suppose that's one thing in your favor. It's stupid as all get-out, but honorable just the same."

He ambled over to the edge of the porch and spit over the rail. Sometime during our conversation, a black woman had started sweeping the edge of her porch next door.

Apparently seeing me looking at her, he said, "She's harmless." He called to her. "May, it's a little breezy out here to be sweeping. You best get on."

"I suppose it is. But there's nothing going on inside."

I stepped up beside him and sat on the porch rail. "I just want to know if he was innocent before I go clear across the country to tell his daughter."

"Let his secrets die with him. Don't be coo-yon." Broussard paused. "That's Cajun for stupid."

I'd heard the word before, maybe even used it. "Calvery said he was innocent."

He hesitated, turned his eyes to May, then back to me. "You say you were in prison. If you listen to cons, they're all innocent. Every last one of them."

"That's what we tell the law, not each other."

Broussard had a redness to his nose that reminded me of Spud. I offered him a pull of whiskey.

He looked at his watch, "I guess it's five o'clock somewheres." He took a swig and said, "What's this guy to you, anyway?"

"My only friend in that darkness."

"I know what you mean."

"You met him?"

"Of course I met him. I wrote the report. Let's go in and talk about it. May has big ears."

We followed the scent of onion, garlic and sausage into the kitchen, where a large pot steamed on the stove. Broussard reached for an oven mitt, lifted the lid and stirred the pot, then opened a cabinet and took out a bottle of rum. "I guess we'll drink like civilized heathens."

"I appreciate this. I know you don't have any reason to talk to me. I can't explain why, but I'd like to keep my word to Calvery."

He poured the rum over glasses of ice and squeezed lime in it. "Only two reasons most men would make a crazy promise like you did—love or money. Which is it?"

Only two reasons? I didn't think so. Neither applied. Calvery had willed me his meager belongings, and far as I knew, short of auctioning Sport on eBay, none of Calvery's belongings amounted to anything. Broussard forgot to mention a third reason for making a promise—the reason I also rejected—God.

"Man, it's like this. He said God was sending him and angel and I was it, and then they killed him. He's in my head, the last wish of a dead man. If he was telling the truth, then…." I lifted my glass. Above Broussard's head a Felix the Cat kitchen clock chimed one o'clock. "I got no choice."

"I don't suppose you do," he said. "Calvery was a stand-up guy. He came down from Washington to do business, that's all. He was in the wrong place at the wrong time, a shame."

Did he just say it was a shame Calvery got executed over a crime he didn't commit? "A shame? That's all you have to say."

"I'm a detective, not a lawyer," he said.

"Let me get this straight. You thought Calvery was innocent, and you let him get executed?"

"It's complicated."

I started at the words. "That's what Calvery said. His identical words."

"I'm not trying to defend myself or anyone else. But in the first couple weeks of my job, I learned that being a cop is not about justice or fairness. I hate to tell you that."

I knew it to be true, but didn't expect a lawman to admit it. Some guy like me, some dope fiend whose contribution to society amounted to zip, gets off with three years. Calvery, an upstanding citizen, a businessman, apparently a good guy, gets framed and executed. Go figure.

Broussard offered me some lunch, and I accepted. From the way the kitchen smelled, it would have been hard to turn down. He placed a scoop of rice in a bowl, dished out a helping of red beans, and topped it all off with slices of sausage.

"Nothing fancy," he said. "That's genuine andouille sausage from Louisiana."

We sat at a Formica-topped table and ate. I dug into the beans and sausage, choked and coughed at a bit of cayenne stuck in my throat. I hadn't had anything so well-seasoned in a long time.

After lunch, we settled in the living room. Broussard plopped into a recliner, reached to a side table cluttered with magazines—Sportsmen Today, Field and Stream, Outdoors—and selected a pipe from his rack. After scraping the bowl with a pipe tool, he pinched a wad of tobacco from the glass canister in his rack and stuffed it into his pipe. Finally, he struck a wooden match on his boot heel and lit his pipe, his cheeks sucking in as he puffed his bowl to a red glow. My eyes were drawn to a collection of pictures on the wall—Broussard standing with a graduating class of cadets, Broussard receiving a plaque from a dignitary.

"What's that?" I asked pointing at the picture.

He turned to see the picture. "That's the mayor of

Seabrook giving me an award for my help when the bikers and the KKK held their Seabrook boat parade protesting the Vietnamese shrimpers. You're too young, I suppose."

"When was it?"

"1981."

"I remember hearing of it. Someone was killed."

"Not in the parade. That happened in 1979. After the protestors had burned several Vietnamese boats and firebombed several of their houses, a white shrimper and Vietnamese one got in a fight. The shrimper died. Vietnamese guy got off for self-defense."

I nodded, sat back into the couch considering all this information. Despite feeling well fed and comfortable, I had this unsettled feeling in my gut, like I was close to putting this all together. Finding Broussard was a good break.

"Anyway, the boat parade could have turned into a blood bath. It didn't. I guess they thought I was to thank."

"Were you?"

He shook his head. "Those bikers were gonna do what they wanted." He paused as if to reconsider. "But I had the place heavily guarded. I guess the Klan wanted to keep things peaceful."

"Sounds like quite an accomplishment."

"Not really."

"I suppose you're the kind of guy who can't take a compliment."

"I reckon I am. You the kind of guy who knows what people are thinking?"

"Not hardly. Lucky guess."

A tabby lumbered into the room, stroked its back against my leg, and then started to claw the end of the couch. Broussard picked up a water bottle and sprayed the cat. "Damn cat. Can't stand them." The cat hissed, then plopped down at my feet.

"Why do you have one?"

"Keep the rats away. Galveston's full of rats."

"The rodent kind or the two-legged kind?" I grinned at him.

He laughed. "You're a bright fella aren't you? I like a guy with a sense of humor."

"Not bright enough to stay out of trouble."

"Why'd you end up in prison, anyway?"

"Dope."

He looked thoughtful as he took a drink of his rum. It seemed all the explanation he needed. "The way I see it, Calvery was at Rossi's at the wrong time. He stumbled onto a dead body and made the mistake of picking up the knife."

I leaned forward. "So who left the knife?"

"I'd look at Duke for it. You read the police report?"

I nodded. "There was no mention of a Duke."

"But there was mention of a man who disappeared as Calvery was walking up."

I recalled the police report. Calvery stated that he arrived at Rossi's mansion around ten at night. As he entered the back yard, he saw a platinum blond man jump an oleander and then the fence. Calvery found Rossi in the house, picked up the knife, put the knife down. I bet Calvery regretted going there that night.

"Yes, I remember," I said. "So you think the guy was named Duke?"

Broussard puffed on his pipe surrounding his face with a blue haze. “I couldn’t prove it. But the guy was Duke Banks all right. He’s a wiry guy, quick on his feet and someone who could jump over a fence or a yucca.”

“Did you talk to him?”

“Of course I did. You know what his alibi was? He was at Gaido’s all night. All his buddies vouched for him.”

“Why would he have been at Rossi’s?”

“He was looking for money or maybe jewels. Some of the Vietnamese smuggled them over when they left Vietnam,” Broussard said. “We used to see a lot of jewels back then. There’s a lot of loot somewhere. Mark my words.”

“Why do you think that?”

“The word on the street was that the Vietnamese paid Rossi to protect them. Rossi hated the KKK, too. On account of the way they treated the Italians.”

“Duke still around?”

“He’s around all right. He heads up the Longshoreman Union, sits in an office on Harborside Drive and watches them load ships, what few we have left. He travels a lot. Probably up to no good. You start sniffing in this, you’re gonna be sorry.”

“You think Calvery has the money?”

“I always wondered why he didn’t fight harder. Appeal the case. He was afraid of someone or protecting someone.”

The sight of Jules going through Calvery’s box came to mind. And that poem. I wasn’t about to bring that up to a cop, retired or not. Broussard said it right, I’d made a crazy promise.

“How would Calvery have taken whatever it was? Didn’t you arrest him?”

“You didn’t know?” Broussard looked at me surprised. “We didn’t arrest him. He was back in Washington when they picked him up.”

“So you met him after he went to Washington? How did he seem?”

"Like you said, he had a way about him."

"You believe he was innocent?"

"I know he was. "The word on the street was the judge suppressed the evidence that would have saved Calvery." Broussard said. "It ended up that the only evidence in a court was a set of prints that matched Calvery. He was the only suspect in a crime that needed a conviction."

That made me wonder what kind of money exchanged hands to keep the judge quiet. Calvery was an unlucky son-of-a-bitch. I figured I had time on my hands and maybe there was some treasure after all. I was broke with nothing to do. I thanked Broussard for his help and headed out.

As I was leaving Broussard said, "Oh, and one more thing, that Duke, his dad was the shrimper killed by the Vietnamese."

Chapter Eleven

Washington was a long way to drive on a Harley, so I went home, told Mother the whole story, except the bit about the money-jewels, and, somehow, I convinced her to drive up to Washington with me. She said it had always been on her bucket list. So we packed up Sport, an ice chest and a few belongings and headed to the Northwest. Calvery had told me Chloe lived in Clam Harbor, Washington, a tourist town on the Washington coast.

On account of mother's health, we only drove a few hours a day. I told Mother all about Calvery, thin places and all the Celtic beliefs I had learned about. Like, I never knew that the tradition of throwing pennies in a well to make a wish came about because the Irish believed wells were like portals to the other world. And the Celts believed that at death the soul crossed a body of water to reach the afterlife. Mother said, she wanted to leave on a wave, she'd always loved watching me surf.

After seven days of sightseeing and talking about life, we arrived in Clam Harbor. It was the end of tourist season, September, so we managed to find a small motel called the Clam Harbor Motor Lodge. All the rooms were tiny log cabins with fireplaces and large windows that faced the Pacific. By the time we arrived, though it was only six o'clock, and in this part of the world still a couple hours until sundown, the vista from our room was obscured by fog. It reminded me of the set in a classic whodunit. Outside our window, a small lawn sloped toward a wall of giant boulders. Beyond the rocks, the earth disappeared into eerie black mounds in the mist.

The motel owner suggested we try Mo's for dinner. As soon as we bunked Sport into a cozy corner, we drove into town.

"What do you suppose she looks like?" This wasn't the first time I had wondered, but it was the first time I had wondered aloud. "I'm thinking she's pretty special, because of her dad and all. She deserves to know he was a good man," I said. "Not all dads are like that. Take mine, for example.

"You're too hard on him," Mother said. "Not everyone is cut out to be a father, or a husband for that matter. I would say, Come to bed, and he would say, I wish I was like other men. There's not a woman in the world that compares to you. I'm not your kind."

"You never told me," I said.

"He always wished he was like those fathers who went to Cub Scout meetings and coached baseball. But he couldn't stay put. When he was home, he wanted to go, when he was gone, he wanted to be home."

The lights of Clam Harbor appeared as I rounded the corner. "I guess this is it ahead."

"He was proud of you, how you went to college. He thinks you're the handsomest boy to walk the earth. And he was proud of the way you could fight. The one thing he could teach you."

I felt a little tenderness towards him, very little. It didn't explain what he'd done. You compare that to Calvery's sacrifice, and it's no contest.

I kept thinking about Lacy, and the way she looked at me from the window. If there was any money, and, after talking to Broussard, I was starting to think there was, then I could afford to go home and take her away from Brooke and Mr. Nice Guy.

We parked on Clam Harbor's main street. Along the

wharf, shops selling candles, woodcarvings, tee shirts and kites lined the street. Tourist season was in its last few weeks. In the summer no doubt the streets were crammed with visitors. Strands of tiny white bulbs like Christmas lights covered the lampposts and lit the edges of the sailboat masts. The glow of dusk and the glint of those miniature lights made me forget all about my misfortunes.

"That's a cute boat there." Mother pointed to a purple and green fishing boat. "Perpetuity."

"Cute, that's the perfect word. I hope they have good insurance." I noticed the years on it. Compared with Jacob's boat it was barely above floatable.

A blond-haired man dressed in a fancy windbreaker, the type one might get at their club, jumped off the boat onto the deck. He waved goodbye to a middle-aged man stowing life jackets and saluted a woman of about twenty-five or so. The blond guy walked briskly down the dock, gave us a hearty howdy when he passed us.

Back on the boat, the woman yelled to the man stowing life jackets. He turned quickly. She stomped over to him holding a plastic cup and made a show of dumping it into the bay.

The girl wore a neon orange windbreaker that stood out in the fog. Beneath it, the tails of a flannel shirt waved about as she moved. Her bottom, what I glimpsed of it, was strong and shapely, definitely sturdy. She pulled her hair off her face and braided it into a thick rope.

"Ahoy," I said, regretting its stupidity right away.

"Did you just say, ahoy?"

"No, it was my mother." I nudged Mother.

"Yes, I said ahoy," Mother said in a very believable tone.

"You're tourists."

"How could you tell?" I asked.

She moved to the side of her boat next to the dock. Up close her unusual green eyes, round like nickels and framed with sandy-red lashes, were wary and hesitant even when she smiled. With one look, I pegged her as a girl who wore hiking boots, chopped wood, tied knots, filleted fish and dressed deer—not usually my type.

She laughed. "Ahoy to you, too."

"It was the first thing that came to mind."

"I thought she said it." She winked a lovely green eye.

I swear I felt a breeze off her eyelashes. It was a warm gust across my face with the smell of a woman—perfumed soap, shampooed hair—suspended in it. My mind traveled off into another direction.

Mother nudged me. "Your turn."

I shifted my eyes to Mother and glared.

"She's right," the girl said. "It is your turn."

The mist on the girl's face took on the lights. She actually glittered, like some of the pictures Lacy used to make for me.

"It's beautiful up here."

Okay, not the most clever comment, but the words just popped out of my mouth. Keep in mind, it was my first conversation with a good-looking woman in an awful long time.

"You're really a whiz at conversation."

I never knew a woman in flannel could look so good. The only skin exposed was her face, neck and hands, but my heart pounded as if she were naked.

"We drove up from Oregon today. We're from Texas."

Mother chimed in and said, "What is there to do around here for a tourist staying a few days?"

"You're in luck," the woman said. "Tomorrow the Clam Festival begins. We'll have fried clams, steamed clams, clam chowder, clam burgers, grilled clams—"

I laughed at the reference to Forrest Gump and added, "Clam sauce."

I couldn't believe my luck. First night in Clam Harbor, and I had already found someone to keep me company.

Chapter Twelve

On the first night of the clam festival, Clam Harbor hardly looked the sleepy town I had seen the previous day. Neon tubes of yellow and blue revolved in the twilight. They belonged to a Ferris wheel that turned lazily over a field of brightly colored tents and carnival rides—the Zipper, the Scrambler, the Octopus—all rides I knew from years ago, perhaps the same flimsy-foldable attractions I had seen on Galveston Island when I was a kid.

We followed the line of traffic into a parking lot where a teenager armed with an orange flashlight waved us into a parking place between an old Chevy and a Toyota.

When Mother and I stepped out of the Impala, the cold Northwest air was as crisp and wet as a stalk of celery. We searched the trunk for warm clothes and pulled on a couple of fleeces before entering the festival.

As promised, first thing, we stepped into the midst of a food court specializing in clams. In addition to an assortment of clam concoctions, there were tacos and burgers, sausage and curly fries, baked potatoes and chicken teriyaki, smoked salmon and roasted corn. There was a selection of fried sweets—fried bread the size of elephant ears, Twinkies and Oreos.

The smell of grilled onions and fried food tempted me into trying a clam burger with onion rings. Mother ordered clam chowder served in a bowl of homemade bread. We elbowed our way to the corner of a picnic table and squeezed in beside a family from Forks. The teenage girl chomped into a hamburger apparently forgetting she was wearing fangs because one of them fell out onto the table.

"Get it," she said, as it rolled dangerously close to the table edge near Mother.

Mother pinched it and presented it to the girl. "Here it is, safe and sound."

"Thank you so much." The girl smiled revealing a mouth full of perfect teeth plus one fang. She immediately set about replacing her second fang by turning to her brother and asking for his assistance.

The father leaned over and said, "I apologize. We're from Forks and this whole vampire thing has gotten totally out of hand. But what are you going to do?" He threw his hands in the air in mock exasperation.

I had already determined they were from Forks because of their matching tee shirts—Native Vampires, Forks, Washington. I knew about Forks from reading the vampire series in Polunsky and, on a fatherly level, sympathized with the bewildered dad. What would I do if Lacy came home wearing a pair of fangs?

After resolving the fang crisis, we discovered we were seated near the stage of the talent contest where a pleasant-looking and very distinguished gentleman demonstrated bird calls. Normally, this kind of thing wouldn't interest me, but when he imitated a screech owl, I felt like the bird was flying right over me.

From another stage, I could hear the sound of The Stones. "Do you mind if I check that out?" I said to Mother nodding to a huge tent across from the food court.

"I'll be right here people watching," she said. "It's lovely."

"I have my cell."

I was hoping to find the girl from the boat. She did say she would be here. When I entered the tent, I was relieved to see the event was restricted to ages twenty-one and older. I didn't figure the girl from the boat was the type to hang out with a bunch of teenyboppers.

Just as the band started in on the classic set finisher—"Jumping Jack Flash"—the girl from the boat appeared dressed in jeans and a black tank top. With her clean, make-up free face, freckles and good looks, she was America's sweetheart and Bond girl all rolled up into one sexy woman. And, in that tank top, she also looked cold.

"Hey," I said, then added cleverly, "Ahoy."

"Oh, Mr. Ahoy. You made it."

"We're here and like you said, lots of clams."

"Where's your mother?"

"Listening to bird calls."

"That would be Ovid," she said. "He's very good."

"I noticed," I said, crouching and covering my head as I added, "I ducked when I heard his screech owl."

She laughed and looking to her side said, "This is Sarah, my best friend."

"Jumping Jack Flash" turned out to be a hit. Everyone was yelling, "Gas, gas, gas."

Sarah said, "C'mon Gallagher, let's dance."

She grabbed my hand and pulled me along with them to the dance floor which was really only a few feet away because the whole house was rocking. I could see the ring on Sarah's finger. Gallagher's fingers were bare.

I'm a decent dancer on account of my mother. She was a rock 'n' roller herself and firmly believed dancing was a spiritual experience. Anyway, the three of us—Sarah, Gallagher and I— were bouncing away, pointing fingers and shaking our hips like contestants on "Dancing with the Stars" without the ballroom touches.

"You're not a bad dancer," Gallagher said. "Most guys are pretty lame."

"Wait until they play a two-step."

Sarah and Gallagher exchanged glances.

Sarah said, "Are you a redneck?"

"Not all Texans are rednecks," I said glancing at Gallagher and tossing my head her way.

"And not all rednecks are Texans," Gallagher said.

Gallagher had the voice of someone who shouted

orders and made snap decisions rather than one who took them. Yesterday, she was certainly in charge of the man on the boat. But there was another guy. Was he in the position of telling her what to do?

"You ever dance the two-step?" I directed the question to Sarah just to play it cool.

Gallagher was out of my league on every level. Whatever confidence I once enjoyed with women, I lost in Polunsky.

Sarah said, "You'll just have to show us."

That I could do. I pushed through the crowd until I reached the band. The lead guitar player was just stepping off the bandstand.

"Can you play a two-step?" I said, slipping him a twenty.

"A two-step? For twenty bucks, I'll play two. Thanks, man."

He pocketed the bill and headed over to the men's room for his break. Giving him a twenty was a little extravagant on my part. I'd explain to Mother later. We were living well on this mission on account of Mother's health. I didn't believe for one minute she was about to die, though she talked of it casually. Rather, ever since Calvery's death, and all this business about thin places, I did have a heightened sense that we were all living on borrowed time.

A few minutes after I slipped the lead guitar player a twenty, The Sea Otters struck the first chords of "I've Got Friends in Low Places", and, still reluctant to get close to this girl Gallagher, I offered my hands to Sarah.

When Sarah and I were dancing, the fanged-girl shoved her way through the crowd towards us. She was flanked by a set of teenage boys dressed in matching outfits of tee shirts, high tops and red cargo capris pants. I was not actually certain whether the pants were called capris on men, probably not. I knew them for women only and thought they were called capris or pedal pushers. No doubt the style had hit the stores while I was in Polunsky. To me, they looked strange, but what did I know?

Despite the band, one of the boys was wired into his I-Pod. He placed a hand to his ear as if a foreign correspondent reporting a news bulletin. The boy spontaneously bounced with a hip hop step I'd seen done in prison.

The fanged-girl was laughing and rubbing the arm of the other boy as she moved her way toward me. "Hey, it's you." She squeezed in between me and Sarah. "I just love you so much."

I pulled back as abruptly as one would pull away from a hissing snake. All I could think was that fanged-girl was underage, and I was an ex-con.

Sarah smirked. "You get around," she said, eyeing the girl and her companions.

"How'd you get here?" I asked the girl.

"You're so phat. Thanks for your help with my fang. You were just so phat about it. I could tell you were...."

"Phat," Sarah said, clearly amused by the conversation.

"I just love you, man." The fanged-girl slid a lollipop between her two fangs.

This action was not meant to be seductive, it was to keep her from grinding her teeth. It was just one hint she was on X. She'd done it before, no doubt, or someone, the capris-wearing twins perhaps, kept a stash of lollipops in their pockets just in case someone wanted to trip.

"What've you been taking?"

Sweat covered her face even though I was still cool in my fleece. I was putting it all together. I'd never taken Ecstasy but knew enough about it to recognize it—the hug drug. She needed to go someplace else. She was bugging out.

"We need to get her out of here," I said, pulling Sarah along with us. "And, I can't go alone."

Gallagher joined us as we escorted the girl out of the dance.

"Who did this?" I took the girl by both her arms and looked her in the eyes.

She turned to Sarah. "You're so pretty. I just love your hair, it's so shiny."

She lifted a hand to Sarah's hair, and then as if she'd taken a hard knock on the head, she dropped to the floor with a hard thump. Her legs flexed into to her chest in a spasm. I touched one and it pushed at me kicking me in the face.

Gallagher knelt beside me. "Just hold her," I said. "It's a seizure."

A crowd gathered behind us.

"Are you sure she won't bite her tongue?"

"Just wait." I turned her head to the side. "Don't vomit. Just don't vomit." The girl's eyes were closed, and her eyeballs twitched under her lids. "I wish I knew who gave her that shit."

"X?"Gallagher asked.

"Looks like it."

"How old is she?"

"No idea. Not old enough." This was the kind of thing even a convict wouldn't tolerate. "If I got my hands on those guys, God help them."

The girl stopped spasming, and just as suddenly, she was still as an opossum.

"Oh, shit." I felt her wrist for a pulse. "You know CPR?" Gallagher nodded. I put my ear to the girl's mouth just as I had learned in Polunsky. She wasn't breathing. "Call 911," I yelled to the crowd.

I pinched the girl's nose and gave her a breath. Her mouth was sticky from the cherry pop. Gallagher pushed on the girl's chest. We weren't counting like they'd taught me. We were just playing it by ear. I'd forgotten all I had learned but figured anything was better than nothing. This went on for a minute or so, me and Gallagher working on the girl like med students in an ER.

"I need to switch," I said, inhaling a deep breath. "Please God, don't let her die."

"Amen," Gallagher said, taking over the breathing.

After Gallagher said "Amen", the air above vampire girl buzzed with ions. It felt like an August evening in

Texas just before a thunderstorm, when the heat gets trapped in the clouds and they spark with lightning. I put my ear to the girl's nose and mouth and felt her warm breath, watched her chest rising and falling. My own chest pounded, I sat gasping. From the goosebumps on my arms, to the throbbing in my veins, I felt like I was the one just given a second chance.

Calvery's voice came into my head. There are places where the thin veil between this earth and the next is lifted, and you will know the mind of God. It only lasts a second, maybe not even that long. But you will remember it forever.

He went on to tell me about the time one of his fishermen fell off the boat trying to land a halibut. Somehow the line got tangled around his feet, and the halibut was so large that it pulled the fisherman out of the boat. Calvery cut the line, jumped in that forty-five degree water, and grabbed his buddy, a guy named Butch, just as he took a huge gulp of the Pacific.

The ocean was still and this gray color pressed down on Calvery, then a moment later it was bright and blue. Calvery had no sense of the frigid water, instead a warmth filled him from deep in his chest. He wrapped an arm around Butch and then popped him so hard on the sternum that a lungful of water vomited from his mouth.

Butch coughed and in a sputtering voice said, "I thought I was dead."

"Keep treading water or you will be," Calvery said. "I can only hold on so long."

"I was headed down this dark tunnel," Butch said. "Then all of sudden everything was sunny. You think I was dead?"

Calvery said he figured Butch was dead or mighty close. He rescued him all right. Calvery said it was the first time he had encountered a thin place. I'm betting it wasn't the last.

In that second, when I was remembering Calvery's story, vampire girl opened her eyes and took a dazed look at the world.

Gallagher said, “You did it.”

When I turned, there was Mother. She smiled at me, and I had the sense I was a young boy who had hit a home run, and that maybe I’d knocked my shame and guilt out of the park.

I wanted to ask Gallagher if she noticed vampire girl’s soul returning to her body, and I wanted to ask vampire girl if she had felt it, but a crowd of people surrounded us. The EMS had arrived and took charge.

Chapter Thirteen

After the crowd at the carnival had cleared, Mother and I arranged to join Gallagher in the morning for her next charter. The Forks family rushed off to the hospital with their daughter; the capris twins got arrested. Miraculously, I was not blamed for any of this, in fact I was a hero. This was a new experience for me, and I vowed not to get a big head about it.

Mother wanted me to rendezvous with Gallagher again. I guess she felt bad for me, being locked up so long, being newly divorced. She also felt I deserved a reward for saving a girl's life.

I was so anxious to see Gallagher again that I spent the rest of the night making up clever conversation. In fact, on the way home from the carnival, Mother counseled me on the art of flirting. After my pathetic display the first afternoon Gallagher and I met, she realized I needed a lesson from Dating 101. It was just dumb luck I had managed to land Brooke. Sure I made people laugh, and as far as looks, some people said I was easy on the eyes. Mostly, I reckon, the competition in Bayport was lame. Though, as I recently discovered, Brooke had found my replacement without any difficulty.

The fact was: Brooke was pre-prison. A lot of things had changed in three years. To say I felt a bit rusty was an understatement. Nothing zaps the confidence from a guy like three years of lock-up.

I welcomed Mother's advice—compliment her looks, show interest in her and everything she says and does, don't talk about me, and whatever I do, don't talk about prison. Yes, it was a little embarrassing to be in this situation, consulting my mother about dating, but pride goeth before destruction. Above all, I didn't want to blow my first shot at a girl in three years."

When I boarded the boat, Gallagher said, "Word in town is you saved that girl."

"Me," I said. "What about you?"

"You figured it out."

The sun broke through the mist and hit her hair. It sparked with red and gold. I wanted to slide my hand through it to see if it was real.

"You flatter me," I said eating it up. "But, hey, I'll take it. That's just the kind of guy I am."

"Puhleeze. Anyway, she's good."

"Glad to hear it," I said. "Seriously. That kind of thing doesn't happen every day. Maybe even every life."

"You may be right about that." She sounded thoughtful as she said it.

I motioned for her to follow me to the bow and passed her a twenty. "I want this trip to be extra special."

"A birthday?" she asked. Her cheeks were flushed with red as if from exertion.

I shook my head. "I wish. She's got this cancer I guess. A bucket list trip maybe." I glanced at mother who was talking to the older man, the Captain I supposed. "She looks good, don't you think?"

"You'll have a wonderful time, I'll see to it." Gallagher started to turn away, then with a puzzled look on her face, she said, "It's sweet. Taking your mother on a charter."

I suppose that was the moment I fell for her. I admit I was easy to impress after three long years of sleeping alone. But the way she looked at me, this woman was different.

She guided me to the wheelhouse where she asked

me to sign in on her captain's log. The captain's log held a position of honor on a small table inside. The girl handed me a pen and opened the cover. On the top of the page it said: Perpetuity, Captain Gallagher.

"That the Captain?" I pointed to the rusty old guy tying knots on deck.

"Why would you say that?"

"You mean it's you?"

She nodded.

"I thought maybe the other guy, I mean I didn't know…"

She laughed. "How's that shoe taste?"

"I'm not the kind of guy that thinks a woman can't drive a boat," I said. "I'm sure women can do it as well as men."

"Keep chewing on that foot," she said laughing.

"Give me a break."

"Just kidding," she said. "You're not the first man, or woman for that matter, to show their prejudice. I get it all the time."

"Sorry." Truly I was. "What do I call you then?"

"You can call me Captain." She turned to leave the wheelhouse, then said, "And you can call him Butch."

I was hoping to find out her first name, but she wasn't biting. But Butch, that was the name of the man Calvery saved. It was a common name I supposed. I looked out over the water, into the morning light and the tide bouncing against the boat. It looked like the pictures I'd seen in the magazines at Polunsky—*Attitudes and Latitudes*—one of my favorites. It pictured all those exotic places we hoped to visit one day. And here I was. I was a lucky son-of-a-bitch. Deep inside I knew I'd made it.

Mother and I settled at the bow, and Butch moved from one post to the next untying the boat. Captain Gallagher climbed up from what I assumed was the engine room. When Butch saw the Captain, he ran over to her. I barely heard him say, "Everything all right?"

She shook her finger at him. He nodded, said "Okay,

okay."

Seated in the cabin, she pushed a button, pulled a throttle and fired up the engine. Her dog, Jazz, followed her wherever she went. This dog was big. I felt like he'd be at home on some long lost voyage with a clan of Vikings. He had an intimidating air of confidence when he looked at me, no doubt considering whether or not he approved of the stranger. A thousand generations of hunting hound made its point in his canine teeth, easily as long as my pinkie finger. The last word I'd use to describe him was hypoallergenic. This was a hunting hound, and he was betrothed to his beautiful master.

As we chugged out of the bay past some other small charters, we all waved. Captain Gallagher was intent on steering through the harbor. Butch kept checking in on her, coming back to us to report: it was a calm sea of two to four feet, they say there's good fishing over at the rock pile, still some Coho in the ocean though some of them have started their run up the river.

Mother said she didn't care much about fishing. Just seeing the sights was good enough for her.

I zeroed in on the water and looked over the side for fish until the shocking cold spray hit my face. Mother zipped up her windbreaker, then pointed to where a great blue heron stood in the shallows scanning the ocean for fish.

When we reached the end of the harbor, the boat tipped port side. Mother squealed and Butch ran up to her, "We're entering rougher waters now, ma'am. You just keep your eyes on the horizon and you'll be fine."

Captain Gallagher gunned the engine. We took on speed, bounced over the waves. When she called Butch, he ran up to the cabin. Mother gripped the side of the boat and grinned as the wind blasted her face, nevertheless, I convinced her to move into an indoor seating area. Meanwhile, Butch had taken over at the wheel leaving the Captain free to talk to us. She had tied a ribbon around her hair but it refused to be contained, its red coils falling onto her forehead and cradling the curve of her neck. I stood, the boat shifted and I grabbed the air.

She caught my arm and laughed. "Your sea legs haven't sprouted yet."

Her clothes smelled of diesel, but a flowery scent wafted off her hair. It was an oddly erotic combination.

"We're stopping in Coho for lunch. It's a cute place. You'll love it. We won't be there too long, long enough to fuel up and eat a bite. Normally I cook. But this time, I thought we'd stop and eat, since we need to fuel up and all."

"You don't normally stop?" Mother cradled a cup of coffee between her palms.

The girl looked up at Butch, then down at the engine room. She glanced at her watch. "It's just that… I thought maybe you'd like to see the real Canada."

"I hope you're not doing this all just for me. I would never want to put you out of the way. I'm sure my son told you I'm dying—."

"You're not dying," I protested.

"We're all dying." Mother glanced at me then turned to Captain Gallagher. "He's kind of protective."

"You're not putting me out of my way. I need to stop there anyway. Now, if you'll excuse me, I'll go check on Butch."

I wondered if I had said the wrong thing, because she didn't talk with us the rest of the way to Coho. I wanted to catch her eye and will her back to talk with us, but she maintained her distance. Then there was Butch. Maybe he was her father. But then why did she call him Butch?

As we slowed into the bay around Coho, Mother and I went back outside. Large ropes of kelp, deep olive green with shiny bulbs, floated in the water. A fuzzy-faced otter surfaced and somersaulted in and out of the kelp bed.

Up in the cabin, Butch and the captain conversed in lowered voices.

A couple of old totem poles stood on a hillside just before we reached Coho. It was much smaller than Clam Harbor and didn't look like a tourist stop. As we approached the dock, I counted only ten boats in port.

A man who looked like a bona-fide American Indian rushed up to us. “Welcome to Canada.”

Canada? Did I need a passport?

“You Chloe Gallagher?” The man held out his hand to our captain. “Millard Free.”

I coughed. Mother started to speak. I elbowed her. I mouthed, “Chloe. Couldn’t be? Don’t say anything. We don’t know her. Got it?”

Mother shook her head at me and gave me the look.

I had a bad feeling about the name Chloe. Lots of girls were named Chloe after all. No reason to believe this was Calvery’s daughter.

Chloe conferred with the Indian, turning her head every few seconds to check in on us. I approached her, but as soon as I got within ear shot, she stopped her conversation.

She turned to me and said politely, “So, here we are.”

It was okay with me. For once in my life, I was at a loss for words. Just being close to her made me nervous.

Chapter Fourteen

Chloe stood face-to-face with Millard. She was conscious of Lucia and Finn, worried about what Millard might say. "I didn't expect…I mean Duke didn't tell me who would meet me," Chloe said to Millard.

"Who'd you expect, Bill Gates?" He had a twinkle in his eye that seemed permanently affixed to his pupil.

"Sorry." She wondered how he had interpreted her comment. Probably exactly how she hadn't wanted him to. He looked like the type of guy who picked up on subtle nuances let alone not-so-subtle ones.

In fact, Millard struck her as the kind of man who stared down bears. His chest bulged under a red and black flannel shirt. When he pushed his sleeves up to his elbows, he exposed the forearms of someone who felled logs.

She headed back to Perpetuity. Chloe needed to lose the tourists, even if she did find that guy Finn more than a little attractive, she couldn't afford to have them hanging around.

"We'll be here about an hour and a half. Why don't you go into town and get some lunch?" Chloe took hold of Butch's arm. She turned to Millard and held up a finger.

Tugging Butch to the end of the dock, she said, "I need for you to keep them entertained. You'll keep your mouth shut, won't you?" Jazz followed at her heels.

"I think I need to be here to help you."

"Look at Millard. He's a nice guy. Nothing's going to happen. Do this for me? I can't be worrying about you right now."

Truth was, either way she worried about Butch blabbing to the guy and his mother, Finn and Lucia Tully. Interesting name, Finn. The way he joked and took care of his mother made her want to know more of his story. If she weren't about to transfer the goods—wasn't that the phrase for it?—she might suggest a walk in the woods, show Finn the sights. She often wondered about her future? Would she ever fall in love? Most women her age had two kids in diapers by now. Chloe shook her head, tossing the thoughts away. Two tanks full of liquor sloshed about in the bilge of her boat. Why on earth had she ever agreed to do this?

Butch and Chloe headed back up the dock. Sun warmed her face and for once they might actually have a day without rain.

Perhaps too cheerily, Chloe nudged Butch toward her passengers and said, "You guys go have a good time. I'll catch up."

"So this is Canada?" Finn said. "I don't need a passport?"

Chloe pointed to the town and laughed. "No, there's no check point here."

"You need some help?" Finn sidled up to her, leaning into her, his face taking in the glow of the sun.

"Uh." Chloe shifted her eyes and stepped away from him, talking past Finn's bright face. "That's okay."

"I'd like to."

"Really, you're a guest."

"It'd be fun."

"Take the Tullys up to town," she motioned for Butch. Seeing the disappointment in Finn's face, she said, "I need to take care of some boat business. You go with your mother."

"I guess I'll see you later?" Finn phrased the sentence in the form of a question.

She hated running him off. Nice guy taking his mother on a trip. If only she could do the same with her mother.

As the three of them left, Butch was already giving them an earful. She heard him talking about the Indians, I mean Native Americans, he said. It was a safe topic, and for that Chloe was grateful. If only he could keep it up.

Millard pushed a big white tank, like a propane tank, up to Perpetuity. He uncoiled a flexible hose, three-inches in diameter, with wire coils covered in rubber or plastic, and handed the end to Chloe. "You need to screw this fitting onto your fuel tank." He emphasized the word fuel and winked. "Do you need my help?"

She looked at the black hard plastic fitting, "You just screw it on?"

"That's it."

Seeing Millard at ease relaxed Chloe. She scanned the tiny harbor. Butch and the others had disappeared; the streets of the tiny village were largely empty. Nothing to be worried about. Just a normal day. A boat captain refueling.

"C'mon Jazz. We got work to do." Jazz jumped onto the boat.

Chloe pulled the hose down onto the boat, down into the galley. She tugged the mattress off the berth to expose the door to the bilge. With a jerk, she lifted it, then lowered herself into the engine room. Her underarms were sticky with sweat. She pulled her windbreaker over her head and tossed it out onto the berth. Just a few trips to get the bills paid. What could it hurt?

The inflatable tank, a rectangular bag of dark green extra-heavy plastic, bulged with liquor. She loosened the cap and screwed the hose into place. That was easy.

Chloe climbed out of the bilge and returned up top where Millard and a small child were tossing bread up to the gulls.

When he saw Chloe, Millard said, "All set?"

"Ready as I'll ever be." Chloe and Jazz stood mid-deck and looked up at Millard. "You've done this before without any trouble?"

"You must keep calm to be invisible."

"That's your advice?"

"If you're nervous the Big Holy can't protect you." He flipped the switch of a pump, the motor kicked on. "And it's always good to have the Big Holy on your side." He laughed and winked at her.

"Are you making fun of me?"

"Maybe just a little," Millard said. "When you white people land in Coho, you expect some of our Native American wisdom."

"All right, all right," Chloe said. "You made your point."

A little girl came running down the dock. He knelt, opened his arms, and she jumped onto his knee.

"Here's my daughter, Happy." Millard stood from his crouched position holding Happy tight against his chest.

It was the perfect name for her. Happy smiled broadly revealing a dark gap where her two front teeth would have been. This confirmed Chloe's estimate that Happy was about six years old. Happy wore plaid shorts and a red-striped sleeveless shirt with a hole near its hem. Her black ponytail matched her father's.

"I like dogs." Happy placed her hand in front of Jazz's muzzle.

"This is Jazz. He likes girls."

Happy started to climb onto the boat, but Millard stopped her. "Not now. You stay up here with me." He grabbed Happy by a hand. "Miss Thomas, you better get back down there and watch the bag. Let me know when it's empty. Then, we'll transfer to the other bag. You do have two tanks, don't you?"

When Chloe returned up top, Happy was waiting on the dock dangling her little brown legs over the edge. Jazz jumped up beside her. Happy pulled back at first, then let him sniff her face.

"All right now, Happy," Millard said. "I guess we're ready to go. Come on Chloe, I'll show you the town."

Coho consisted of two paved roads—one running

along the bay and one down the main street making a "T" in the village. It had the shabby look of a reservation—a cluster of manufactured homes in an area just to west of town, a pot-holed main street and a rusted pick-up abandoned on the shore.

"Nice town," Chloe said.

On main street, four of the eight businesses were boarded up leaving a saloon, a grocery, a hardware store and a gas station/auto store. The words—Everything Must Go— were painted on the window of an out-of-business furniture store.

Millard was silent as they headed down the dock. Chloe regretted her sarcasm.

"We used to have a nice village here," Millard said.

"I'm sorry," Chloe said. "I didn't mean to insult your town."

"You can't insult a man with words unless he allows it."

"Good," Chloe said. "I mean, Clam Harbor is looking pretty shabby these days as well."

"Can't cut the trees, the salmon are leaving, and the tourists all go to Victoria," Millard said. "That's why I'm doing this smuggling with you. I'm doing it for Coho."

"I'm doing it for me."

"I believe you're hiding part of the truth. You're a good person, I can feel that." He pulled the tank along behind him. "You're our only business now, you know."

Chloe brushed it off. This man knew enough about her already. Happy and Jazz ran ahead, then circled back. Coho was a pathetic place in the foothills of a rainforest covered in madrone, Douglas-fir and manzanita. The branches of the trees and bushes, damp from the morning fog, glistened in the sun. At least it had that going for it. She wondered if the Tullys were disappointed, if they were asking each other why she would take tourists to this place. And Butch, what was he saying? Please let him keep his mouth shut. She wasn't the nervous type, she reminded herself. No one would suspect her. No one would suspect alcohol. She could make a thousand a trip.

That would go a long way to fixing the boat and helping her mother. She had sent Spud Olson her last thousand dollars to get her father's ashes. It was only fitting she should turn into a criminal to pay for it.

Happy ran up to her father. "Jazz loves me."

Millard picked her up, "Well, I love you more."

Chloe looked on, trying to push away her envy. Vaguely, she remembered having a father. How he came home from fishing, how she rushed to the door, arms waving in the air, her little legs competing with themselves as she ran. Inevitably he lifted her up against his Mackintosh still slick and cool from a day of fishing, like a wet balloon rolling over her skin.

Most of all, his smell stuck in her mind. To this day, every time she landed a fish, the smell of her father came to mind, the scent of fish so linked to her father's memory that when she pulled in a catch it was impossible to tell whether she was actually smelling the new salmon on the boat or calling up the olfactory memory of him.

"How are you, my little green sprout?" He always said. For that was what her name meant—young, green sprout. Chloe always responded with a giggle, "I'm not green." Then, he tickled her and said, "Oh yeah, you look green here and here and here." The two of them laughed until finally her mother intervened with a stern admonition such as, you'll ruin her dinner.

After Chloe helped Millard stow the tank in a pump station at the end of the pier, Millard gave her a tour of the village. Main Street started only a few steps off the dock. They passed a post office, a café, a grocery, a general store. In front of the store—Eaglefeather's—stood a small totem with beavers, salmon, bear, eagles and elk carved into it. A laughing Indian with an elaborate headdress crowned the totem. Next to the carving, the store window displayed a collection of neon beer signs: Olympia, Henry Weinhard's and Labatt's.

The centerpiece of Coho—a church with a tall white steeple—butted up against a forested hillock at the far end of Main Street. The church looked old, maybe a century, maybe built by missionaries, and its construction was far superior to the other buildings on the street. Fog had lowered onto the church steeple, softening its pointed tip. The scene might have qualified as scenic except for next to the church some misguided city planner had planted a cinderblock building, the Marmot Brewery and Bottling Company.

"This all there is to the town?" Chloe asked.

Millard shrugged. "Disappointed, eh?"

"Not at all. I just wondered where Happy goes to school." She watched as Happy led Jazz down the boardwalk in front of the town's few stores.

"I'll show you." He led her into The Coho Inn. She motioned for Jazz to stay, but Millard waved her on. "Bring him in."

Before stepping inside, Chloe conjured up a picture of a quaint inn with knotty pine walls and western furniture. However, instead they stepped onto the entryway of a hotel built from thin plywood and rolled linoleum. To her right, there was a small sitting room with two over-stuffed chairs, their armrests threadbare and the upholstery scarred by frequent visits from cats. Jazz started his way around the room, sniffing.
Chloe followed Millard through the café and into another room at the far corner of the café.

"This is my house." Millard waved his hand over a large square room. He kept walking through the room and Chloe followed. They reached another door leading into what looked to be a converted garage, at the back stood a potbelly stove and at the front of the room was a blackboard. "And, here's the school."

"You run the school?"

"My wife does." He took a piece of chalk and drew a beaver on the board. "I've got the dubious honor of presiding as the hyas tyee, the great Chief, around here. That's why I'm smuggling. How about you?"

His honesty surprised her. Compared to this, she was rolling in it. She felt just a little bit guilty. Millard had mouths to feed and apparently a school to run. No wonder he was smuggling alcohol.

"Just broke, that's all," Chloe said, walking toward a bookshelf .

"You don't want to tell me. That's fine," Millard said, sketching an elk next to the beaver. "We all got our troubles. But you're helping us. You should know that."

"I didn't sign up for that." Chloe pulled the Tales of Paul Bunyan from the shelf. Looking at Babe the Blue Ox and Paul put a smile on her face.

"You are, all the same," he said.

"How do you know that guy Duke?"

"He used to like to come fishing up here. Maybe he was smuggling marijuana, I don't know. When the Canadian taxes on liquor got so high, he approached me with this scheme."

"You trust him, then?"

"As much as I'd trust a drunk to set chokers." He laughed at his joke. "But what're you gonna do?" He took hold of her elbow and led her out of the room. "C'mon now. Let's get your lunch."

"It's all right, really."

"My wife will be waiting for you."

As promised, Millard's wife was standing in the café waiting for them. "We have fish and chips or fry bread sandwiches."

"I'm looking for my friends. Two men and a woman. She was—."

The woman merely motioned to the chalkboard menu, the oil-cloth covered tables, the kitchen door, "I know, I know. They went on up to the falls. You better eat." She ushered her to a table. "What will you have, the fish or a sandwich?"

Chloe glanced at her watch. "Where is it?"

"You eat."

The woman hustled through two swinging doors into the kitchen and muttered in a Native American tongue. A few minutes later, she returned with a sandwich wrapped in wax paper.

When Chloe tried to pay for it, Millard's wife said,

"My husband told me to take good care of you."

In the course of the last hour, Chloe had risen in the ranks, promoted from broke boat captain to the savior of Coho. The trip hadn't been that difficult. After all was said and done, the transfer of the alcohol was as easy as fueling up. Not a bad day's work. And now she was sitting in a café in Canada, the wife of her co-conspirator hovering over her, topping off her tea glass, handing Jazz bits of smoked salmon, and, finally, presenting her with a slice of wild blueberry pie. She was a rum-runner. She was a criminal. She was royalty.

Chloe grinned as she closed the door to the hotel-café-schoolroom home of the Free family. So this was how it felt to have a little money: strangers deferring to her, her every need attended to. A nice change from people feeling sorry for her, she had to admit. Now, she could feel sorry for them.

She jaywalked across the main street and headed toward the church and the brewery. On a path between them, a small wooden sign said: Whitehorse Falls .25 mi. Jazz trotted down the path ahead of her about twenty feet, then returned.

Chloe said, "Let's go."

Reaching beyond her normal stride to keep up with Jazz, she soon heard the roar of the waterfall. Chloe stopped to catch her breath and smooth her hair. When she saw Tully again, she didn't want to seem out-of-breath. His hazel-colored eyes, and toothy, child-like smile made her breathless enough.

Jazz barked at a rustling in the sword ferns, then ran into the woods to follow whatever it was. The trail curved around a boulder and immediately the grade turned steep.

By the time she reached the top, the temperature had dropped a couple degrees. Chloe took a deep breath. The air tasted like gin and the spray from the falls was the tingling tonic. From her elevated view, Whitehorse Creek tumbled along, bypassing boulders for calm, deep pools where trout nibbled on algae-covered rocks, or twisting into eddies where swirling bubbles disappeared into rapids. Finn, bright and animated, with his arm on the back of the bench behind his mother, took it all in. She watched the scene and felt a pang of jealousy. They turned to look at her.

Butch rushed over to her. "Everything all right?"

"Of course, why wouldn't it be?" She gave him a look that said, You idiot, please stop talking. Butch often missed subtle nuances.

She noticed Finn looking at her and straightened her spine. He stood and walked toward her, combing his slicked-back hair with his fingers. This only succeeded in messing his hair further. However, the effect was sexy and looked straight out of GQ.

"I guess we'd better go," Chloe said in a loud, clear voice.

Finn stood beside her now. She felt the heat of his body, or she imagined she did. This was ridiculous. It was physical. An attraction she hadn't experienced since high school when she first kissed Jay Brenner in the backseat of his Jeep. For a woman alone in a small town, it was easy to have your pick of men, and easier to stop a waterfall from crashing over a ledge than to say no to their advances and go home to a cold, empty bed. It never felt right, but a warm body next to her didn't feel wrong either.

The thought of going to bed with Finn caused an uncomfortable sensation starting in her chest and surging down inside her. She glanced at him and caught him looking at her, and there was no mistaking his expression. He looked at her with complete admiration. She quickly turned away, embarrassed for him, embarrassed for her.

"I'm glad you brought us here." Mrs. Tully interrupted Chloe's thoughts.

Chloe plopped onto the bench, pushed thoughts of Finn away, felt the weight of the day slough off her as she stared at the spray and mist. How long had she been sitting there saying nothing? Chloe made eye contact with Mrs. Tully and noticed the woman's eyes moist with tears.

"Are you all right?" Chloe said finally.

"It's just so beautiful. The world is so beautiful." Mrs. Tully wept. "Don't mind me. And please call me Lucia."

Finn joined in. "She cries at everything. You get used to it."

Lucia pulled her hood off her head and revealed sprouts of very short gray hair, the all-too-typical breast cancer cut. "He's right. Some of us around here don't cry enough," Lucia said. "It'd do him good to have a good cry sometime. That's the whole problem with him. Tries to act tough—"

"Mother, I'm sure Chloe is not interested in hearing about me and my problems."

Actually, Chloe wanted very much to hear about them. She laughed. "Oh, but I would. Please do go on, Lucia."

Finn positioned himself in front of his mother, pointed his finger at her in mock irritation. "Okay, let me put it another way, I don't want to listen to you talking about my problems. Like you said, this place is beautiful."

Lucia slapped Tully on the hand, "Go play on the rocks." She turned to face Chloe. Leave us girls alone."

Tully shrugged and ran down to the creek where Jazz and Butch were examining a dead trout.

"So how is it you ended up a boat captain?" Lucia locked eyes with her. She had the earnest look of those anti–death penalty people, that let-me-help-you look.

"My father left it to me."

Lucia nodded. Silence followed. If Chloe had it her way, the conversation would stop there. But she knew the next questions would be about her father: Is he dead? How did he die? How long has he been gone?

Lucia cleared her throat. "I'm so sorry. Are you on your own then?"

Chloe snickered at Butch and Finn as they checked out trout beached on the rocks. They looked like a couple of junior high boys. "No, my mother lives here."

"How nice," Lucia said. "Does she come out on the boat with you?"

"She's ill."

After a minute, Lucia said, "What's your mother's name? I'll pray for her."

A rainbow shimmered in the spray of the falls, and Chloe stared into it. "If you like, if you believe in it. Her name is Sally."

"I've always liked that name, a happy name," Lucia said. "I was just sitting here thinking of all the people who have gone before us." Lucia watched the falls with a dreamy look. "How many have there been do you think? As many as the drops of water in the waterfall?"

"I suppose so," Chloe said.

"Maybe one day your soul lives in the waterfall, the next in a cloud." She turned to Chloe, her eyes were matter of fact and nonjudgmental. "I'm dying. I want to believe I'll end up wherever I want to go. Indulge me."

"I agree, it's a nice thought."

"You believe we have a soul?"

Chloe paused. She never wasted her time thinking about such things, things you could never know the answer to. "Maybe."

"Think about it, when you die, all that energy has to go somewhere," Lucia said. "It's physics. You believe in atoms and you can't see them."

Chloe wanted to believe that her father's spirit might be floating nearby. But it was too far-fetched. "You're right, I do believe in atoms."

"You don't need to see them or even understand them to believe in them, right?"

"I suppose I don't," Chloe said.

"The spirits bring comfort to you, if you let them," Lucia said. "Have you ever hiked alone in the forest, or ran on the beach, and then all of a sudden felt connected to every living person and every living thing. Maybe you even turned around to see if anyone else was with you, but no one was there—it was only the whole universe opened up to you. And you knew that no matter what happened to you, you'd be all right. That's the way I feel right now."

It had been a long time since Chloe had felt like that, but she knew exactly what Lucia was talking about. When Chloe was younger, before she knew her father was on death row, she had known happiness or at least peace. Out on the boat with Butch when all was tranquil and nothing existed but the sound of water lapping against the hull and a cool breeze drifting up from the sea, she had always felt at peace.

She had experienced the same sensation climbing the steep trails to Cat's Paw or hiking along the Humptulips River. How pleasant to have her chest tight with exertion, to watch her breath form miniature clouds in the brisk air, to enter into the silent forest, dimly lit like a cathedral, air heavy with the incense of fir boughs.

But then, that was years ago.

Chloe pulled up her sleeves and glanced at her watch. It was one o'clock. "We need to go."

Finn stayed uncomfortably close to Chloe while they hiked up the trail leading away from the falls.

"How about showing us more of the sights tomorrow? We'll fish." He ran a few steps in front of her, pivoted and grinned. "We've got cash."

She shook her head. "I can't tomorrow."

"Then, how about dinner? Tonight?" Finn put his hands in prayer position. "Oops, I mean…" He quickly brought his hands apart and put one on his heart.

So she hadn't turned him off. She found it touching that he was so considerate of his mother. Dinner with a good-looking man might be a nice way to end the day.

"I don't usually—"

"Life is too short for I don't usually." He put his hand on her shoulder. "Look, I don't blame you. I've been there myself. I just thought maybe we could get together. We might have plenty in common."

Butch and Lucia passed by them. An awkward quietness filled the air.

"I guess you're right. Life is too short. Dinner it is."

She whistled for Jazz who was down at the creek lapping at the foaming water. He bounded up to them. “Watch out,” she said as Jazz shook, and a shower of Whitehorse Creek descended upon them.

Chapter Fifteen

I took a new razor blade out of the package and slid it into my Trac II. In prison, the thing I missed most was the bathroom. Imagine being under surveillance day in and day out, twenty-four seven. You can't take a crap alone, never mind take the time to steam up a mirror for a good shave. I pushed my cheek out with my tongue, sliding the razor over the stubble of my face and creating a nice path down the middle of a thick layer of shaving cream.

Chloe seemed like a nice girl. She couldn't be the real Chloe. She didn't look like she was grieving. A memory gnawed at me. It was just too much of a coincidence.

I ran out of the bathroom to the box of Calvery's belongings where Chloe's picture was stowed in the Bible. "Mother, hey, look at this." Picture in hand I rushed out to the couch. "Does this look like the same girl?"

Mother examined the picture, then looked up at me with a puzzled expression. "Where'd you get this?"

"It's Calvery's daughter." I paused a moment to catch my breath. "I mean, when she was a little girl. The last time he saw her."

"Same girl."

"You sure?"

She nodded.

"I thought so, too." A sick feeling came over me. "What do I do now"

"You tell her about her father," Mother said. "That's why we came here."

"What if she didn't even know where her father was? Some parents do that. They hide things from their kids. What right do I have to be the one to tell her? Besides, I need to know if she even knew he had been executed. Calvery didn't say I had to break the news to her. You think she even knows her father was on death row?"

"You're just making excuses."

Mother always knew the truth.

"Okay, I don't want to tell her," I said. "I want to see where this goes."

"You'll have to tell her sometime. It's always better to put it on the table." Mother stretched her legs out on the couch and put her pencil to her mouth. "I guess you better get some lettuce for Sport while you're out. What is a four-letter word for Jazz's home?"

"You're asking the wrong guy."

"Seems like I've seen this on a crossword before." She erased her crossword.

"Maybe I don't come home," I said.

"Maybe you better tell her before you do anything like that. It'll backfire on you. I'm telling you," Mother said. "Sure as a four-letter word for "stretches the truth" is liar."

My mother had warned me many times in my life, and like all the other times, I ignored her again. A man flooded by hormones often ignores wise advice. This time, I felt my cause more worthy. Instead of sneaking off to a dark alley to buy drugs, I was taking a girl on a date, in front of the whole of Clam Harbor, and I felt more than a little proud of myself.

I dabbed some whitening toothpaste on my brush. My teeth had lost a little of their sheen while I was in Polunsky. I'm not whining, just stating the facts. I brushed three minutes, counting one Mississippi, two Mississippi, with a steady beat until I reached one hundred eighty. This was another luxury I had missed while I lived at Polunsky. After rinsing, I flashed my teeth in the mirror. They were improving, the yellow tinge gradually disappearing.

"Utah," I said. "Jazz's home is Utah."

"Of course, the basketball team. That solves my puzzle," she said, placing her paper aside. "Would you like me to iron your jeans?"

Yes, I would like that, I thought, but I was not such an ingrate as to ask my dying mother to iron my pants. I shook my head. Anyway, I opted for the more relaxed look, a pair of stretched-out Levis my father would not be seen dead in. Another reason for me to rebel and wear them.

Chloe lived on a mountain outside of town, well, a mountain by my standards. Up here, they called it a foothill. By four o'clock the fog had descended and from the earth to the sky everything was gray, and wet, not as wet as the waterfall, but damp and moist with air that fizzed like Seven-Up. When I knocked on the door, Chloe's dog barked. She appeared at the door wearing a red sweater and jeans, un-pressed as well. I followed her into the living room and, at her direction, plopped onto a white couch in front of a piece of driftwood shaped liked an overturned armadillo. She'd turned the wood into a coffee table by covering it with a rectangular piece of glass. Her coffee table books included: Waterfalls of the World, Sailing Ships, The Pacific Northwest.

On her hearth lay three anchors—small, medium and large. Up on the mantle, I noticed a collection of pictures, but I resisted the temptation to inspect them.

After we shared an Anchor Steam, we drove into town. Chloe wanted to take me to a Mexican restaurant, but I knew better. Mother and I had stopped at one in Nevada and vowed not to eat Mexican again until we returned to Texas. Instead, Chloe and I ended up at an Italian restaurant named Luigi's.

We sat in a wooden booth in the back corner. A waiter greeted Chloe by name and lighted the candle—a long taper stuck in a fat jug of Chianti covered with drippings of multi-colored wax.

When I ordered a bottle of Prosecco, Chloe seemed pleased. It seemed a lot like a date. So far, I was doing all right.

"You all on your own?" I asked.

She acknowledged by inclining her head. Candlelight reflected from the tiny silver sea shells on her ears.

"How much time does she have?" Chloe asked in a voice just above a whisper.

"Huh?"

"Your mother."

My mother? How much time did she have? I had no idea. "She won't tell me. She looks good. Don't you think?"

"She does. You'd never know."

A sconce, etched in scarlet and gold, shone above her head. I was staring at her. She looked away.

I pointed to the light above her. "Sorry. It's like you have a crown on your head." She looked up into the light now illuminating her face. She was beautiful in a captain-of-a-boat way, all natural and hearty, not afraid to show the freckles on her face. "You look like the queen of Clam Harbor."

She laughed, picked up her glass and took a drink. "Not many men can just take off with their mother like that."

I was glad she changed the subject. Otherwise, I might have crawled under or over the table and kissed her. My mission seemed impossible. If I were to tell her who I was, it would ruin everything—this moment, and other moments.

"Let's just say I made the time."

It was true in a way. I had made the time.

"It's beautiful all the same. I love my mother. Do you remember when you thought your mother was the stupidest person on earth?"

"I don't," I said.

She pulled a piece of bread from the loaf on the table. I admired the way she buttered it. Brooke had always shied away from food, reluctant to let on she enjoyed it. Chloe stabbed at a cherry tomato in her salad and it jumped from the bowl and rolled across the table. I flicked it back to her side with my middle finger. She stopped it, like a seasoned soccer player, and then carefully aimed it to my side of the table. It rolled past my net and onto my lap. We laughed. I picked up the tomato from the bench beside me and set it on the table.

"So how did you get to be the captain of a boat?"

"I was born into it. My father sold fish. This was the only boat left when he died." Chloe leaned to the side, allowing the waiter to place a plate of eggplant parmesan in front of her.

Did she really not know what happened to her father? Maybe her mother never told her. Maybe they kept it a secret. After all, how do you tell a kid her father is on death row? She had to be only twenty-five, twenty-six at the most. How was I supposed to come in and drop this bomb on her? I couldn't do it.

"I like the name."

"Mother said my father named it."

"Where is your mother?"

"She's here in Clam Harbor."

I stabbed a clam and lifted it to her mouth.

"You should try this. I haven't had a meal like this in a long time."

She opened her mouth and then closed her lips over the fork. I watched as she chewed and swallowed it.

"Would you like to come over?"

"I have a daughter," I said. "I'm divorced."

"She here?"

"Yes, I'd like to come over."

Out the window, the harbor lights blinked on. When I looked back at her, she was leaning on the table resting her chin on her hand. "You ready?"

When we got back to her house, Chloe invited me into the kitchen to make drinks. She handed me a glass tumbler and pointed to her refrigerator. I opened the freezer, looked for the ice cube tray. It was hidden beneath several packages wrapped in butcher paper. For a single woman, she had an impressive freezer.

"You could live a month just on the food in the freezer."

"I cook. That's what I do. I cook for my fisherman, most of the time. You missed it, since it was a trip to Coho. But most of the time I cook lunch, grand gourmet lunches."

I took her in my arms, "I had a good time today."

She stood a few inches shorter than I, I guess she was close to five nine or ten, and we fit together nicely. Since she hadn't bolted, I kissed her, and while we kissed she reached a hand up under my shirt and slid her hand across my back. I opened my eyes and looked at her, tried to read her eyes. I needed to take this slow; I wanted to take this slow. My body was saying, Hurry up.

A hand had reached my chest and she squeezed my pec muscle, I flexed it.

She laughed and said, "Impressive."

I had a hard-on a cat couldn't scratch. But I wasn't about to make a move for the bedroom. Let's play this out nice and slow, I said to my pecker. It wasn't listening. Then she backed up, moving the hand to my belt buckle and tugging me toward her, we eased our way out of the kitchen, down the hallway and into her bed.

I kissed her again, rolling on top of her, pressing myself against her. "You are amazing," I said.

"I bet you say that to all the girls."

While she was unbuttoning my shirt, I thought if only she knew how wrong she was. I rolled this way and that to get my shirt off, tossed it on the floor.

From the darkness, a growl broke the silence. I jerked. "What the hell?" The muzzle of an Airedale was staring me in the face. It wasn't a particularly unfriendly stare, but when a seventy-pound dog stares you in the face, you pay attention. "Could you call off your dog?"

Jazz licked his lips, my concentration shifted from Chloe to this dog with the incisors of a lion.

"Place," she said. Jazz obliged and left the room. Just like that. She was not only a boat captain, but she knew how to talk to dogs. Also, I had the feeling he had been sent out of her room before. But that didn't matter. Not one bit.

A small night light shone down on her and reflected off her wet lips. I kissed her again and slipped my hand under her blouse to her breast just like she'd done to me. A moan escaped from her mouth. I swallowed it with my tongue and realized how impossible a task it was going to be to break the news about her father. I needed to keep things just like they were. But if I didn't tell her, no telling what Calvery might do. It was a helluva position to be in.

I pressed her against me and squeezed the cheeks of her beautiful behind. Her wild red hair tickled my chest. She moved her hands all over me, all the while whispering in my ear, and I felt lucky as a hound lost in Petco.

Chapter Sixteen

At five the next morning, Jazz licked Chloe's face. Finn was curled up like a cat, snoring slightly. It had been a wonderful night. She would want to see him again. Just her luck, he was from Texas. Never any decent men wanting to stay around.

She needed to be on the boat by six o'clock, so she might as well wake him up. Chloe went about her morning routine as usual, hoping the noise would rouse him. After letting Jazz out, she ran the shower. As she waited for the water to heat, she listened for Finn. His smells—sweat and a faint menthol—lingered on her skin. She stepped in the shower and soaped up.

"Hey, what about me?"

She flinched, dropped her soap. Chloe peeked out of the curtain.

"You're up early."

She looked down at his penis, which was anything but limp. "So are you."

"Mind if I join you?"

Chloe pulled the curtain aside, waved her arm for him to enter. Around Finn, she felt at ease. Maybe it was because he would be leaving soon. After last night, all her anxieties had disappeared. At least for the time being.

"I've got to get to work, so you'll have to make this quick."

"What if I go with you?"

She thought over her schedule. Another load of

alcohol, she couldn't risk him finding out about it.

"What about your mother? You did bring her up here to see the country. Why don't you take her on a drive around the peninsula, to Lake Quinalt?"

"I'll see you tonight?"

"I might need a rest."

"We could just take a walk on the beach."

After their shower, he joined her in the kitchen for coffee. This, too, felt comfortable, like they had shared many mornings. She packed her lunch and Butch's—four Albacore sandwiches on Ciabatta bread—and filled one thermos with raspberry tea and one with coffee. Tully stood bare-chested before the toaster watching two slices of Muesli bread. She admired his body—his well-developed pecs, his chiseled abs—and wished she hadn't given up her morning exercise routine.

"Who will be on your boat today?"

"Just me and Butch."

"Don't you have a charter?" He turned her around to him and kissed her. Still with his mouth on her lips, he said, "Then why do you need to go?"

"I…" She glanced at her watch. Chloe pushed him away with a playful shove. "I really need to get going. You're a bad influence."

"You trying to get rid of me? I don't see why I can't go with you."

"I thought we decided. You need to be with your mother."

"But I'll see you tonight?"

Maybe this had been a mistake. He didn't seem the clingy type, but his persistence made her nervous. On the other hand, if he disappeared today and she never saw him again, she would notice. She reached her hand down to his crotch and held him, the weight of his equipment pressing against her palm.

"I will see you tonight."

"What time?"

"Eight."

"That's too long." He grabbed her hand and pulled it

upward over his hardening penis. "Can't you be back sooner?"

Tully moved his lips all over her face. If he didn't stop soon she might have to cancel her trip.

She finally made it outside and into the truck. When she pulled away, she saw Tully in her rear view mirror. He lifted his hand to his forehead and saluted her.

The truck hit a pothole. She jerked, reached over to Jazz to keep him from falling out of the seat. She really must get him a doggie seat; the road crew couldn't seem to keep up with the potholes. By now she had memorized them, for the most part, and she weaved skillfully down the road. Finn must be hitting them all, she thought. And the rain, it was its usual relentless self. The drops plopped on her windshield in dull splashes of crystal and gray, and the road ahead was like one long Slip 'n Slide.

It was time to forget about the evening and focus on another day at the helm of Perpetuity. If all went as planned, she would arrive at the boat and it would have been refilled. This trip she would have another thousand dollars. Tonight, she and Finn would make love again. Life wasn't so bad after all.

When she pulled into the parking lot she saw Duke's car, a Hummer. It was an obnoxious thing and the sight of it repulsed her. What did he need with a rig like that? Duke was suited up in camouflage rain gear and it took her awhile to see him. He was talking with Butch on the stern of the boat. Oh, lord. What was Butch running his mouth about? And, why was Duke at the dock? Chloe parked her truck, and grabbing her groceries, she and Jazz ran to the boat.

"I didn't expect you." Through the rain, she doubted Duke could see her irritation. "I thought you were going to take care of everything last night."

"Take it easy, little lady. Just a friendly visit."

So he did notice her irritation. She wasn't sure how to play it with him. Treat him like a boss? She'd never had one before.

"I don't think it's a good idea for you to hang around

here."

"Keep your cool. But I won't argue with you. There're two theories to arguin' with a woman. Neither one works." Duke winked at her, pulled a caramel out of his pocket, offered it to her. When she declined, he unwrapped it, and stuck it in his mouth. "I'll see you when you get back."

"Somethin' about him don't seem right," Butch said after Duke left.

"You think? Maybe it's because he's a criminal." She released the stern line. "Let's just get the hell outa here."

"No need to get sassy with me. This wasn't my idea."

"That's right. It was my idea. Now let's just get underway."

"Okay, okay. Hold your horses." Butch pulled a bumper onto the boat. "I guess they like everything big in Texas. You see the Hummer Duke's driving? A tank. Looks like your fella likes it, too."

"Huh?"

Butch pointed out to the wharf. "Isn't that Finn out there? He sure is a nice kid. Him and his mother both."

Chloe threw the line down. "What's he doing here?" Sure enough, Finn stood next to the Hummer drinking a cup of coffee and talking to Duke.

"Maybe he wanted to see you again."

She started to say, I just left him, but Butch didn't need to know she had already slept with Finn. Maybe Butch was right. Finn had a whole day ahead of him. He probably just wanted to see her off. Sweet, or weird? She wasn't sure which.

"Like I said, let's cast-off."

"Now don't be running that boy off. I can tell. He's a good one."

"How can you tell? Besides, they're just visiting, remember?"

"I've got a feeling it's more than that. You know my feelings is always right."

He did seem to have a sixth sense. For one thing, he always seemed to know just the right time to gaff a fish.

She remembered when Butch's hair looked brown as fir bark, his face smooth and handsome. That had changed quickly. When her father disappeared—it was not until her grandmother died that she learned the truth—Butch took over the boat. He became a surrogate father attending her ballet recitals, helping her mother and grandmother around the house, watching out for her all through high school. When she turned twenty-one, he turned the boat over to her reluctantly, but voluntarily. That was when he stepped up on the drinking a little. Maybe because he knew what was about to happen to her father. Alcohol was a poor substitute for a friend, but it was better than thinking about her father, she supposed.

They motored out in silence, Butch pouting in his first mate's chair in the wheelhouse. Finally he said, "How long we gonna do this rum-running?"

"Don't start." They passed out into open waters. Ten-foot waves and white caps lunged toward at the boat. "Right now we just need to get across to the island without capsizing."

"Not too late to go back in."

"We've been out in worse weather."

The sea was a caldron of foam stained cinnamon by the fir bark and logs it tossed about. She agreed with Butch; they had chartered in all kinds of weather.

The radio whistled and the scratchy voice of the Coast Guard came on. "Perpetuity, come in." It was a voice she recognized—Scooter.

"This is Perpetuity, come in Scooter."

"We have a storm warning for later this afternoon. Confirm your destination."

Her destination. Great. Now she had to tell the Coast Guard she was going to Coho.

"Victoria. I should be there in an hour."

"Roger."

Butch joined her in the cabin. "Maybe we should turn back."

"Not with two hundred gallons of alcohol in our boat. The storm won't be here until this afternoon."

He worried about everything. For a drunk, he managed to maintain a high level of alertness. Chloe steered toward Coho. She noticed Perpetuity struggling a little with the excess weight, but she was well within the limits.

Chloe relinquished the helm, and as the boat lurched port and starboard, she worked her way to the stern. Off in the distance, the color of the sky had turned to slate. The storm still needed to travel a ways to get to them. They should have enough time to get to Coho. It was a good feeling, to be out of debt, and with a little luck she soon would be flush. With yesterday's load, she was even with her advance. With today's run, her bank account would be back in the black. It wasn't such a bad way to make a living. She prided herself on her ability to survive anything. So what if she lived alone with a dog.

She went back to the cabin and poured cups of coffee from her thermos. Butch took one, then she went back to the stern, to watch for the storm. She liked the feel of the rain falling on her skin like a silky wet powder and the sense of flying over the ocean like a great bird. The Pacific came at her with long swells. Huge and unforgiving, the waves rose into great quivering mounds. The stern lifted, a ten-footer passed and the bow rose. Perpetuity pitched and yawed.

"Keep her northwest," Chloe yelled.

"She doesn't want to stay on course."

"Just do it." Perpetuity slid down the backside of a wave, and icy water poured over the stern onto the deck.

The frigid water splashed into her boot and her toes burned from the icy shock. Chloe ran up to the cabin, grabbed the wheel. Best to run with the storm. She steered Perpetuity down the face of a wave at an angle towards the trough, careful not to bury the bow in the next wave. When she reached the bottom, she let Perpetuity ride up to the crest of the next wave. She needed to keep at twenty knots so the wind wouldn't poop the deck.

Butch stood behind her. "You better call the Coast

Guard."

"Just what we want, Scooter out here nosing around." Perpetuity smashed into a wave. Chloe urged Perpetuity through the swells. "That's my girl. You're a good old girl."

It was only five miles to Coho. Her teeth chattered and her calf muscles cramped.

The sea kept coming at them in big rollers, while she held tight to the wheel sending Perpetuity's bow right into the middle of it. Rain blew across the cabin window at a slant. Ahead of her she saw the tip of the rock outcropping guarding Coho's bay.

She slipped past the rock. A gale came at her from the southwest, a wave smashed the boat from the stern and tipped her starboard. "That's all right, old friend."

She patted the wheel and turned port. Perpetuity righted. Chloe's heart raced and her whole body tingled with excitement. The friendly harbor of Coho awaited her. In the distance, she saw a man standing on the edge of the dock. Hundreds of Western and glaucous-winged gulls congregated on the shore, the estuary and the dock. They were smarter than she was, she supposed, already settled in for the storm.

The man waved and she could see it was Millard. A ray of sun managed to break through the dense cloud cover and it beamed on the dock, illuminated the puddles of rain with a glossy sheen. All was silvery and polished, ready for company.

She throttled back and glided smoothly into the dock. Millard ran next to her, jumped on the boat. He grabbed a rope and tied it to a mooring. "I am glad to see you. The birds beat you here."

"I got here as quickly as I could."

Millard pulled his tank up to Perpetuity. "We need to do this before the storm hits."

This time Chloe let Butch help. She had no choice. They moved about the boat and the dock as if they had done this hundreds of times. Rain blew in diagonally stinging her face and pelting her with tiny wet needles.

With the pump on the tank of alcohol, all they could do was wait. They sat in the cabin and watched as the downpour increased. She offered Millard a drink, he refused. Don't mix business with alcohol, he said, and it struck Chloe as an odd thing to say, but she knew what he meant. Butch said he would have one, but Chloe told him no.

"You have a leak," Millard said. "Greyfeather will fix it. A leak in the bilge and the weight can sink you." He stepped down into the bilge and disconnected the pump.

Butch placed his belly on the floor, perched to get a good view of the action in the bilge. "I think I can fix it."

"It's best you let Greyfeather do it," Millard said.

"I know this boat well."

"Not so well. You let it leak."

To that, Butch sat up. The way Millard talked, it was hard to be offended, and Chloe knew that Butch was not.

Chloe checked the damage to her boat. Like Butch had said, it wasn't too bad. For an old boat, Perpetuity had held up well.

Millard handed her the pump, and climbed up from the bilge. He wore his hair pulled back in a pony tail. Normally, she detested men in pony tails. Either they were old hippies, people who had missed the sixties and seventies and decided to make up for it, or Casanovas trying to stay young. Millard fit into a different category. He wore it naturally. Like what else would he do? Gray streaks ran through his black hair and his pony tail reached to the middle of his back. It appeared nothing less than authentic.

"You'll stay in the Inn," he said.

"They'll wonder about me."

"Yes, you will call them. The Coast Guard. Tell them exactly where you are."

"I told them I was going to Victoria."

"The waves were rough. You decided to stop here. It's nothing unusual." His expression was firm, like a father telling a toddler to stay out of the street.

She called the Coast Guard. Scooter answered the radio. "This is Perpetuity," she said.

"You picked a fine day to go out in it. How is it?"

"We stopped at Coho. Had a couple waves hit the stern and it leaked into the bilge. We're fine. Over."

"You want me to send someone over to fix your boat?"

"I've already got it set up. Thanks for the offer."

"Anything for you, Chloe."

She and Scooter had dated long enough for him to ask her to marry him. He was a sweet kid, for that is the way she thought of him, a kid, even though they were the same age and had grown up together. But his was a neat and tidy life—officer-in-the-Coast Guard dad, stay-at-home mom and two sisters, both cheerleaders. People like that didn't understand what it was like to grow up otherwise. So Chloe had turned him down.

"I'll check in tomorrow before I head back," she said. "Over and out."

The three of them strolled up the dock. Millard pushed the tank to the end of the dock and secured it in the shed. The gales were probably thirty or thirty-five knots. Chloe leaned into the wind.

When they reached the Inn, Mrs. Free had hot chocolate and chowder waiting for them. It was only one o'clock, but felt like six. She hated to spend the night, but outside the wind blew the rain horizontally. By now, the waves were probably fifteen footers at the least and thirty footers at the worst.

Millard dug into his bowl of chowder. "You cook, Chloe?"

She nodded and told him about the lunches she served on the charters.

"That's good, a woman should cook."

"Now Millard, don't tell me you're one of those kind of men."

Chloe took a bite of the chowder. It was just how she liked it, with carrots, potatoes and lots of black pepper. There was another spice, maybe celery salt and a little rosemary.

After lunch, they showed Chloe and Butch to their rooms and both of them decided to take a nap. In fact, the whole house grew quiet. Chloe fell on top of the bed, a queen covered in a bright yellow Chenille spread. The wind knocked against the shutters outside her window and the rain crashed against the glass. It lulled her into a deep restful sleep.

When she awoke, it was already six o'clock. She jumped off the bed and rushed to the window. The rain fell in slow, heavy drops. The gutters of Main Street swelled with water. She grabbed her rain coat and went downstairs.

Happy and Millard were sitting at a table drawing eagles.

"Have you seen Butch?" Chloe asked.

"He went over to the bar. It's just there, by the post office, Fisherman's Cove."

"I better go get him."

"We'll have dinner in a half hour."

Chloe donned her rain jacket and headed out into the storm. The rain had turned to drizzle and the lighted sign of Fisherman's Cove, missing its "C" and "V", blinked in the distance.

A bell rang overhead as she opened the door, though, in the din, no one noticed it. A split log, bark intact, hoisted onto two stumps, served as the bar. Water rings spotted the unfinished surface. At one end of the room, a small linoleum dance floor, buckled slightly at the edge, hosted a couple slow-dancing to a country song. The rest of the room consisted of eight small tables placed in no particular arrangement on the fuzzy green indoor-outdoor carpet.

Butch, perched at the end of the bar, half on the stool, half hanging over a native woman, leaned over and whispered in her ear. The woman looked up at him and nodded. Chloe cringed. What was he saying to her? The bartender poured Butch another drink. Butch reached into his pocket, the man waved him off.

Chloe stormed up to Butch, grabbed his shirt and pulled him away from the bar. “What did you say to her?”

“Nothing, I swear. Nothing.” He scanned the bar.

“Why is the bartender giving you drinks?”

“I’ve only had a few.”

Someone played “I’ve Got Friends in Low Places,” on the jukebox and a couple rushed to the dance floor. Chloe followed them with her eyes.

“This isn’t meant to be a party, Butch.” She put a finger to his chin and turned his head so she could look him straight in the eye. There’s a lot at stake here.”

“I didn’t do nothing. I swear it.”

The woman staggered up. “We thank you Miss Chloe for coming to our village.”

She took Chloe’s hand, flipped it over to exam Chloe’s palm, then turned it back, as if Chloe’s hand were a pancake and the woman’s leathery hand a spatula.

It was as Chloe had suspected. Butch, the dear, unreliable drunk, famous for diarrhea of the mouth, always looking to impress a woman no matter how haggard and worn the lady— for after all, wasn’t he haggard and worn as well—was no more responsible for his behavior than a two-year-old was for spilling milk.

Chloe was to blame. She waited for the woman to loosen her fingers, then when politeness allowed, gingerly pulled away. “It’s…” She had started to say lovely, but it wasn’t lovely, it was a town in ruins, only two paved streets, both pot-holed, and only two decent buildings, the church and the Marmot Brewing Company. There was the one waterfall, but it was hardly enough to drive tourism. “…nice of you. I’m afraid I must take Butch to help me.”

The woman complied. “Of course, of course.”

She hustled back to the bar for Butch’s slicker. Pulling up onto her tiptoes, she helped Butch into the rain jacket. He crouched down to meet her half way.
When he was suited up, Butch turned to the woman.

She patted his face with her hand and he bent down

to kiss her, then turned to Chloe and grinned broadly. "I didn't say nothing, I tell you."

Chloe and Butch left the bar, entered into a dark, wet fog.

"It's only six o'clock and look at you. You're going to get the Coast Guard after us."

"Ain't no law against having a few drinks when a storm's at sea. You got no call treating me like that. Your dad wouldn't like it one bit." There was a loud plop, a spray of black water, Butch staggering to catch his balance. "Damn potholes."

She let the comment about her father pass. Chloe resented Butch for knowing her father, knowing him as a friend and equal. It was the same reason she loved Butch so much. If anything ever happened to Butch.... Well, nothing could happen to him. Her family was shrunk down to a woman in a nursing home, a drunk and a dog. But it was still family.

When they reached the Inn, Happy greeted them at the door. She had set the table, she said, and where did they want to sit. Her father always sat at the head of the table, she said. Happy ran from one ladder-back chair to the next until the seating arrangement was all decided.

Happy's two older brothers, handsome teenagers with smooth bronze skin, joined them. The Frees had a tradition of eating together and telling stories about the day. The boys had chased a marmot out of a woodpile behind the brewery. The storm had flooded some of the houses at the end of town. Everyone worried about mudslides.

Mrs. Free entered the room carrying a cedar plank with a large salmon filet on it. On another platter she presented a pile of roasted vegetables—potatoes, carrots, squash. Chloe felt at ease with this family. Her appetite had returned and the plain but hearty food comforted her. After dinner, against Mrs. Free's protest, Chloe helped with the dishes.

A little after eight, Millard appeared in the kitchen. "Coast Guard is on the phone."

Chloe's heart raced. She analyzed Millard's face for some clue. "What is it?"

He shrugged. She followed him out to the reception desk to the phone.

"This is Chloe Gallagher." She hoped he couldn't hear the fear in her voice.

"Hey, Chloe, it's Scooter again. Just wanted to make sure you were okay. Some guy name Finn Tully's been calling about you. Said you were supposed to have a date tonight. He was worried about you."

"And?"

"And I told him you had to stop in Coho."

Chloe clenched her hand into a fist. Inside her chest her heart bounced against her ribcage as if it were the ball in a junior high dodge ball game.

"I wish you wouldn't go reporting my whereabouts to strangers."

Scooter laughed. "He didn't sound like a stranger."

"Give me a break." Chloe drew in a breath and deliberately slowed the pace of her speech. "I just met the guy."

She wished she hadn't said that. It was too close to the truth and Scooter would know exactly what she had done. Gawd, Clam Harbor was a glass house. She needed to get the hell out of there. And if it weren't for the boat, the boat she loved, she'd have nothing. Chloe clenched the back of a chair.

She could hear the faint snicker of Scooter at the other end of the line. Perhaps he was whispering to one of his mates. No doubt she was the joke of the town. Did you hear about Chloe's latest? He was calling out here looking for her.

"You know the funny thing." Scooter's voice was filled with sarcasm. "He said you were going to Coho all the time. Not to Victoria."

Finn Tully, you will die. Who was this idiot? She smiled into the phone. Chloe had read once that if you smiled when you spoke you could disguise your anger.

"He's mistaken."

"That's what I thought." His voice sounded less accusatory now. "As long as you're safe."

"Thanks, Scooter. And if he calls again—"

"I'll tell him we can't give out information."

Chapter Seventeen

When I got home the next morning, I caught Mother throwing up in the bathroom. Her body was limp and pale. I just looked at her, quiet, wondering where this thing came from. I imagined a million little PacMans chomping away at her bit by bit. Calvery would say dying is a natural part of living. That may be, but you hope to avoid watching it.

I patted her forehead with a damp washcloth. She grabbed my hand, and when I pulled her up from the floor her legs buckled. I put my hands around her waist to give her an extra boost to straighten her legs.

"Got it," she said. "I can do it." Her voice was sharp.

"How often does this happen?" I stood close to her as she rinsed her mouth in the sink.

"Every day."

"Don't they give you medicine for it?"

"It'll pass." She grabbed the doorjamb and stepped from the bathroom. "Let's go outside."

"I could get you some marijuana," I said as we settled out on the patio.

"Don't you dare."

"Kidding."

We settled into the two chairs outside. It was cool, but with no wind and the sun beaming down over the roof, it seemed all right for Mother. As she promised, whatever caused her vomiting passed, and soon she seemed back to her old self.

"I can't figure out why Chloe told the Coast Guard she was going to Victoria." Except for the wind beating at us, it was a fine day, the fog already lifted at eight in the morning. "She really didn't want me to go with her."

"She had a life before you showed up here, you know." Mother was wearing a fisherman's hat, the floppy kind with a string to keep it from flying off her head.

"And that blond guy that hangs around. This is twice I've seen him at the dock."

She lowered her red sunglasses from her eyes and smiled, "We could nose around a bit. The Mystery of Clam Harbor. I like the sound of that. Solving a mystery before I die."

"You need to stay out of it."

"Since when did you start bossing me around? I'm still your mother."

"I have a bad feeling about this guy."

"Oh, like you're so good at staying out of trouble," Mother said, standing up from her chair. "We'll go into town, I'll ask around, see what I can find out. Ladies love to talk. I'll find out where the talking goes on."

Funny thing. It made sense. I certainly wasn't getting anywhere. The guy at the Coast Guard told me she was going to Victoria. I wanted to find out what was going on before I told her about her father.

"There's always Butch," I said. "I have the feeling he could tell us a lot. Like whether or not Chloe knows about her father."

"We could visit her mother."

"That might be pushing it," I said, following Mother back into the room.

"We'll look at the organizations in town. I'll get the phone book." She opened the sliding door and stepped back into our room. Mother returned with the Clam Harbor phone book, pen and paper.

"This should be a good one," she said. "The Quilting Society."

When Mother went on a tear you could forget about

stopping her. But reality forced me to point out one thing, "You don't quilt."

"What's there to know? A needle, a thread, I can learn."

"How about an ALANON meeting? Or AA?"

I knew the information in one of those meetings was confidential. But maybe we'd hear the skinny on Chloe and Butch.

Mother dismissed the idea. "We have our ethics. We are not going to go about sleuthing at an AA meeting. It wouldn't be ethical. There's gotta be another way." She now wore a pair of red rhinestone reading glasses. "This is it. The local Audubon Society." Mother dialed the number. As she listened to the message, she updated me. "They meet today at 10:00."

Birds. Just great. I pictured a group of studious types, traipsing through the woods, scouring the shorelines, binoculars bouncing on their chests, calling out, "There it is, do you see it? A red-winged, blue-tufted dodo bird."

I wanted to see Chloe. Had Calvery considered I might fall for his daughter? Did he even know what a beauty she was? I know he would want me to keep her safe, which is a laugh, me keep someone safe. But somehow, I guess he thought I could.

We arrived at the birdwatcher's group a little before ten. Mother worked the room—all ten of them—for us. We recognized the president from the Clam Festival Talent show. He was the bird calling expert. He introduced himself as Ovid Northcraft Pugis, a retired professor from Washington State. All soft, and rounded, his stomach extending pleasantly over his canvas belt, and dressed in matching khaki shirt and pants, Ovid wore a broad smile on his face. His cheeks—orange-red like the smooth, feathered breast of a robin—puffed out from his face and bounced when he talked.

When Professor Pugis insisted we call him Ovid, Mother and I blew a sigh of relief. He had inherited his name and his love of birds from a long line of British aristocrats. Best of all, and most pertinent to our mission,

Ovid talked. Within two minutes of arriving we knew: He had moved here to live on the ocean, his wife died a few years back, he loved Clam Harbor and best of all—he knew everyone.

When he revealed that juicy tidbit of information, Mother said, "You do? Of course, such a likable gentleman as yourself, I'm not surprised."

To that Ovid's puffed cheeks swelled with pride.

Though Ovid probably could have given us all the information we needed, Mother also chatted with the women in the group. The minute she mentioned breast cancer, they all started in on their own stories, their exuberance so intense with remedies, Mother's true story and certain fate faded from the focus. I cringed as I listened to the anti-carcinogenic powers of exercise and fresh air. I wanted to stop them with their yada-yada. But Mother joined in happily.

We set out for a walk to an inlet where we hoped to find a red-throated loon. I followed close behind Mother and Ovid, stomping deliberately on the giant ropes of kelp covering the shoreline. We came upon a log, half-buried in the sand, with a moat of clear water surrounding it. Three Double-crested Cormorants sucked the water through their orange beaks, prompting Ovid to launch into a dissertation about their feeding patterns. Mother stuck close to him, hung on his every word.

"Now who would have ever thought. How on earth do you know so much about birds? I find it fascinating, don't you, Finn?"

Anxious to get to the news about Chloe, I nudged her and mouthed, "Chloe, remember?"

With that, Mother reached into her pocket and pulled out a tube of lipstick. She applied it, looking into a small mirror on her lipstick case. Flashing me her teeth, she said, "All clear?"

I gave her the thumbs up. She laughed and rushed up to where Ovid examined a nesting area in the midst of a thicket of vines—heart-shaped and emerald—crawling over the sand. "We were out on the boat with Chloe

Thomas and saw three herons. You know Chloe, I suppose?"

Ovid nodded, waved for the group to follow him down the shore. "She's had a hard life from what I've heard. Don't know how the poor girl manages."

The tide surged up to where Mother stood. She hopped away from it, splashing both Ovid and me in the process. "I'm so sorry." She knelt down and brushed a clump of sand off his cargo pants. "Chloe seems to be quite self-sufficient."

"I don't want to speak out of turn," Ovid said.

"Oh, no. Of course not," Mother said, thumbing through her brand new bird book. "It's just that Finn here has taken a liking to her and she seems such a lovely girl, but I could tell she is not at peace."

The rest of the group had wandered up the shoreline.

Ovid's face sobered. "You do know what happened?"

"I know her mother is ill."

"This might come as a shock to you." He lowered his voice. "Her father was executed." Ovid looked Mother straight in the eye. "For murder."

"Oh, my, the poor dear." Mother acted as if she was hearing the news for the first time. "I thought maybe Butch was her father. Or, I saw this man at the boat talking with her. I've seen him a couple times. I wondered who he was."

"From what I understand Butch knew her father. He looks after her. Or, he did until she grew up and started looking after him. He tends to imbibe in excessive amounts." He lifted his binoculars to his eyes and watched what I learned was a killdeer take off from the Oregon Grape. "I do go on, don't I? You must forgive me, I'd hate for you to think I was loose-lipped. I can't abide gossips."

"And I don't mean to pry. I just wanted to help her, with her mother, if I could. But now here is this news. It's too much." Mother fumbled for her borrowed binoculars, peered through them. "I suppose the other man is just a businessman in Clam Harbor."

"Are you referring to the Texan who came into town?" Ovid bent over to examine bird scat on a piece of driftwood.

"I'm not sure. Finn, was the man from Texas?"

It made sense. The man certainly didn't seem like a native. Chloe had made it clear she wanted me gone when he was around. But that might not have had anything to do with the man. Maybe she got to work and started having second thoughts about us.

I shrugged. "He did say howdy to us."

"Smallish man, middle-aged, over dressed." Ovid pointed to a trail leading away from the shore and into thick hedges. "It's a belted kingfisher." His hand pointed to a bird—black and white with a long, sharp beak—perched on a dried branch. The belted name was probably derived from the white line around his neck.

The group rushed up, some pointing their binoculars, some their cameras, just when we were getting somewhere with Ovid. Here I stood on the beach, walking along with my ears tuned to Ovid's every word, the gulls squawking and tiny gnats swarming around me, listening to Ovid expound on the feeding habits of the belted kingfisher.

From the thicket, we traveled to an inlet where a small stream flowed into the Pacific. Never mind the droning of Ovid lecturing about marbled godwit and black-bellied plover, never mind my shoes—a new pair of Nike's—drenched and covered in sand, never mind my toes-turned-popsicles.

A blue heron flapped down before us and strutted about the inlet like it was walking the runway. All of us pointed at it, its long black bill, its head and eyes scanning the water. The great bird dipped its bill in the water and came out with frog legs squirming in its mouth, then with one beat of its wings, it flew off into the forest behind us.

I pulled Mother aside and reminded her of our mission. "We're here to find out about Chloe, remember?"

"I'm just being polite," she said.

"If I hear about one more bird I won't be responsible." I glanced over at Ovid who was still spouting off at the mouth.

"You don't think this is fun?"

She turned away and hurried over to Ovid's side. I repositioned myself behind her. Edging closer to him, I stood in the midst of the Audubons in the thicket of what I learned was Oregon Grape, salal and red flowering currant. Maybe he'd keep talking about Chloe, maybe if I just hung in there with this bird-watching expedition, Ovid would tell me everything I wanted to know about Chloe.

After Ovid finished, the group thinned. Mother managed a segue back to Chloe.

"Maybe we could get Chloe to take us out on her boat to do some bird watching."

"It would be nice to motor along the shore." Ovid helped Mother over a rivulet.

"So what did you say the guy from Texas looked like?" My patience had long ago waned.

"Nicely dressed and well-groomed, athletic looking but small, big diamond on his finger."

"I did see him. That's the guy I saw with her."

"I believe his name is Duke."

Chapter Eighteen

After the birder outing, I replayed the conversation with Ovid a thousand times, and even though I knew it was coming, each time my mind landed on the name—Duke—dread swelled within me. All my talks with Calvery hadn't prepared me for this.

I began to see the whole picture, the image of Julius in my cell, rifling through Calvery's belongings, the sense of danger that rose in my heart, upon seeing Duke, then hearing the confirmation from Ovid. It was all coming together, though I couldn't quite figure how Chloe fit in. She was mixed up with the very man who framed her father, and she had lied to the Coast Guard. It was not what I had planned, and I did not want to see how it fit together.

After taking mother back to the motel, I drove around Clam Harbor killing time until Perpetuity was due back. I found a quiet stretch of sand next to the dock and waited. It was one o'clock. I imagined/hoped/prayed Chloe had left Coho early. If I told her about Duke, which I had to do, I had to tell her about her father. When I told her about her father, she would wonder, rightfully, why I had waited so long to tell her. I was pinned in, no doubt about it, pinned into the corner of the ring, hugging the ropes.

Then the purple hull of Perpetuity appeared at the far end of the harbor. My heartbeat revved. The only things keeping me grounded were my shoes, still wet and heavy from the morning's hike.

Perpetuity grew larger and more purple, its hull pushing a frothy wave, and I recall the regret that lashed at me as I watched, for anyone with any sense knew I should have spoken up earlier. Calvery had given me the opportunity to do something decent, but I was weak, overcome by desire, and now I had to uphold my end.

Though I dreaded the encounter, I already felt some relief. I'd spent recent years harboring secrets, the drug use, and now that I was clean, now that my life was an open book, I wanted to be free again. I could hear the engine now, the sound of it lowering its RPM's. Butch ran to the bow and positioned himself for docking—one foot balanced on a bench, one on the hull. When I yelled at him, he smiled and waved. Butch seemed to like me, for all that was worth. He threw me the dock line, and I wrapped it around the piling.

Chloe appeared from the wheelhouse. Her look was not a pleasant one. Her lips were clamped together so tight the skin around them was blanched. Boy, did I know that look.

"Hey." My voice cracked. I wasn't even sure it carried over the squawk of gulls.

She stomped right past me, dropped a bumper off the starboard side of the boat.

Butch was rooting for me. "I don't think she heard you."

"Hey." I tried again.

"I'm not deaf," Chloe said. "I heard you."

"Then why aren't you talking?" This retort came from Butch.

She grabbed a back pack from the bench seat, and climbed up onto the dock. "Be sure you get the cabin locked up."

Butch looked up at me and shrugged his shoulders. Chloe brushed past me.

"C'mon now," I said, my voice pathetic and desperate. "You can't do me that way."

"Maybe you should call the Coast Guard," she said, her words terse.

"Is that what this is about?"

Chloe turned on her heel, put one hand on her hip and shifted her weight. "Let's just say, I've never, ever, had anyone call the Coast Guard about me. You think they don't have anything better to do than answer phone calls from my one-night stands?"

I sucked up a hefty breath of air. My hand felt cold and heavy as mallet; I willed it out of my pocket to touch her, to see if she was as cold as she sounded.

The hand jerked about and finally landed clumsily onto her forearm. "That shot straight to the heart. I got to be honest. I didn't see it that way. Is that how you saw it?"

It seemed an honest enough question. Chloe backed away from me, and my hand fell from her arm. Behind her stern expression, I looked for signs of hope but came back empty.

She shifted her backpack to the other shoulder and turned. "I'm tired. I just want to go home."

"C'mon…" I quickened my pace to keep up with her. "I have to come clean with you. It's important. Serious." I felt helpless, my ineptitude packed with consequences—a failed mission, possibly danger for Chloe, and worst of all, pardon my selfishness here, a lost love.

"Right. Like I said, you might try calling the Coast Guard."

"I was worried about you," I said.

"It embarrassed me," Chloe said.

"I need to talk to you."

"Okay, so tell me." She whistled for Jazz.

"Here?" I said, reaching out to her. "It's personal."

"If you're trying to do this just to get over to my house, forget it." Jazz trotted up beside her.

"It's not like that," I said, putting my hand down for Jazz to sniff. "I should have told you sooner."

"So, tell me, now," she said.

"It's not the kind of thing one blurts out on the dock," I said.

"Now you're being discreet," Chloe said, the irritation in her voice lessening. "A little late for that."

"I have a message for you. We came here to find you."

"Why would you want to find me?" She tilted her head, put her hands on her hips and stared at me.

"Someone sent me," I said to her.

"Okay, so here I am," Chloe said. "Who sent you?"

"I was in prison." I want to take it back—tell her never mind. Mother and I could leave now, go back to Texas. I didn't care about the money, not now. But if I left, she would be alone with Duke. That, I couldn't tolerate.

She dropped her lower jaw. "No. I can't…" Chloe put her hand to her mouth.

"In Texas," I said. Here I paused for her reaction.

She just shook her head.

"In Polunsky." My throat felt full of rocks. "I was a porter. I cleaned, and I cleaned on death row."

Her chin quivered. She looked up and blinked, a trick mother often used to keep from crying in church. "On death row?"

I had four more words to say, and she was waiting for them. She wasn't moving and I took a chance, I pulled her close to me. I could feel her tremble.

She pulled away violently and ran off.

"I knew your father," I said, yelling into the wind.

Chapter Nineteen

As she ran toward the truck, Finn called after her, his words pleading, but she felt as if someone had punched her in the gut, and though she first felt the pain of the blow, before she had time to recover, she filled with rage toward this creepy guy, toward her father and toward herself—not necessarily in that order. Jazz followed her, thinking it was a game, barking happily. So this was the inmate Mr. Olson had talked to her about, the one her father "had taken a-liking to." Now, she had slept with said inmate. A chill passed through her.

Chloe jumped into the truck and burned rubber as she squealed out of the parking lot. Out of the rear view mirror, she saw Finn running after her. If she could just get some distance between them. She merged onto the main road squeezing the wheel. She had slept with an ex-con who knew her father, the murderer. Actually, it was funny when she thought about it. So funny she burst out laughing.

Finn was following her now, tail-gating her. The thought of being alone with him made her cringe. He had seemed like such a nice guy, what with his mother and all. But now this.

In front of her, an SUV made a sudden turn. Chloe slammed on her brakes and honked her horn before waving the finger at them. "Shit!"

Finn swerved to miss her bumper. Chloe gunned the engine, passed a sedan in a no-passing zone and took the first right headed up onto the hillside. Jazz fell over on the seat as she swerved round a curve. He whimpered. If anyone, anything, could tell when she was upset, it was Jazz. She swerved the truck back the other direction, and his hind quarters dropped off the seat. When he struggled back into his place on the passenger side, he whimpered.

Then she stopped abruptly at the rusted iron gate of Clam Harbor graveyard where the afternoon sun threw shadows of tombstones across the clover. Now it was quiet, except for her rapid fire breathing, and the noise of regret in her head.

Jazz raced across the hilltop, his paws tossing up the red clay or fir needles. Just her damn luck that this latest attempt at a leading a normal life had failed miserably. Looking at her behavior, any outsider would grade her record poorly. Don't even bother to look past her history in relationships, just look at this one—ex-con, liar, loser. Chloe settled in front of her grandfather's tombstone and looked out over the hill. She couldn't get their night together out of her mind. It was hardly the kind of lovemaking she could forget. That night Chloe thought Finn might be a keeper, she had felt an unnamed kinship with him, a connection she and Scooter never shared.

A car skidded into the parking lot. She jerked and watched Finn's tires toss gravel as they slid in next to her truck. One thing about him, he couldn't take a hint.

He stepped out and opened the door to the back seat. When he emerged from behind the door he was holding a box. She knew what it was, of course. This was the inmate with her father's belongings. Finn stepped forward slowly.

"Leave," she yelled at him.

"Look, I should have told you sooner. My bad. But you have to listen to me. You're in danger."

"Yes," she said. "I think most people would agree."

"I don't mean me." Finn sat down the grass leaving a good six feet between them. "This is important. You've got to listen to me."

She thought it was impossible that this man, this young man straight out of prison, knew anything very important. He had been staring straight ahead, deliberately avoiding eye contact, as if she were a stray dog of indeterminate temper. Then a gust of wind filled the quiet with the noise of the rushing air and brushing of fir boughs against each other. The air cooled her face. She pinned her shaking hands between her knees. All she wanted was to go back to the night of their date and make another decision—go home alone.

He spoke, finally. "I think Duke is the man who framed your father," Finn said, his voice turned sullen. "I don't know why he is up here…" He waited, as if the wind— now stirring every living plant on the hilltop—was speaking, and he was politely waiting his turn. "What does he want from you?"

She felt a jolt of fear, and her heart fluttered as the realization formed in her mind. Now there were two men who had played her for a fool. Chloe looked to her pickup, patted her pockets for her keys. I am all alone on the mountain with one of the men. Instinctively, she grabbed Jazz's collar. There was no need. Jazz was sitting next to her intently watching Finn.

"Look," Finn said. "I'm not a bad guy. Look at me, I came up here with my mother. Your father trusted me."

"I didn't know my father," she said, her voice sharp. "He was nothing to me."

"You were very special to him." He pulled out his wallet and opened it, then leaning toward her he stretched out his arm to hand her his billfold. "Take it."

The wallet was thin, like one of a man just out of prison. She flipped it open and took in a sharp breath—her kindergarten picture. She remembered the dress, its white Peter Pan collar had been a constant irritation on her neck.

He pushed the box gently toward her. "Let me just give you this. It's yours."

When he handed her the box, she stared at him for a

long while before saying anything. "I don't want it."

"It's your father's belongings."

"I know what it is."

"How could you know?"

"When Captain Olson called me about my father, he said that an inmate had my father's belongings."

"You talked to Spud?" Finn looked excited. "He was a good guy. And what did he tell you?"

"That my father took a-liking to an inmate."

Finn smiled, and in that moment he looked like the ideal man, perfectly built, a rugged yet handsome face, an all-American guy. No one would suspect he was an ex-con. How was she to know?

"I didn't expect to find you," Finn said, his words rushing from his mouth. "Your father told me you lived in Clam Harbor. I wasn't going to come. I was just going to blow it off, but I kept hearing him talking to me." He stopped and looked up to the sky. "I wish I'd given this to you sooner," he said.

Chloe stared at the box, her heart pounding. So this was it, the father she'd never really known. On the side of the carton was a Del Monte logo. Inside, on top, she found her father's tee shirts. She lifted them to her nose. They smelled like pine. Had he worn some kind of aftershave, or was it the soap? She fumbled through the shirts, seven in all, her fingers stiff wooden appendages. Then, she found a book, *Sacred Places*, and she held it as one might hold a small, whimpering puppy.

Chloe found other items, Finn told her, and a Bible, and then a scratching startled her. She jumped and Finn laughed. "Go ahead. It's a surprise."

At the bottom of the box, she saw the humped-shell of a turtle, its dome covered in ringed rectangles, its plates the almost black looking green of a river bottom. She resisted smiling as she pulled the creature from the box. "He had a pet?"

Finn nodded. "Sport. He's good company," Finn said, then looking to Jazz he added, "I mean, not a dog. Mother made him a terrarium, I've got it in the car."

"Jazz, look here."

He sniffed at the turtle. Sport's head retreated into its shell. It was alive, this thing, and her father had raised it.

"Your father wanted you to know, he didn't do it," Finn said.

Everything was so complicated all of a sudden.

"I'm sick of people saying he was innocent," she said, watching Jazz paw the turtle. "That information is coming to me a little late, don't you think? It's like a surgeon telling an amputee he could have saved his leg."

Finn nodded in agreement. "He didn't want you to live your life thinking he was a murderer."

"I want to know the truth, not have some ex-con come tell me he said he was innocent," she said. "I never really knew him, remember."

"He used to give me his homemade wine. I would give him the sugar, and every week I'd get a new batch from him," Finn said, talking about her father as if he loved him. "He made the best wine. The last time I saw him, he said, This is my best batch ever. And it was. It tasted like imported wine right out of a restaurant. He liked Pinot Noir and always talked about how Oregon had the finest Pinots."

She put up her hand for him to stop, trying to decide whether Finn was crazy or pulling some kind of con on her. "You can make wine in prison?" Chloe turned away.

"You can. It was hard to get the sugar, but I had connections." Finn looked up as if remembering good times. "Wasn't a whole lot to do there," Finn shrugged. "Especially for Calvery." Then there was a long period of silence before he said, "Your father trusted me. He felt like God had sent me to him to find you."

"It sounds like you're both crazy."

"I thought so, too. Like I said, I was going to blow it off, but I got out, went over to my girl's house—except my girl isn't my girl any more. She divorced me. I thought if I just saw her once, she'd change her mind...."

He's playing on my sympathies. "Didn't go well?"

"She was with this other guy. He looked like a nice

guy and all that. I even shook his hand like I was some big shot grown up about the whole thing. But inside I was falling apart. Not because of her, they wouldn't let me see Lacy," Finn said. He sounded sad, and when he said "they wouldn't let me see Lacy" there was the tiniest crack in his voice. "I left her house and went to see my father. I needed to punch someone. When I was a teenager, I used to listen to the Beatles and smell the after shave he had left at the house. It made me feel close to him. Then, I just got angrier and angrier, started doing drugs, and I didn't listen to the Beatles anymore. So by the time I got out, I was ready for a fight. He was never there for me. So I went over to his place to give him a mouthful of knuckles." He paused. "All that did was make me feel lousy. I've lost everything. Except mother and she's not long for this world. So I came to find…."

Chloe shook her head, trying to sort out the truth of the story from all this. "I'm not some helpless girl you can con into believing your ridiculous stories."

"Your father said the truth is always unbelievable," Finn said. "Look, I wouldn't blame you one bit if you never wanted to see me again. But not yet. Now that I'm here, I have to tell you everything." He pulled folded papers from his jacket. "It's the police report. Have you ever read it?"

No, she had never seen it. No one ever told her anything. Now she was hearing the story from a complete stranger.

Chloe read the report and after a couple of minutes, she sucked in a breath of air and placed her hand to her mouth. "So someone else killed this man Rossi? They set my father up?"

"That's what I needed to tell you. When I was in Galveston, I talked to the detective on your father's case. And this is important." He waited. "The guy who set up your father was named Duke."

Chloe recognized a sensation of falling, her mouth down to her neck, her neck to her chest, her chest to her knees, and she stayed there in this limp mound waiting for the strength to hear what Finn was saying.

"So the guy I saw you talking with at the wharf, his name is Duke?"

She tasted a burning liquid in her throat, and her stomach spasmed. Then, she took a breath and straightened herself. "I don't believe you," she said. "Why should I believe you?"

"You can't have anything to do with him," Finn said. "You hear?" He raised his voice to make his point. "Why have you been meeting with Duke?"

"Business," Chloe said. "It's not the same guy. It couldn't be the same guy."

"Read the description."

"Blond, wiry build." She set the paper down. "Could be anybody. I'm telling you, you've got the wrong guy."

"What are you doing with him?"

"Look, you've done your duty. Thank you very much," Chloe said, putting two and two together in her mind. Why had Duke come to her? What did he want? "But you can't butt into my business. You can't go calling the Coast Guard on me."

"Why do you care about the Coast Guard?" Finn came over to her, his brow wrinkled with worry.

"I don't like my boyfriends calling the Coast Guard," Chloe said, folding her arms. "That's all."

"So, I am a boyfriend," Finn said, his brows relaxing from their intense furrows and moving into an expression of surprise.

"It was a figure of speech," she said.

"What are you doing with him? I need to know. I've come all this way. Do you think I don't care about you? Especially now." He grabbed her shoulders. Jazz jumped up and growled at him. "Call off your dog."

"I don't think you're in a position to tell me what to do," she said, her voice firm and determined.

Jazz bared his teeth.

"Let him bite me." Finn said, squeezing her arms gently. "I don't care. I need to know you're safe."

"Down." Jazz responded to her voice. "He's helping

me with a business deal. I'm broke. If you must know, I'm flat broke."

Finn's mouth fell open. He moved quickly up onto his knees and sat on his heels. "You've got to believe me. Duke is dangerous." He looked at her intently, his eyes pleading. "Maybe there is money. Your father said there was a treasure. The detective in Galveston, he felt there was some money," Finn said, and with a look of excitement in his eyes he added, "And that's why Duke's here."

So now Chloe understood why Finn had come to Clam Harbor. A picture of her father came to mind: his face was behind a cell door, his turtle in his hands, Chloe's picture by his bunk. Then, Finn passed by, and they talked, and her father told fairy tales about treasure to keep Finn interested.

"I'm not a fool, you know." But the words sounded false.

"I can prove it to you. Just give me a chance," Finn said. "We could talk to the man who arrested your father here in Washington."

"Who was it?"

"He lives over in Port Angeles."

Whether her father was guilty or not, finally someone was talking to her. It was a relief to have these bits of knowledge, the truth cracking out of its twenty-year-old shell like an overdue chick. And now, after all these years, her dad had returned, what was left of him, his books, his pet, little pieces of him to hold inside her. She petted the tiny head of Sport.

"So, we'll go?" The worried expression on Finn's face turned hopeful.

"I don't know why it matters at this point, but, yes, we'll go."

"Everything cool with us?" Finn was standing in front of her with his hands stuffed in his blue jeans and his shoulders slumped in submission.

He dropped to his knees in front of the gravestone and studied her grandfather's tombstone. She turned to follow his eyes: Owen Thomas, b. Yachats (Oceanview), Oregon, 1910, d. Clam Harbor, Washington, 1986.

"Yachats," he said, a look of recognition in his eyes. "Your father told me to ask you where your grandfather was born." His voice had filled with excitement.

"My father said that?" Chloe said, her voice cracking with the realization that Finn might actually be telling the truth. "When my grandfather was born, Yachats was named Oceanview. That's why it is in parentheses on the tombstone. I wonder if that means something."

Finn shrugged. "Your father said that this grave will lead us to the treasure. You can't show this to anyone, understand? That's why Duke is here."

"And why you are here," she said with an accusing tone.

"I know it sounds crazy." Then he lowered his voice and said, "I didn't have anything else."

The inflection in his voice, the emotion of loss almost imperceptible, caused her to question her anger and fear.

"And now, you still have nothing."

"You're wrong," Finn said. "I have hope."

Chapter Twenty

Chloe and I drove the Impala to Port Angeles, a forty-five minute drive from Clam Harbor. The Federal Marshall who had arrested Calvery, Hal Snodgrass, lived across the street from the beach on a cul-de-sac with four houses built in the fifties—small ranch style homes with sprawling yards and, I imagined, a fleet of riding lawn mowers. An army-green wooden salmon, posed as if he was jumping upriver to spawn, greeted guests to the Snodgrass House, 101 Beachside Drive. He omitted his name from the mailbox, not unusual, I supposed, for someone who could potentially have hundreds of convicts seeking revenge on him. However, when we called and asked to talk to him, he didn't sound at all concerned for his safety.

When we drove up, a thin man, over six feet tall with a bootcamp-style haircut, was outside dead-heading a hydrangea bush. If you've never seen a northwest hydrangea, you can't truly appreciate this task. His bush started on the right side of the porch and sprawled the length of his eight-foot picture window. Blue blossoms, round clusters the size of homecoming mums, covered the shrub. With a wilted one in hand, he pointed us to our parking place, as if we were driving into the parking lot of a huge event.

"I guess this is Hal," I said.

Hal opened the car door for Chloe and offered his

hand. She climbed out, and as I was walking to their side of the car, she introduced herself. Hal looked at her with a sorrowful expression that I knew she hated. When I stuck my hand in between them, Hal seemed surprised to see me.

He led us into the back yard and motioned for us to sit on the patio. Like Chloe's yard, Hal's butted up against a forest.

"I read about the execution in the paper," he said, his voice soft and sober.

I had to give it to Hal, he didn't pussyfoot around.

"It wasn't a surprise," Chloe said, not attempting to disguise her sarcasm.

"No, I suppose it wasn't. I didn't have anything to do with the case, you know," he said. "I just arrested him for the State of Texas."

"When I was growing up, they kept everything from me," Chloe said, offering more explanation than I felt necessary. "My mother felt it was for the best. I thought he was dead until just a few years ago."

"I don't know how I would handle a thing like that."

"I guess they thought they were doing the best for me." She looked up as if to clear her eyes. "Finn's the one who told me my father was arrested here."

Hal poured us each a lemonade and handed us a glass. "It was an interesting situation." He paused and seemed to muse for a minute to collect his thoughts. "I received a call from a fellow named Broussard. He asked if I could make the arrest. He said he thought I'd find Calvery in Clam Harbor."

"How many days was that after the murder?" Chloe asked, scooting to the edge of her Adirondack chair.

"It was at least a week later, as I recall."

Plenty of time for Calvery to come to Washington and dispose of money. I wondered if he used it to buy Perpetuity. In fact, I wanted to ask right there in front of Snodgrass, but I held my tongue.

"Was my mother there when you arrested him?"

Hal gave Chloe a sympathetic look. "No, it was an

interesting situation. I went over to Clam Harbor, met your mother and grandmother, neither of them had seen him. At least that's what they said."

"You didn't believe them?" I blurted it out. Chloe was supposed to be running this show, but I couldn't help myself.

"Normally, in such circumstances, I wouldn't have." He spoke softly, a certain air to his voice like a kindly priest. "But I believed them. They were worried sick. They hadn't seen him since he left for Texas. That would have been two weeks prior to the murder. Your mother said it was not like your father. Even though it cost money to call long distance, he always called every day at 6 o'clock."

"How did you find him?"

"I followed this guy named Butch," Hal said. "After I talked to your mother and grandmother, I went down to the dock. I knew Calvery owned Perpetuity."

There went my theory about Calvery using the money to buy Perpetuity. "So Butch worked for your father way back then?" I asked Chloe.

Chloe nodded. "I thought you knew that." She focused on a hummingbird feeder at the edge of the patio, then turned to Hal, "You were saying about Butch?"

"I asked around the dock. A few folks said they heard Butch talking in the bar," Hal said. He seemed to be choosing his words carefully. "I guess he gets loose-lipped when he's drinking."

"You could say that," Chloe said, her words drenched in sarcasm.

"The folks in the bar overheard Butch talking about going down to Newport, Oregon to see Calvery," Hal said. "I drove down to Newport, stopping in all the bars on the way, you'd be surprised at how many of them said they had seen Butch, and he was heading south. When I got to Newport, I found Butch's truck parked at this bar on the bay. I went inside, confirmed he was alone, then waited in the car for him."

"Butch and his damned drinking," she said.

Hal continued. “Later that evening, he drove to a little motel called The Paddock. I watched the room. It was summer and it stayed light until nine o’clock and even after the sunset the twilight lingered until ten. Your father showed up about ten. He was wearing rubber boots, carrying a shovel and a clam bucket. I just walked up to him and asked if he was Calvery Thomas. He said, ‘You here to take me in?’ I said, ‘Yes.’ He said, ‘Your timing is perfect.’ I asked him if he’d had any luck, he looked at his clam bucket. It was empty. It was the funniest thing, he said, ‘The air was too thin for clams.’ Now what do you think of that?”

I glanced at Chloe. Good old Calvery. Always the enigma. “Maybe referring to the humidity,” I said. But I knew he wasn’t talking about the weather, and by this time, I assumed Chloe did as well.

“Then I drove him to Portland and flew with him to Texas,” Hal said.

“Did he tell you what happened?” Chloe asked, obviously starved for details.

“No, mostly he just talked about fishing and how he would miss seeing his little girl’s smiling face,” Hal said.

“Did he really say that?”

“He really did.”

Hal had the most sincere expression on his face that I believe I’ve ever seen. Chloe was glowing herself. I couldn’t imagine what was going on in her head and couldn’t wait to process this in the car ride home.

“One thing,” Hal said. “He seemed resigned to being convicted.”

We left Hal with hearty handshakes.

On the way home, Chloe said, “Damn, Butch. If he hadn’t been such a drunk, they’d have never found Daddy. On the day Daddy was executed Butch kept saying, If only,” Chloe paused. “Then he would never finish his sentence. I guess he feels guilty about all this.”

“A hell of a thing to carry with you all these years,” I said, removing my sunglasses and wiping the lenses with my shirttail.

"What if he hadn't been caught?" Chloe asked.

I recalled the stories I'd heard from guys who'd been on the lam. It was expensive, bad on the blood pressure, and a life of always looking out the window.

"I don't guess your life would've been much different," I said, feeling bad for Butch. "He would have been on the lam. That's not easy."

"So what do you think he was doing in Oregon?"

"I think he was hiding the treasure from someone," I said, thinking of the poem and the treasure. "And he hid it in a thin place."

Chapter Twenty- One

When I returned from our trip to see Snodgrass, I told Mother the whole story. “I’m convinced this guy Duke really set up Calvery.”

“You don’t need to be involved with this,” she said so firmly that I felt twenty years younger. “You’re fresh out of prison.”

“What am I going to do, leave Chloe all alone with this guy?”

“What do you think she’s doing with him?”

“I don’t know, but I’ll find out,” I said. “I think it has to do with the boat. She’s going to Coho again tomorrow, and I’m going with her.”

“Oh, exciting! I’m going too,” Mother said, her eyes shining with excitement. “You’re in my custody, remember?” She had a point. I was technically in her charge. “And I’m going to call your father.”

“No!” I shouted at her. She just returned my shout with silence. “What does he have to do with this?”

“Maybe he can help,” she said, searching through her purse. “It’s his turn to help you. Besides, he knows about these things.”

“What things?”

“You know, con men, thieves and murderers.”

“You forget,” I said. Then stating the obvious, I added, “So do I.”

"Just the same, maybe he could help." Mother wasn't looking at me. She'd made up her mind.

"Don't do it, I tell you. I don't need or want him around." The very thought of him up here meddling in my business irked me. "You're not calling him, understand?"

Mother nodded.

The next day, Mother, Ovid and I just happened to appear at the dock at sailing time. Chloe didn't protest. By now, the two of them appeared an unofficial item. While we motored out of the harbor, Ovid and Mother stood side by side at the stern, binoculars in hand. A morning fog, thin and drier than most mornings, blurred their images—Mother in her baggy Levis and sweatshirt, Ovid in a khaki safari shirt and nylon cargo pants—so that their bodies looked like the work of a depressed impressionist, the colors gray and tan and muted.

I sat by Chloe in the wheel room. She used a GPS to steer the boat and had a display screen beside the navigation table. Smooth teak, soft like a well-worn shirt, paneled the console. When I first touched it, I thought of Calvery and how he must have enjoyed this boat.

Chloe tucked Sport's terrarium in a corner of the wheelhouse. Down below might make him seasick, she said.

As Perpetuity sped into open water, it rocked from starboard to port. I fell against Chloe and grabbed her butt as I corrected myself. At the same time, I noticed Mother leaning onto Ovid, laughing. It was a romantic sight, Mother and Ovid, Chloe and I. I wondered if Butch felt the odd man out, though he seemed to like me. In fact, he paid more attention to me than anyone else. Maybe he thought I was good for Chloe. I hoped so.

We all drank strong coffee. Along with our speed, the wind picked up and chased Mother and Ovid inside. They settled in the galley where Chloe had left a coffee cake.

Half an hour later we were out on the Pacific with no land in sight. Chloe steered Perpetuity northwest. I knew she knew what she was doing, but with nothing but the wide-open sea, I felt the opposite of claustrophobia, which I learned later was known as agoraphobia. Just as I entered into the middle of a string of what if's—what if the engine failed, what if a whale hit our boat, what if Duke came abreast of us—the radio crackled. Chloe adjusted the squelch knob and picked up the radio handset.

"This is Perpetuity, over."

"Free here. Switch to 71."

She switched from the emergency channel with a look of panic on her face. Free came on again. "The Coast Guard is looking for you. You all right? Copy. Over."

"Copy. Over." Her jaw dropped and she looked below. "Butch!"

"What's going on?" I said, already putting together that Chloe was in a world of hurt and I was sitting smack dab in the middle of it.

She ignored me while pacing back and forth in the wheel room and rubbing her chin. Now, I can only imagine what raced through her mind. Chloe looked off to the sea, just briefly, her eyes glazed as if tuning into a force field. I was calculating the time I would serve in prison. What were the odds the Coast Guard heard that conversation? After all, the Sound was full of boats. They couldn't possibly listen to every conversation on every channel.

"Tell me, what's happening?" I said, half afraid to ask the question, afraid not to.

"We're about to get busted," she said, her voice firm.

"For what?"

"Smuggling," she said. "Look, I'm kind of busy right now. Perhaps later we can talk about how crazy stupid I was, but for now, Butch, get your butt up here!"

Butch had a handful of cards and was sorting though a deck on the middle of the table. He lifted his eyes from the card he had picked. "We're playing Go Fish."

"Now!" Chloe screamed at Butch. Mother took his cards and shooed him away mouthing, You'd better get going.

The radio crackled again. "Perpetuity. Are you there? You don't have much time. Over."

She stared at the microphone. "This is Perpetuity. Out."

"Run down to the bilge and get the hose and the pump." Chloe pushed Butch toward below and told me to drive the boat.

Butch said, "I told you this would happen."

"Just go," she said, hurrying below.

"Hey, what am I supposed to do?" I asked.

"Just hold her steady," she said. "Don't run into anything."

I looked around. Nothing but blue. It was a safe bet that I wouldn't hit anything. I'd never seen Butch move so fast. In moments he was topside with a hose in hand. Ovid and Mother followed him. I tightened my grip on the wheel. Before me the path was still clear, the water smooth. Chloe had disappeared down into the engine room.

Butch put a hose over the sides of the quarter deck.

Chloe yelled from below. "You got anything?"

Butch looked at the nozzle. "Not yet."

Just then, the hose squirted him in the face, he opened his mouth and took a few gulps, then started a coughing fit. The hose was pointed into the air and I was going thirty knots. Its contents sprayed all over the deck and the distinct smell of alcohol filled the air.

Ovid now sidled up next to Butch.

After the contents of the hose sprayed Ovid in the face, he licked his lips and said, "It's whiskey."

Mother took charge. She put the hose in the water. "Chloe, should we slow down or keep going full speed ahead?"

"Are you sure it's working."

We all yelled. "It's working."

"Change course. Go east. We need time."

"How the hell do I go east?"

Ovid said, "I do believe Ms. Thomas is smuggling alcohol. And if my palate is correct, it's whiskey, good whiskey." He looked over the boat, pulled up the hose to see if it was still running.

Mother was standing next to me. "She said turn east."

"Mother, I can do it."

"Isn't this exciting? The Coast Guard is chasing us." She took over the wheel and turned the boat starboard. "I'll drive. See about Chloe."

Down in the bilge, Chloe sat next to the inflatable tank—a giant black plastic bladder. Her face was flushed bright red. Other than that she looked the same old tough Chloe.

I squatted next to her. "You're smuggling for Duke."

She nodded.

I'd heard about this in prison. On the east coast, the Mafia were big into it. Why would Duke come to Chloe to smuggle alcohol? Did he know who she was? Maybe he was a different Duke.

Then, I thought of a bigger problem—my record. If the Coast Guard looked into it, they'd pull out the handcuffs. Even someone as convincing as my mother couldn't talk her way out of this mess, especially if they found me on this boat next to four-foot long bladder of liquor big as a bloated cow.

"Who's driving the boat?" Chloe pressed on the inflatable tank, as if pushing the air out of a mattress.

"Mother's going east."

Chloe set her beautiful bottom on the bag. "Maybe this will get it out faster. We need some time."

"Just this bag?"

Oh, the expression on her face when she shook her head. My stomach filled with worry.

"All we can do is pray," I said.

"Go topside and see what's happening," Chloe said, looking anxiously at the two tanks of alcohol in her bilge.

I took one last glance at the bladder. Its gigantic size had hardly changed. "How long does this take?"

"About thirty minutes per bag," she said.

"Per bag?"

Chloe nodded to another bag tucked into a space on

the port side of the bilge.

With that news, my stomach heaved. I felt little difference between it and the pitching of the boat against the waves. It occurred to me, I might want to go ahead and follow through with the prayer mentioned earlier. The way I figured it, God probably didn't care much about the alcohol, though there is that troublesome verse, "Render unto Caesar that which is Caesar's."

I quickly pushed the verse away and returned to my own version of God, one where God allows extenuating circumstances to overrule the law.

First of all, I offered up Chloe in prayer, then brought up my own delicate situation. I didn't ask for anything in particular, like: Lord, please don't let us get caught. Rather, I gently reminded God how Calvery was a man of faith, a man who believed I, Finn Tully, had been sent by the Almighty to help Chloe. I hate to admit it, but to be totally forthcoming, I added how I trusted God, packed up my dying mother and headed to Washington, just like the Israelites trusted God and headed to the promised land. Now, I realize I may have elevated my importance and my mission's importance, but that's what I talked with God about, and by the time my conversation ended, the pitching in my stomach had as well.

Chloe just stared at the inflatable tank shaking her head. "Get Butch down here to watch the tank. I need to find some place for us to dock."

Up top, Mother's face beamed over the steering wheel. "I'm burning up the ocean, had her up to thirty-five knots until Butch told me to slow her down."

Butch and Ovid sat out on deck—Butch manning the hose and Ovid with binoculars in hand. When I stepped out onto the deck, the wind and the rocking of the boat pushed me off balance.

I slid quickly onto the seat. "See anything?"

Ovid scanned the sea from port to starboard. "Not a thing."

"Butch, Chloe wants you down in the bilge," I said.

He left me and Ovid watching the hose.

"How far away can you see with those binoculars?" I asked Ovid.

"As you know, you can't see farther with binoculars than your own eyes," Ovid said, gazing out into the Pacific. "But I might be able to determine if a boat in view is a Coast Guard boat."

I didn't know that. But Ovid had a knack for education and I didn't feel the least bit dumb when he explained it to me.

"We do need to know if it is a Coast Guard boat," I said. "Good thing you brought those."

"However, the speed of our boat and the motion make it difficult." Ovid said, his voice as calm as a senior professor delivering a lecture. "My advice is to head to shore. As a matter of fact, I believe I'll discuss it with the Captain."

This could be bad. Chloe climbed up into the wheelhouse and stood in front of her navigational charts. Ovid edged beside her and together they drew their fingers along the map. In a few minutes, Chloe nodded, took the wheel from my mother. Immediately, the boat veered slightly to port.

Butch yelled from below, "One down."

"Switch it over," Chloe yelled. Then, after giving instructions to Mother and Ovid, she went below.

Within minutes, the alcohol started pumping out of the hose again. Ovid joined me back outside. "We're going to try to find a little birding place I know of, Cook's Inlet. At this speed, we should be there in twenty minutes. I can't imagine that the Coast Guard could find us there."

He seemed rather nonchalant about the matter. In fact, both Ovid and Mother acted as carefree as teenagers on a date. Realizing he wasn't the type to panic, or worse yet, a guy who believed it was his civic duty to report infractions, a strong bond of fraternity swelled within me.

This feeling lasted only seconds before I heard Mother yelling, "The radio! Someone's calling on the radio."

Chloe appeared from below. Ovid and I rushed into the wheel house. "Perpetuity, copy?" Chloe answered, her voice flat. "Copy."

Turns out it was Free checking on our progress.

Chloe rushed off the airway and began issuing orders, "You," pointing to me. "Get back out there with the hose. Ovid, find Cook's Inlet. Lucia, I'll take the wheel."

We left for our assigned watches and rode in silence, except for the wind rushing past and the engine with its annoying roar. The blue of the water gradually turned lighter, grayer, and Ovid confirmed land was close.

When it appeared, we all celebrated with cheers. Ahead, to starboard, a large sandbar jutted out from the shore, and a more substantial peninsula dotted with fir trees lined the port side of the inlet. Chloe lowered her speed. I left my post and wobbled up to the bow, stood next to Ovid and Mother. Chloe followed the swath of dark, and therefore deepest, water into the cove. The color bent into an elbow at the end of the inlet. Perpetuity eased into the bend, and Chloe turned off the engine. Perpetuity rocked and glided over the water. Chloe and I set anchor, then Chloe checked below. The bag was almost empty.

Mother said, "All that excitement worked up my appetite. Let's have our picnic." Mother set fried chicken and macaroni salad on the table, pulled Ovid from the stern where he searched the inlet for rare birds, and Chloe, Mother, Ovid and I settled in the booth. Relieved of his watch over the tanks, Butch decided to go topside.

"You're hungry?" My own stomach, though better, felt in no shape to hold food.

"How about you, Chloe?" Mother said, sliding a plate of food toward Chloe.

"I'm sorry that I got you guys involved in this," Chloe said, staring at the food and shaking her head.

"I'm not." Mother pulled a piece of chicken breast off its bone. "It's just the adventure I needed."

"All's well that ends well, I always say." Ovid pulled a second drumstick from the platter.

With Perpetuity settled and the engine quiet, our quartet looked like a happy family settled down for lunch. Chloe stabbed a macaroni and placed it in her mouth, then took a sip of water.

After a few moments, Chloe looked around the table and said, “Wonder what Butch is up to?” She tossed her napkin onto the table and stood quickly. We all followed.

Up top, Butch knelt on the starboard bench with his torso leaning over the boat, his right hand grasping the hose, while his left held a plastic cup catching the stream of whiskey flowing out of the hose. After filling his cup, he lowered the hose. The alcohol rushed into the Pacific with a hollow sound and the whiskey-laden sea lapped against the hull with a bump and a splash. At first, Butch remained oblivious. Chloe put a finger to her mouth. Butch took a sip, shook his head the way one does when they taste strong liquor, then raised the hose and examined the stream of liquid. He put his thumb over the tip and created a spray of amber whiskey as if watering the sea.

“Ahem.” Chloe cleared her throat.

She winked at me. I was glad to see she had a sense of humor despite our situation. We would have to deal with the fallout from Duke later. For now, we had dodged a bullet.

“What is this?” Butch asked. “Wait,” he said, making no apologies. “Don’t tell me. Jim Beam.”

Chloe shook her head.

“No, you’re right,” Butch said, taking another gulp. “It’s better than that. Crown Royal. No. That would be the worst thing, wouldn’t it? Smuggling Canadian Whiskey into Canada. American or foreign?”

Ovid stepped forward. “I pride myself on my discerning palate. I’m sure I can tell,” he said. “Do we have any tumblers?”

Mother disappeared, then returned with four hard plastic glasses. Butch poured a couple fingers full into each of our glasses.

Mother took a drink. “Perhaps I’ll become a drinker.

I've always envied them their tony ways," she said, sipping her drink with her little finger extended politely. "All those smart cocktails in long-stemmed glasses."

"You jest, I'm certain of it," Ovid said.

"You never know," she said.

Not an expert on whiskey, I was sure to lose this little game, but I played along. "Okay, who's first?" Then, I looked at Chloe. "You do know?"

"I do," she said.

Ovid took another drink and swished it about his mouth. "I believe it tastes of mountain heather and seaweed. Glenfiddich it is."

Mother guessed Jameson. Probably because Irish whiskeys were the only ones she would be familiar with.

To me it tasted like fire. I figured only the Americans would make whiskey that harsh, and I guessed Old Overholt.

Butch returned to his original guess of Jim Beam. Just as we were about to hear the origin of our contraband, we heard the sound of a boat.

Chloe said, "I'm disconnecting the pump." She ran downstairs.

A smaller stream of whiskey ran out of the hose, so maybe the bag was nearing empty. For all we knew, it was a fisherman, or a birder. But my stomach was telling me it was the Coast Guard.

The engine sound grew louder. The hose still drained. It had to be about finished.

Chloe came back and pulled the hose out of the water.

"Was it empty?" I asked.

"Not quite," Chloe said, quickly looping the hose to stow it.

"How much, not quite," I said. "If it's the Coast Guard, we'll pretend we pulled over to do a little partying."

A red and white striped hull came into view.

"Butch, go get an empty bottle or two." Chloe pushed him toward the ladder.

"Now, that's a first," he said.

Mother started singing, "As I went home on Monday night as drunk as drunk could be, I saw a horse outside the door where my old horse should be. Well, I called me wife and I said to her, Will you kindly tell to me, who owns that horse outside the door where my old horse should be?"

"Everybody now," she said.

It took awhile for us to get the tune, but after a few verses we had the hang of it. Perpetuity sounded like an Irish pub. In fact with our voices raised, each of us trying to outsing the other, the blare of the horn blended into our quintet with an off-key tenor. When it blew again, louder, I turned toward it. Our voices trailed off. There she was in all her glory, a fully outfitted Coast Guard patrol boat, one of the smaller ones, eighty-seven feet—flags blowing at bow and stern, a manned black cannon at mid deck.

Obviously, I've had my run-ins with the law, but this boat topped them all. Immediate discomfort settled in my abdomen, and I felt a sudden urge to visit the latrine. I couldn't let anything ruin my chances to get back into Lacy's life. Shortly after the boat came into view, a bright orange quick response boat appeared at the elbow of our cove.

"It's a short range patrol boat—SRP—26-foot CB-OTH-IV," Ovid said, peering through his binoculars. "Aluminum hull, speed up to 40 knots, inboard diesel with water jet propulsion."

This guy Ovid knew everything. This time, it came in handy.

"Great," I said. "40 knots. At that rate, they'll be here in one minute."

"The Coast Guard added these boats for counter-drug operations," Ovid said. He spoke with his usual calm and confidence. "It's armed with a M240 7.62 mm machine gun."

"Perpetuity, Captain Thomas. Permission to come aboard."

Chloe waved at them all friendly and nice as the SRP edged toward us. "Scooter, what're you doing out here?"

"Chloe, we need to take a look at your boat," Scooter said. "Sorry to have to do this."

"What's the problem?" She asked with all her wits about her.

Scooter jumped onto the boat. He was a handsome fellow in a clean-cut sort-of-way. Everything about him looked sanitary and inspected—hair as white as his starched uniform, knife blade creases on his trousers, and, of course, shiny, even teeth.

"Do you have any weapons?"

"Just a pistol. You know that." She started to walk to the wheelhouse.

This was the first I knew we had a gun on board.

"Stop!" Scooter yelled with his best 'police' officer voice.

Chloe jerked around. "You think I'm going to fire at you? What is this?"

Chloe knew very well what was going on, of course. But if I hadn't known myself what a world of trouble we were in, I might have bought her act.

"Just step back while we search the boat."

Scooter assigned a boatswain to watch us and set about inspecting the boat.

"Look," Chloe said. "We stopped for a picnic. Had a couple drinks so we thought we ought to wait a while before heading back."

"That your story?" He lifted the bait box and stuck his hand in it.

With the end of a fish net he poked into the ice, tossed it out by the handfuls until he was apparently satisfied it was empty. I figured this would have been a logical place to haul liquor and maybe, just maybe, he wouldn't think of the gas tank. He slammed the lid shut and stomped into the wheelhouse, then peered down below.

"Anything down there?"

"No, this is it," Chloe said. "This is our sinister party. Scooter, for God's sake, you know me."

"I knew you. Lately, I'm not so sure," he said.

"You're acting funny."

"Well, I have had some major events lately," Chloe said.

"That's no excuse for breaking the law."

"Of course not," Chloe said, shooting him a look of total bewilderment. "That's why we're stopped here."

He disappeared down below.

"Your mother must be very proud of you." Mother addressed the young boatswain guarding us. "What an impressive boat. I imagine you must have had years of training to do what you do. Are you hungry? I believe we have some chicken left. Chloe, do we?"

"I'm on duty ma'am," the boatswain said. "Thanks all the same."

"I've been reading about the dangers of the crabbing industry." Ovid joined the conversation. "Do you spend a lot of time enforcing the stability rules?"

"That and watching out for smugglers."

"Smugglers," Ovid said. "Of what sort?"

"Marijuana, sir. Canada grows a lot of marijuana."

"Now I thought that was a Mexican import, didn't you, Lucia?" Ovid touched Mother on the elbow.

Together Ovid and Mother handled the situation like a pair of seasoned grifters. I watched, marveling at their dumb-tourist routine and wishing the Coast Guard would leave so I could visit the head.

Scooter came back up. "Looks like you got some new inflatable gas tanks since I last boarded your boat."

"They've been helpful on long trips." Chloe smiled at him. "You find what you were looking for?"

He shook his head.

My need for the head dissipated immediately. Instead, joy overcame me. I wanted to scream out but restrained myself. In fact, just as I had seen Calvery do one time in his cell, I looked to the heavens and whispered a sincere thank you.

Chapter Twenty-Two

Later that evening, Chloe and Finn returned to her house. Everything looked as she had left it, two half empty coffee mugs on the kitchen counter, a bag of unpacked groceries, Jazz's bowl licked clean. She passed by the dining table strewn with her father's meager belongings. What a fool she was. A broke fool.

She dropped onto the couch, Finn plopped next to her. He kissed her. "I've been waiting all day to do that."

Chloe pulled away from him. She would have worried about involving Finn in all this, how close he was to going straight to jail, but instead she thought of Duke. She wondered if he carried brass knuckles in his pocket and, if he, in turn, owed someone the money. Maybe he reported to a fat Don with a list of completed hits the size of a dime store novel. Surely Finn knew about crime, how to deal with thugs.

"I shouldn't have done it," she said.

"No, you shouldn't have," Finn said.

Finn had removed his boots at the back door. His feet smelled of day-old wash and his clothes of whiskey; she smelled just as bad.

"I'm broke. And now I owe Duke." She rested her head on Finn's shoulder. "What now?"

"He'll be over here wanting his money, and I'm not leaving your side."

"What an idiot I am." Chloe pulled her hair away from her face, twirled it into a knot at the back of her neck. "You know, don't you? I'm in big trouble."

"We're," Finn said.

"What should I do?" She looked up at the curve of his chin.

"We're not just talking about money here," Finn said, his voice serious now. "We're talking about the man who killed your father."

The statement hung in the air. This was the aftermath of the proposal Brian had brought to Mo's that she and Finn now shared: this quiet, this mound of debt, this story unfolding.

She reached for Finn's nearest hand and squeezed it. "I'll tell him I'll pay it back."

"Where's the pistol?"

"I left it in Perpetuity."

"Shit," he said. "You got anything here?"

"You don't think he'll come here?"

"Hell, yeah. You think he's going to wait around for you to show up back at the boat?" He had raised his voice, but seeing her reaction, he added, "It's all right. We'll get through this." He looked around the house. "We've got that anchor."

"Geez."

"That's right," Finn said. "I'm not trying to scare you."

She could feel Finn's breath on her neck. If they left now, they could be in Canada before daybreak. When she proposed the idea to Finn, he pulled her closer.

"I'll figure out how to pay him back. Somehow."

"What about the treasure?"

"You don't believe that."

"There was that poem in the Bible," he said. "We could at least take a look. You got a better idea?"

"What poem?" Chloe looked over to the table.

Finn popped up from the couch and ran to the dining table. He lifted the Bible from the box, opened it and showed her a tiny slit on the back cover. "There's a poem he wrote. It's in there."

"Now I'm stupid and crazy." She went to the kitchen and found a pair of tweezers. Her fingers shook as she tried to reach the paper with the pincers. Finally, she grasped it and pulled it out. They settled back to the couch and read the paper.

Chloe stared at the poem, then set the paper on the table. Then she picked it up again. "I can't imagine."

"I agree. But think about it," Finn said. His mussed up hair, and the excitement in his eyes, made her forget that he was some tough ex-con. "After your dad died, I caught this guy Jules in my cell looking through your dad's stuff. I didn't know what to make of it. Maybe there is a treasure. Why else would Jules be rifling through your father's stuff?"

Chloe stared at the poem, the printing of her father, perfectly-formed block letters, a bunch of silly rhymes. "This doesn't even make sense."

"There's money somewhere," Finn said. "Why else would Jules be snooping around in your dad's stuff? And your father always said that Rossi told him to take the jewels. Rossi didn't want anyone else to get them."

"I seriously doubt there are any jewels," she said.

"What if there are?"

Chloe examined the poem once again. She had heard about Thomas the Rhymer before, from Father Hollybrooke. "I can't make sense of this."

Finn read aloud. "'Rhymer Tom on a grassy bank/Sang songs for a crop of flowers fair/A turtle crawled inside the ring/To finish the race before the hare.'" His face gleamed with such hope it almost filled her as well. "Where's Sport?"

"A turtle is not exactly an animal you'd expect to read about in a Celtic poem," Chloe said. "Unless the turtle is—"

"Sport," Finn said, looking at Chloe in disbelief. "Why didn't I connect this before?"

Chloe rushed over to the terrarium and interrupted Sport who was making his way toward the greens of a carrot. She lifted him to eye level and examined the bronze and coffee colored scutes on the dome of his shell and the three letters—DCC.

"What does it mean?"

"I have no idea," Finn said. "Someone's initials? Dear Chloe and Calvery?" Finn shook his head dismissively. "It has to be a place. Do you know a place with the initials DCC?"

"What does it say next?"

" 'Upon his shell; the answer lies/The door to that fine thin place/Where nearby the horn echoes its sound/Pitting fear on the sailor's face.' "

"The fear on the sailor's face?"

"The horn is by a place too dangerous for ships," said Finn. "Unless…."

He tilted his head as if suddenly remembering something.

"You think you know what it means?"

"Why did your father want me, us, to know where your grandfather was born?"

Chloe saw the eagerness in Finn's eyes, as though that hope he had talked about was now taking form. There were moments today when she thought that maybe, just maybe, she had a future too, that her life was not going to end up a pile of crap after all. Finn had thrown himself into this project, convinced his mother to help him, brought this turtle to her, painted everything with this bright picture of hope. Now it was all here in front of her, her father was leading her somewhere, and it was too unbelievable to dismiss.

"He wants us to go to Yachats," Chloe said finally. "That's why you were supposed to ask where my grandfather was born."

"I think so, too. You want the next verse?" Eagerness enveloped every pore of Finn's face, sparked his eyes, gleamed from his teeth and it was contagious.

Finn read on. " 'Amidst the boughs of ancient firs/A cape named for a saint ever bold/She gave up all for Christ the King/Before thrown into the gladiator's hold.' "

Finn scanned the room. "Do you have an atlas?"

"Yes," she said, placing Sport on the floor. Then, standing, she added, "And, I have the calendar."

She fumbled through her father's box and pulled out the calendar.

"Is there a Cape?"

Chloe flipped through the pages until she found a picture of Cape Perpetua. Tracing her finger along the caption, he read, "Captain Cook named the cape Perpetua because it was sighted on St. Perpetua's Day."

"You're not going to believe this, but my cellmate, he used to draw saints on the wall, he drew her. Weird that he would draw her. Just a coincidence, I suppose. And, look at this picture, there's no way a ship would be able to come to shore around there. Fear in sailor's eyes. That has to be it."

"And guess where it is," Chloe said.

"Yachats?"

"That's right." She read through the stanza again: a cape named for a saint ever bold. "Let's Google Perpetua." Chloe hurried over to her desk and signed on to the computer. She drummed her fingers on the desk, waiting for the internet connection. "Come on," she said, resisting the temptation to press 'enter' again.

Finn peered over her shoulder. She felt his warm breath on her neck.

"Finally. Look at this," Chloe said. "St. Perpetua refused to renounce her Christianity and was sent into an arena with wild animals. So Cape Perpetua is named after a saint."

"I'm telling you, my cellie knew his saints," Finn said, handing her the calendar. "And, the only page in the calendar with any writing on it is this page. I thought it was because he was executed…" He glanced up, paused for a moment, just looking at her, "But maybe not. It's too many coincidences."

Finn grabbed the poem from Chloe. "Of course, the huge grassy hill, every other hill is covered in trees. Now you know where Perpetuity got her name. Had you ever wondered?"

"Not really. I just thought perpetuity meant perpetual. This cape must have been a special place to him." Chloe looked back at the poem. "There's more. The next verse says, 'The saint abides above the sea/Her hair a hillock of grass so fine/At the foot of the lady's mane/Devil's cavern fifty yards and nine.'"

"Devils Churn is at the bottom of Cape Perpetua," Finn read from the calendar. "It says here it is a sea cave."

"Devils Churn—DC—," Chloe said, turning the letters over in her mind.

"What's the other C?"

"Cape?"

"Devil's Churn Cape," Finn said. He studied the picture on the calendar. "Devil's Cape Churn." Finn screwed up his face. "Devil's Churn Calvery. The order is not right."

"Listen to this," Chloe said, " 'True Thomas I removed my load/And laid it down at the ladies knee/My God is good and always true/Surprised me at the places he'd be'. Interpretation, Finn?"

"Ladies knee- Cape Perpetua is named after a saint, a lady. The knee would be under her, right?"

"It goes on to say, 'A portal clear to show the way/To nether worlds far beyond the sea/Left for you dear a treasure true/By the door left open all for me.'"

"I know this," Chloe said. "A cave is a portal. He left the treasure in the cave."

"That's what it looks like," Finn said.

"There's one more," Chloe said. " 'Seek low to find my legacy/For you the future's yet to unfold/Where the Devil and Saint collide/I left for you a pot of gold.'"

"The cave is at the end of Devil's Churn and at the base of Cape Perpetua," Finn said. "Devil's Churn Cave or Cavern." He high-fived Chloe. "That has to be it."

"Wait, not so fast. I'll get a map." Chloe ran over to the coffee table and pulled a map from its drawer.

She unfolded the map, smoothed it flat onto the

dining room table. Her heart picked up its pace as she traced the coastline from Washington to Oregon with her finger. Heat rose to her neck. It was her tell as they said in poker games. She knew she was ablaze with red.

"Snodgrass said he arrested Daddy in Newport." She pointed to it on the map. "And, here's Yachats and the Cape right next to it." Chloe twisted her head to see Finn's reaction.

"It's all adding up." Finn studied the map. "Wouldn't Butch know about this?"

"Remember, Snodgrass said Butch went to meet my father. If there was money, Daddy wouldn't have told Butch. Anyone who knows Butch more than one day knows not to tell him anything you don't want the whole town knowing."

"I can't believe it." Finn didn't look up, his mouth hung open. "Spouting Horn."

"Where?"

"Right by the Cape." Finn pointed to a place on the map that said Spouting Horn. "The poem said, 'Nearby the horn echoes its sound.' Spouting Horn is right there by Cape Perpetua. That has to be the place. Remember what your father told Snodgrass—the air was too thin. You know why Calvery said that? There are at least three thin places here—the Cape is a hilltop, and you've got the shoreline, the cave, that's three right there. If it was sunrise or sunset, the place would have four. That's why your father said the air was too thin."

How was it possible that her father did all this before he was caught? Why didn't he go to her mother and wait for them to arrest him? Her father had planned it all, and it occurred to her, it might have been because of her. This man Finn was proof of it. How did her father know Finn would come along? How did he know he could trust him? She imagined only one explanation, one so far-fetched no one would believe it, especially not someone like her. Her father loved her, her father was innocent, and her father gave his life to leave her all he had.

Someone pounded on the front door. Chloe jumped.

Jazz barked.

"I'll get it." Finn started for the door.

Chloe gripped Finn's arm. "No, let me."

She opened the door. Just as she had feared, it was Duke. When he saw her, he took off his dripping hat, one of those safari-type canvas rain hats like Indiana Jones always wore.

"Where's your car?" Chloe took the hat from Duke.

"I left it halfway down the mountain." He unzipped his jacket, pulled it off and held it out to his side.

"Let me get that." Chloe grabbed it.

"I need to talk to you," Duke said, walking into the room.

"I'll just put this in the kitchen." Chloe ran into the kitchen with the dripping coat.

"What're you doing here?" She heard Duke address Finn.

"I could ask you the same thing. I met you down at the dock, remember?" Finn offered his hand, and Duke shook it.

"Oh, yeah," Duke said. "Still trying to make time with Chloe."

"Something like that," Finn said.

"It's all right," she said. "He was with us today." Chloe stepped next to Finn. "Look, I know I lost your money. Somehow, the Coast Guard found out about us."

"So what happened. Did they find anything?"

"Nothing," Chloe said, shaking her head.

"He saw the tanks, though?" Duke asked.

Chloe shrugged. "He saw him, they were empty."

Duke ambled over to the table and checked out the map. "Going somewhere?" He pulled a pair of reading glasses from his pocket and examined the map. "You wouldn't try and run out on me now, would you?"

"Finn's up here with his mother," Chloe said. "They're driving back to Texas."

"Finn? Unusual name," Duke said. "What did you say you were doing up here?"

"I didn't," Finn said.

Chloe shot Finn a look. No need for him to get cocky.

"Mind if I sit down?" All of a sudden, Duke's voice sounded overly polite. He pulled a wooden chair from the dining table and sat. Jazz followed him and let out a barely audible growl.

"I figure if we do two more runs, I can make it up to you." Chloe's voicc sounded desperate. "Maybe day after tomorrow?" Chloe sat in the chair next to him. "Another run?"

"So how is it the two of you met?"

Chloe flashed a smile. "The way I meet anyone. Finn and his mother came down to the dock, and I sold him on a charter."

"You never knew him before that?"

"Never saw him before that day," Chloe said.

Duke raised his eyebrows. "Y'all need to get rid of that drunk you have aboard."

"What about him?"

"I figure he blabbed down at the dock."

"He didn't have anything to do with it." Chloe dropped her eyes, reached down to scratch Jazz behind the ears.

"That's not what I hear. You better leave him home," Duke said, eyeing Finn as he talked. "Maybe this Finn guy can help you. I think ol' what's-his-name—."

"Butch," she blurted his name out in a harsh tone.

"I think he got loose-lipped in a bar. But you're right, they won't suspect you now," Duke said. "No one would be stupid enough or have cojones enough to try it again after that."

"Besides, I feel like the Frees are counting on it." She fiddled with the curls in Jazz's coat.

"They are." Duke fidgeted in his seat, looked around the room. Then he looked to the floor where Sport crawled about in his terrarium. "Where'd you get the turtle?"

"I've always had it," said Chloe.

"I didn't know they had this kind of turtle up here. I've never seen any. Of course, I haven't been out on the rivers much, but I thought they liked warmer weather." He picked up Sport and examined him. Sport disappeared into his shell. "Funny you're so willing to go out again, after all you been through. Must have been quite a day."

He practically dropped Sport into the terrarium. Duke inspected the room, examining the books, the shells and the driftwood, as he made his way to the fireplace. He wore a pair of denim boat shoes—the kind with a leather string woven into the top of the quarter and vamp—soaked navy blue by the rain. Not exactly hiking shoes.

"The Coast Guard came on board the boat and all?" Duke examined a piece of brain coral on the mantel.

"Searched everything. We made like a bunch of Irish drunks. You should have seen it. It was good, wasn't it, Finn?" She laughed, a forced laugh, but maybe Duke didn't catch it. "Anyway, about your money. Maybe we do another run day after tomorrow."

"I'll give you another crack at it. Seeing's as how you owe me. Give you a chance to pay me back." Duke pulled his lower lip tight until it looked like a smile. "Maybe you can figure out a way to convince your fella here to help out." He stepped to the door.

Chloe followed him, handed him his coat, then edged in front of him to reach the knob. She twisted it until she heard a click and the door swung open. "Okay then, day after tomorrow it is."

Chapter Twenty-Three

Chloe and I agreed our first move was to take care of Duke, so the next morning we drove over to Clam Harbor Motor Lodge to get Mother and headed to the Coast Guard station. Chloe and I had agreed that Mother might help our credibility.

Golden Boy Scooter greeted us. "Sorry about the other day." He flashed his pearly whites our direction.

"That's what we're here to talk to you about." Chloe smiled at him, and I felt the hair on my neck perk up. "Are you in charge of policing the waters around here?"

"I am." Scooter squared up in the chair, his spine as straight as a West Texas highway. "We are." He corrected himself.

The guy made me feel inferior, I will admit. He was handsome, built, had a steady job, and no doubt, was neither an addict nor a felon—a real Eagle Scout.

"And if we were to tell you about someone breaking the law, you wouldn't hold us responsible?"

"Uh." He stammered, looked around.

This might have been the biggest thing to hit Clam Harbor since he and Chloe went to the prom.

Mother stepped over to the wall and admired a certificate. "So you're the Chief Petty Officer. My, my, my. You are in charge. If you heard word about illegal activity going on and you stopped it, I suppose your superior would give you a—what's the word—

commendation."

He looked as if he were pondering this idea, in a positive way. Maybe Scooter even daydreamed about the ceremony when the Admiral pinned a medal to his chest.

"Of course, we only know this information second hand," Chloe said. "But in the interest of Clam Harbor, we feel it is our duty to report illegal activity. Oh, hell, Scooter. Here is the long and the short of it. I was broke. I didn't even have a thousand dollars to get my father's ashes. This guy told me he would give me a thousand bucks every time I smuggled alcohol over to Coho.

"Man," he said, shaking his head. "I never took you for…."

Chloe kept her feelings close. I realized I was staring at her and turned away. A reminder dinged on the computer. I wondered what movie-star man thought about all this.

Finally, Chloe broke the silence. "I don't want the Native Americans touched. If you won't give me your word, the deal's off."

"Indians?"

Chloe sat down and explained the whole scene to Scooter. His movie-star eyes fixed on her face. I saw how much he wanted her, and it burned me to see her sitting so close. However, I kept my cool.

When Chloe finished, I said, "What now?"

"I'll need to run this by my superiors," Scooter said.

Mother pointed to his certificate, "I thought you were in charge."

"I'll have to run it by the senior officer."

"You don't think there will be a problem?" Chloe scooted forward in her chair. "I don't want to put you in a difficult position."

"I wish you wouldn't have gotten mixed up in all this," Scooter said. "You're asking me to ignore the fact that you were breaking the law." He paused, looked out the window. Just outside, his crew mopped the deck of Clam Harbor's one cutter. "And, you're asking me to keep the Indians, the Nootkas, out of this."

"It would be the right thing to do," Chloe said. "This could be a big case for you."

"I don't care about that," Scooter said, and then paused to study Chloe before adding, "I'm doing this for you."

I felt like a guy on a double date without a date. Judging from the way Scooter looked at Chloe, I suspected there would be no problem convincing his superiors.

He stood and stepped toward the door. "The Nootkas are in Canada. They're also Native Americans. They have their own laws."

"Surely you work together on things like this," Chloe said.

"I'll see what I can do," Scooter said, his cartoonishly handsome face sober.

We waited for at least fifteen minutes. Mother and I predicted the answer would be yes. Chloe predicted no.

Finally, he returned. "This is how it's going to go down. We'll keep a man posted at the dock and wait for Duke to come fill your tanks. You…" He fixed his eyes directly at me. "Chloe will wear a wire—"

"No way!" I stood up. "She can't do that."

"It's the only way."

Rage swelled up in me, and I imagine my face showed it. I knew he was right. They couldn't pick Duke up for loading liquor in the bags, that liquor had to cross into international waters.

Let it go, Calvery used to tell me when he saw me puff up like a junior high bully. Anger is only fear coming out. I was afraid, all right. Now that I'd come clean with Chloe, I couldn't let anything happen to her.

"We don't know about these guys," Scooter said, his voice calm and deliberate. "They could be dangerous."

"Guys?" Chloe asked.

"We've received word that Duke Summers was seen meeting with another man outside of town."

"Another guy?" I said, watching him sort through a stack of papers on his desk. "That settles it. The deal's off."

Chloe put her hands on her hips and cocked her head. "It's not your decision."

"It's one girl—"

She put up a hand and pointed at me, "Don't you dare say it."

So I realized I'm not going to get anywhere. I threw up my hands and backed away. "My bad."

"It's probably Brian," Chloe said, her voice softer this time. "He's harmless." She waved a hand in the air like we were talking about ordering lunch.

Scooter turned down the corners of his mouth and shook his head. "It's not Brian."

"You know Brian?" Chloe tilted her head to Scooter and shot him a suspicious look.

"I do," Scooter said. "Clam Harbor is a small town."

"He's not from here," Chloe said.

"He comes down often enough."

"Would somebody please fill me in?" I asked.

"Just a guy," Chloe said.

From the way she said it, I figured she had meant it. She did seem pissed that Scooter seemed to know just a little bit too much about her.

Even though Scooter smirked, he looked worried.

I was downright scared for her now. I had the sense that Golden Boy Scooter was in over his head. After all, how many times does something like this go down in Clam Harbor?

"So who is it then?" I asked.

"We don't know, and you don't care," Scooter said, scowling at me. "You came to us. You turned this over to us. You stay out of this. You stay with your mother. I don't care. You just stay away. Understood?"

Real hard-boiled, he wanted me to know. But I saw right through it, all the way to his chest full of Scout badges. He was the big catfish in the pond all right, but after three years of dodging great whites and killer whales, in this one respect, I had the edge.

"All right, Boss." I said with a cool sarcastic tone.

Chapter Twenty-Four

After the meeting with Scooter, I immediately contacted my connections—Butch and Ovid. Scooter had a point about wanting me out of this stakeout; he wanted to keep things neat. Me, I needed to see this going down. I didn't like Scooter's plan, but there was no other option. If Chloe was going to wear a wire to meet Duke and this unknown man, I was going to keep an eye out. That's where Butch and Ovid came in. In addition to his other talents, before he became a birder, Ovid had spent years shooting ducks with aristocrats in England and happened to be a crack shot. And shooting harpoons for over thirty years, Butch's aim had been perfected. If the set-up turned bad on us, between the three of us, we would be a tight team.

Friday evening I assigned myself to keep a lookout for Duke, and stationed Ovid and Butch at opposite ends of Main Street. I parked Mother's sputtering Impala behind the tuna packing company and secured a spot on a cinder block strategically located behind a dumpster filled with whatever fish remains hadn't made it into the can. After thinking about all the tuna I'd eaten in Polunsky, it was a relief to see fish guts in the dumpster.

The alley teemed with feral cats loaded up on Omega 3 and reeking of fish. Their coats gleamed like mink. My hideout stank of cat spray, rotted lettuce and tuna heads.

Fog crept in through every alley and passageway, crawling like a snail under every bin and building, leaving a slick, wet trail on every surface it touched. I convinced myself it was the fog, not the cat pee, seeping through my jeans.

Perpetuity had long ago lost its color to the brume, it was merely a formless object on the dock, the sixth in line. I had no idea when or if Duke would show up. If he didn't come, I wasn't sure what I would do next.

After two hours of watching felines fighting over fish guts, I finally saw him. He jumped off the dock and onto the gangway leading to Chloe's boat. I texted her, "He's here."

As Duke scanned the wharf with a flashlight, I caught sight of his face, ghostly pale skin, eyes narrow as coin slots, his lips clamped onto a toothpick. The light zeroed in on the gas tank, one of those big white drums on wheels like you might see behind a trailer out in West Texas. It was parked at the shore end of the dock. Duke grabbed the handle on the cart. That's it. Take the tank, fill Chloe's boat. That's all you need to do.

The beam from Duke's flashlight jerked back and forth as he tried to position the tank to roll down the dock. Duke had come alone. That was good for Chloe. A cat meowed and landed exactly in front of me. I fell back onto the cinder block wall behind me. Of all the luck. The tom stood there, its yellow eyes staring at me, a hiss pressing through his clenched teeth.

Dammit, this cat's gonna get me killed. I edged into a shadow. The light jerked to the wharf, to the dock, to the boats. I held my breath. Freezing cold burned in my chest as if I'd swallowed an ice cube. I folded up as small as I could and waited for the light to pass over me. I was starving for air but afraid that when I finally gasped for breath the noise would be deafening. My heart pulsed against my kneecap. It felt like a phone vibrating. Wait, it was my phone. I ignored it.

The beam of light stopped at the entrance to Chloe's dock, then illuminated the whale-watching ticket kiosk before pausing at my dumpster. The pressure in my chest was about to blow. Duke caught the cat in his spotlight, its fur spiked and glossy with fog, glowed orange and white. The tom looked straight at me, arched his spine and let out an alley-cat-sized roar as it ran away. I exhaled, a puff of my warm breath disappearing into the fog. Duke's light returned to its position by Perpetuity.

Stakeouts required steady nerves. Currently I was about as calm as a tom chasing a molly in heat, the molly leaping from one garbage can to the next, the air heavy with her scent. I needed to take a break, go home, lap up some milk, lick my wounds, and take a nap.

Time hadn't lurched to a halt so much as teetered like a car with its front wheels hanging over a cliff. I listened, straining to hear someone talking even though I was well out of ear shot.

A footstep sounded, then a split second later, a hand landed on my shoulder.

I jumped.

The hand moved over my mouth. "Don't say a word."

Even though it was a whisper, it was a familiar voice. I jerked around and ended up eye to eye with the man I hated most in the world—my father. "Damn, of all the—"

He put a finger to his mouth. "Your mother called me. Now I know you'd just as soon wrestle with a javelina, but here I am, and I aim to offer some tactical support."

Then we heard the hum of a big motor. Lights appeared in the bay, then the red and white flag of the Coast Guard. Despite the fog, the lights of the interceptor illuminated the entire wharf. A crewman climbed off the boat and jumped onto Perpetuity. Behind him was another man, someone standing so straight it had to be Scooter.

Duke appeared at the stern of Perpetuity. He held his hands up in the air like, what's happening? Chloe stood beside him. The crewman followed the hose down into the boat and left Duke up top with Scooter. A few minutes later the crewman reappeared. They talked a minute, then Scooter shook Duke's hand and climbed back aboard his interceptor.

"What the hell?" As much as it pained me to admit ignorance to my father, I looked up at him hoping for an explanation. "Why didn't they arrest him?"

If what I was thinking played out on my face, I must've looked a sight, even in the fog, because Dad said, "You better fill me in and fill me in quick."

My eyes met his. "They were supposed to arrest him for smuggling alcohol."

"You setting him up?"

"He killed Chloe's father."

I looked back at the dock. Duke had rolled the hose back onto the gas tank and left it in front of Perpetuity. He was talking to Chloe, and as soon as the cutter moved into the bay, the two of them strode off the dock.

"I don't understand why they didn't arrest him."

He shrugged. "Maybe the Coast Guard's dirty."

"Not a chance, that guy is so clean he squeaks when he walks."

"Then Duke wasn't doing anything wrong. He was pumping gas into the boat; he didn't say anything on the wire."

"That has to be it. But how did he know?"

"Must be slick." Dad motioned me away from the dumpster. We moved back around the fish cannery to Main Street. "And he's already figured out who set him up."

"And he's got Chloe," I said. Terror bore down on me and all the way down to my balls, every hair on my body stood on end. Only one thing calmed me—the thought of Scooter's face at the end of my fist. I wanted to pound some character into him, flatten his nose and fatten his eye. To top it off, my no-good father was here to rescue me. All that would have to wait. "You got a car?" I asked Dad.

Dad motioned to a black convertible Mustang.

A message from Ovid popped up on my phone:

"Hummer passed Main and headed out the coast highway."

"It shouldn't be hard to catch up with a Hummer," I said.

We jumped into the Mustang, a poor substitute for Dad's usual Corvette, but I supposed the sportiest car available for rent. Dad cranked it up before I even closed the door.

"Where's the money?" Dad asked.

"Huh?"

"We haven't got time to fool around here. You know this guy's gonna want the money."

"We haven't got any money. We had to dump the alcohol. Exactly what did Mother tell you?"

"She said the Coast Guard almost arrested the two of you and that the girl owed money to a very bad guy."

"That about sums it up."

"She also said the guy was with the Bandidos."

After I told Dad the abbreviated story of inheriting Calvery's belongings, and about my encounters with Jules in Polunsky, Dad said, "I should have told you to keep away from them."

"I didn't exactly invite him in. Anyway, Duke was the one who set Calvery up. Jules wasn't involved."

"You're telling me Duke set up your girl's father?"

I nodded and clenched my teeth. "Not good, right?" I checked my phone again.

Dad shook his head, then pointed his finger to the road, asking directions. I motioned him toward the main highway. The tires skidded around the corner as he gunned the Mustang.

After we drove a mile or so, I caught a glimpse of the Hummer's giant rear end. "There it is!" I yelled.

Dad gunned it. The Mustang fishtailed into the left lane, then flipped back into the right lane just before an Acura appeared.

He said, "Two reasons why people do things—sex or money. Which do you think it is?"

"Money," I said.

"Where is it?"

"I don't even know if there is any."

"Don't give me that," Dad said. "I didn't raise no idiot."

I thought about saying, you didn't raise me at all. But thought better of it. "There's all this nonsense about a treasure. But it doesn't make sense. It could just be all some crazy thing this guy made up on death row."

"Does she know where this treasure is?"

"Not exactly," I said.

"Does she know where it is?"

"Okay, okay," I said. "It's in Oregon. If it is. It is in Oregon."

"Then, that's where we're going."

An RV obstructed our view of the Hummer, irritating Dad. He kept inching over the line to see if he could pass. Finally, he whipped around it. I grabbed the handle on the door frame.

It was a six-hour drive to Oregon. When we reached Seaside, Oregon, the Hummer pulled off at a gas station. We kept our distance and waited at a Shell station down the street. I could tell there were three people in the car, and I thought of all the things that could happen to Chloe. Death was not the worst of them.

When we got back on the road, I started thinking about Lacy looking at me from behind the curtain, her eyes wide with fear, and a typical worthless feeling twisted in my gut. That worthless feeling made me want to ask Dad where he'd been all these years, all those Sundays Mother and I waited for him, all those nights Mother and I watched baseball alone, but when it came right down to it, I didn't care. If I could just get through this night with Chloe safe, I felt certain everything would be all right between us. I'd have done something right for once and could finally cut him some slack.

The whole drive seemed familiar, maybe some time long ago we had taken a Sunday drive, and maybe stopped at the beach and had a picnic. Except I knew I remembered every moment I had spent with my father, and I knew that there was such a thing as false memories. I went back in my mind to the last time I'd been civil with my father. It must have been before I'd grown hair on my balls.

"Do you think we should've called the Coast Guard?" I said. Then thinking it through, how Chloe had a wire on, I reconsidered. If she had indicated she was in danger, the Coast Guard would have followed her. Hell, maybe they had beaten us here. "I guess there was no need, on account of the wire."

"Unless she pulled it off."

That seemed exactly like the kind of crazy-ass thing Chloe would do, if she could. "Always the optimist, Dad."

After six hours of some skillful driving on Dad's part, we finally reached Yachats, Oregon. I knew we were doomed when they stopped in Yachats. It meant Chloe had told them where the treasure was, if there was a treasure. What horrible thing had they done to her to make her tell them?

It was early morning— about two—and the Hummer pulled into The Sandcastle, a two-story motel overlooking the Pacific, or so I assumed. At least the sign promised ocean views.

We pulled into a roadside rest area and waited for the Hummer to unload. For a moment, we were quiet. In the distance, lights from the motel winked on and off. When we finally moved the Mustang to the Sandcastle parking lot, we saw the Hummer parked at the back entrance. I wondered how Duke had managed to get Chloe inside without looking suspicious.

We parked the Mustang at the opposite end of the lot from the Hummer and in the closest spot to Highway 101. The Sandcastle looked like the kind of place frequented by families on a budget or retired couples. Its redwood siding had weathered to a driftwood gray, and its landscaping consisted of mulched flower beds with more dog poop than flowers. Economy-sized rental cars filled less than half the parking lot.

“We’ll get a room,” Dad said. “Next to them if we can.”

“Leave the keys under the mat,” I said. “You don’t want to be fumbling for keys while making a getaway.”

Through careful bargaining with the night clerk, Dad managed to rent a room just down the hall from Duke. Its room amenities included the musty smell of too much parmesan, orange indoor-outdoor carpet and a balcony overlooking the Pacific.

“I don’t know anything about this guy Duke.” I said. “No telling what they’ll do to her to make her talk.”

“If she tells them where the money is, they won’t hurt her.”

“She doesn’t exactly know.”

“That could be a problem.”

“I’m not sitting here until dawn to find out.” I checked out the sliding glass door to the balcony. Outside, the western sky was black as a cast-iron skillet, and the wind whipped up a wet breeze from the Pacific. The air dances around me with icy blasts from below and above. “I’ll go in from the balcony. This guy I knew at Polunsky said hardly anyone ever locks their back door or their balcony.”

“That’s what you learned?” Dad said. “I wish to hell you hadn’t had to go there.”

“Yeah, well, right now that information comes in handy.” I sat on the other chair, across from him. “You stand guard by the ice machine, and I’ll jump the balconies.”

“Not a chance.” Dad lifted his bag onto the kitchenette counter, unzipped it, pulled out a couple paperbacks, a box of bullets and a .45. “I have the pistol; I’m going in after her.”

“Not now. There’s no time for your bull—.”

“This is not bull shit. I was the Ranger in ’Nam, I can do this.” He paused while he examined the chamber of the .45. “I want to do this.”

“You’re pathetic,” I said. “It’s always about you, isn’t it?” The waves rushing and the wind sounded like the constant din of Polunsky. I heard Calvery talking me down from many a metaphorical cliff—Time is too expensive to be spent in anger. And if time was too expensive then, it was Ferrari expensive now. I dropped it and said, "We'll both go."

Dad shot me a thumbs-up.

Our second floor room overlooked a deserted beach. Duke, his buddy and Chloe were two rooms over. A concrete wall separated the balconies, so it was no big deal to climb around, but one wrong move and we'd crash onto the rocks below. No sweat for me, I was light on my feet. But my old man was, well, old. I had faith in him, I had to. It was go time. Time to punch in and play hero.

When I helped Dad across them, he scowled at me. He would have managed just fine without me. The blinds on their patio door were closed. On the television a man said, "Up next, CSI Miami." Pressing my face to the window, I looked through the fraction-of-an-inch holes in the blinds and saw Chloe with her back to us, tied up in a chair.

Dad chambered a round in the .45, and I unfolded my pocket knife. With a nod to each other, we eased open the door. Dad stepped in first and immediately shifted left, covering the two doors in the room with the pistol. The water in the bathroom was running. As soon as Dad took his step, I filed past to Chloe. The tension on her face eased the minute she saw me. Since I kept my knife sharp, I cut through the tape with ease—first her wrists, then the ankles.

Chloe's eyes widened. I knew another person was in the room, the air suddenly suffocating from their presence.

"Don't move, Finn, or I'll smoke your game."

Dread filled me. I hadn't heard the voice in a couple of months, but I recognized it as if it were yesterday. "Jules, you're a long way from Polunsky."

"You're late." Jules eyes went to my dad, then to Chloe, then back to me. "We've been expecting you."

"Long drive from Washington," I said.
Jules shifted on his feet and glanced behind me. I turned just in time to see Duke step out from behind a drape.

"You've met Duke, I believe," Jules said.

I guess we'd interrupted Jules cleaning up, because he was bare-chested, his abs cut up like a bad bag of dope, and his skin covered in twenty years worth of prison tattoos. All those times he had sashayed into my cell laden with lettuce for Sport, the fried-egg sandwich, it had never fit together until now. He was the other man. Why? Because he knew Calvery gave me more than a turtle. Because he was searching for something in my cell. Because the world of prison gangs and free-world gangs are not all that far apart. Duke and Jules and the Bandidos, it fit together somehow, and I was close to figuring it out.

What we had was a Mexican standoff—Jules pointing a gun at Chloe, Dad with his sights on Jules, Duke aiming at Dad.

"You got parole," I said. "Funny you'd end up so far from Texas."

"I hear they have good crab up here." Jules backed up toward Chloe.

"Cut the chatter." Duke repositioned his revolver and motioned for Jules to move toward Chloe.

"I've underestimated you, Tully." Jules put an arm around Chloe's waist, and pulled her up to his chest so that she was standing in front of him. "I'll take your knife."

"What's your plan?" I handed him the knife.

"You know the plan," Jules said. "We're just here to get what's coming to us. Help us out. It's not like you ever cared for your father anyway. Tell him to back off. No one needs to get hurt."

"I'll do whatever you want." Chloe spoke calmly for a girl in the arms of a murderer.

"That's a good girl," Duke said. "We can work this out all nice and easy."

"What's all this about?" I said.

"It's about money," Jules said.

"There isn't any," I said. "That's why Chloe got involved with Duke in the first place."

"You really are an idiot, aren't you?" Duke waved the gun back and forth.

"I've been told that before."

"Calvery left it up here somewhere. You know that," Duke said, examining the trigger of his revolver. "Then, we're done."

Duke bared his teeth at me while he pressed the gun into Dad's head.

"You haven't taken enough from her?" I asked.

"You think Duke here offered to help Chloe with some cash because he wanted to get her into the smuggling business? C'mon." Jules spit a piece of tobacco from his mouth. "Calvery took our money the night he killed Rossi. She's our social security."

I knew it was the Vietnamese who had left the money, and I bit my tongue, literally stuck it between my molars and chewed on it as if it were a piece of gum. Glancing over at Duke and my father, I recognized a look in Dad's eyes.

Jules followed my gaze. With an abrupt jerk, he turned just as Dad tackled Duke and started in on him. Dad looked stronger than Duke, but Duke was younger. Duke's revolver slid across the floor. Chloe dove towards it and ran from the room.

Cursing, Jules aimed the pistol at my father. Desperate to spoil his aim, I grabbed Jules' gun hand. Gripping his wrist, I twisted with all my strength. Jules went to his knees, clung to the weapon. Clutching, twisting, heaving, I forced him backwards and, frantic to deflect the gun barrel, I fell on top of him.

He squeezed the trigger. With the semiautomatic's silencer, the shot sounded like a door slamming, not even loud enough to draw attention. The stench of gunpowder burned my nostrils.

In the corner of my vision, I thought I saw Dad hit the floor. Duke looked out cold. I started to turn, but the pressure of the gun against my forehead, the reminder that it was pointed directly into my frontal lobe, halted me. Jules' breath, heavy with beer and Slim Jim's, blew into my face. Not a smell, not a sound, not a movement, seemed unimportant to me.

Jules sounded calm and in control when he said, "Don't make me kill you."

Another shot rang out, and the cool gun barrel slid off my skin as Jules fell. Blood gushed out of one of his thighs. I grabbed the gun and made the count—Duke was still knocked out, Dad had a gun, and Jules was hit.

"Get out of here." Dad mouthed the words and pointed to the door.

I shook my head and said, "I can't leave you here."

"Go," he said.

I knew we needed help and fast. Jules was hit, but Duke would wake up eventually. He wouldn't hang around with Dad, he'd be after us, after Chloe.

Not looking back, I ran for the stairs, and when I reached the parking lot, Chloe jumped from behind a car and hugged me. "Thank God."

For an instant—time enough to feel her cold hands and see the determined I-will-survive look on her face—we waited, both breathless.

"The Mustang," I said, not a split second later, and pointed toward the car.

We bolted toward the Mustang. I cranked it up and gunned it, spitting gravel as I left the parking lot and merged onto 101. Chloe glanced at the speedometer, then back to the parking lot.

"He'll be following us," I said.

"He?"

"Duke."

She didn't ask any questions beyond that. Knowing Chloe, she was putting it all together in her head. It was easy enough to see who was missing—Dad and Jules.

"Watch for the Hummer," I said.

Chloe turned sideways and kept her eyes on the road behind us.

Patting at my pockets, I pulled out my phone and tossed it to Chloe. “Call for help,” I said. “Tell them two men have been shot. Don’t tell them who you are.”

She called 911 and while she was talking she kept an eye out for the Hummer. The operator wanted to keep her on the phone, I could tell, but Chloe worked it just right. She had experience beyond her years, and I only knew the half of it. Someone with a regular life gets their fair share of troubles, but most of the time, they ride them out, have some good times with the bad. Then some people, like Chloe, never catch a break at all.

Though it was cold, sweat dripped into my eyes. I looked at the gas gauge. We were just above the reserve. “We’re running on fumes.”

“I think I see the Hummer,” Chloe said, turning to me.

“Where is it?”

“A couple cars behind us,” she said. “Turn off this road.” She pointed to a gravel road.

I whipped the car off the highway, and when the Mustang was well into the roadway, I turned off the lights. “I don’t know where this is going, but it better be good.”

Before I turned off the lights, I got a good look at the road—narrow, muddy, and, in about five-hundred feet, steep. Chloe rolled down her window, and the air turned moist and slick as oil.

“You’re okay on this side,” she said, just before we hit a pothole and bottomed out.

“You think this is far enough?” I knew we had reached the hill. This had not been a good idea.

“Go on,” she said. “Maybe there’s another turn somewhere.”

We passed a white post with a number and company symbol on it. Chloe must have seen it at the same time because she said it was a logging road.

“That good or bad?” I asked.

“Bad,” she said. “It’s going nowhere, that is unless you want to cut some trees.”

“Shit.” I pounded on the steering wheel. “Of all the

shit to get into. We got to back out of here."

I put the Mustang in reverse. Backing up, the rear end slid towards the shoulder. When I put it back into first gear, the tires spun and the driver's-side rear wheel fell into the ditch.

"Of all the luck." I grabbed Duke's pistol from under the console. "Chloe, take the gun and get us some sticks out of those woods. We can wedge them under the tires for traction."

She turned her head towards the forest, and when I handed her the .45, she said, "You keep it."

"No, you." I waved her off. "Hurry, I can get us out of here. I used to go muddin' in Texas all the time. Get me some sticks while I dig."

I searched the trunk for some kind of tool. Finding one measly lugnut wrench, I dropped to my knees and tore into the mud with it, "Shit, holy fucking shit," I said, scooping the thick heavy earth, looking for a solid bottom, for gravel, a rock, finding nothing but black wet mud. I kept at it, clawing at the mound until from behind me in the trees, I heard a voice.

"Ah, Finn, look at you, digging in the mud," Duke said. "When you gonna get it? Guys like us weren't meant for a pedestrian lifestyle. That girl's all in your head, little brother, I mean, we could find this money and head to the sunny weather. Instead, you have me chasing you through the rain, getting all dirty."

"You just leave Jules to die?" I said. "Too bad, the ambulance is on their way."

"You never know how things will work out," Duke said. "That's why you have to look at each situation with fresh eyes. Take you, for example, one minute you've got a girl and a father, the next minute you don't. But that's okay, because I'm here."

"And Jules?"

"Don't worry about him," he said, huffing. "Worry about you. Me and you can get this treasure."

"How do I know you'd keep your word and not kill me?"

"What choice have you? Your girl ran off, as they always do," Duke said. In the headlights, his hair gleamed like milk. "It's just you, me, and my pistol. You ought to pick the winning side."

I pretended to consider it, hoping Chloe would have sense enough to stay away. As if I would ever do business with someone like him. "If I show you, you'll whack me."

"If you don't show me, I'll whack you."

"If I knew where it was, I'd have it by now."

"You don't know yet. It's still sorting itself out in your head. But it's in there. Somewhere in your mind, you hold the secret. In your mind, and in the mind of that cunt that's run off on you, you know. You're right to assume I won't split the money with you. What I will do is let you live," Duke said. "If you don't give me that loot, I'll kill you and get the girl, who will show me. Then I'll kill her. What will it be, Finn? Live or die? Choose correct, cause in three seconds you could be dead…Three…Two…One."

In an echo like God's own voice, a deafening blast roared over the hills and back, and my only regret was that I would die having failed Chloe and Lacy. There was no pain, only a sense of a lurching stop.

Duke's gleaming hair fell out of view and into the rising morning mist. The mist gathered over him and buried him before floating over to me. It softened the ringing in my ears, it pricked my skin with cool effervescent bubbles. And then, I realized I was still standing.

Chloe was frozen, arms still extended with Duke's pistol. A lick of smoke rose from the barrel, and a tear slid over her cheek. Not fear. Not sadness. It was the resolve of a little girl's pain from a fatherless childhood—retribution for a stolen patriarch.

Chapter Twenty-Five

After the police took Duke's body away, a detective asked Chloe and me some questions, then let us go visit my father in the hospital in Newport, about twenty miles from Yachats. Chloe and I drove there in silence.

When we reached Newport, it was six in the morning and low tide. The waves fell limply onto the shore and pulled away with a hushing sound. Even the seagulls seemed to be using their inside voices. The ocean swam in a pearly light extending from the sky, where the clouds hugged the horizon, to the shoreline, where hand-in-hand a couple explored the beach. I looked out on it all like a soldier home from battle—relieved, proud, perhaps even certain.

I left Chloe at the Sylvia Beach Hotel, where she could get some sleep and wait for Mother and Ovid. She made me promise I'd see her as soon as I finished visiting Dad, and for the first time, I felt like we were a couple.

Walking up to the hospital, I prayed. I realized I was the worst kind of believer, the kind that only dials up God when his ass is on the line. This time, there was a life at stake. Dear God, let my Dad live. I mean, if it is your will and all. And, if you wouldn't mind, between now and when I see him, would you give me the words to say? Because I've got nothing.

In the intensive care unit, I faced a paler version of

my father, his face whitewashed, his skin wrinkled and puckered like the peel of a shriveled apple. An IV bag hung from a pole beside his bed, a yellow bag of urine dangled from the bed frame, and a plastic rectangular box with a rubber tube connected to it sat on the floor. It turned out to be a chest tube. His left lung had collapsed.

"You alive?" I asked.

Dad opened his eyes. "I've been better."

"Close call."

"Glad to see you're all right." He locked eyes with me.

I looked at his thin face. "Me? You're the one who got shot."

"You're the one who killed Duke." he said.

"It was Chloe," I said.

"Well, I'll be damned," he said, making a face. "She all right?"

"In shock, I suppose," I said. "She didn't talk much on the way to Newport." I pulled up a chair and collapsed into it. "What happened to Jules?"

"He's here."

"He's alive?"

"I figure Duke gave us both up for dead. He grabbed my pistol and ran out of the room. I wish I'd shot Duke instead."

"I think I'll have to pay Jules a visit."

"I imagine he's got a guard."

"We'll see."

After we finished replaying the night, Dad seemed to perk up, his deathbed pallor replaced by a hint of color in his cheeks.

"Mother shouldn't have called you up here," I said, giving him a look that showed him I was glad Mother had called him.

"Your mother's a good lady. She was always the smart one. Except for marrying me." He reached toward a tiny jar of lip balm on the bedside table. "Only two good things came out of that. You and Lacy."

I opened the lip balm and dabbed it on Dad's lips.

The lights of the ICU twinkled Dad's eyes. He was right about Lacy.

"Maybe only one," I said.

Nevertheless, I appreciated the nice reference to me. Thinking back, I guessed it was the nicest thing he had ever said to me.

"You were always a good kid," he said. "Until you got into the junk. I blame myself."

I knew enough about AA to protest. "It was my own fault, Dad."

"I should've been there for you."

"It would've been nice to have you around," I said.

"I haven't got much of an excuse. Maybe Vietnam," he said, then paused thoughtfully for a second. "I never got over it."

Not prepared for an apology, I made a just-bit-into-a-lemon face. "You don't need to do this. You're not dying." The IV let out a whirring sound. I stood up against the window and considered the view of Yaquina Bay. It looked like someone had fired a bird rifle full of sunbeams across it. "It's okay, Dad, really."

"I wished I could have been a dad to you. I really do. It wasn't in me."

"I guess it's about time to let it go," I said.

Dad replied with a question. "Forgive me?"

I didn't commit entirely, though I had the sense I would someday. You know the feeling, it comes in smaller versions like running a mile one day and knowing you'll run two the next. Dad launched into a coughing fit, causing the hose in his chest to bounce like a poltergeist beneath his gown. Figuring bouncing tubes were a bad thing, I pressed the call light.

The nurse rushed in, shot me her best look of annoyance and said, "He needs to take it easy."

Finally, Dad recovered from his coughing fit. "You gonna answer me, Son?"

Calvery once told me, "We're all bastards, but God loves us anyway." Those were the words of a smart guy named Will Campbell who was asked to define

Christianity. Incredibly, I'd forgotten I was a bastard, too. Not a surprise, as I look back on it. My ego had often barged in and attempted to ruin things for me.

"Sorry I was such a jerk all these years," I said.

The light over Dad's bed illuminated his face. His cheeks were wet. A sight I never thought I'd see.

He shook his head. "No. I'm sorry." His apology whirled about the room like a note struck and held—breathy and vibrating—a full two measures.

"I love you, Dad."

"I love you, too."

I stayed with Dad for another hour or so, just watching him dose. After I was convinced he was truly out of danger, I left his side. I had a piece of unfinished business with Jules, who was just down the hall, an armed guard sitting outside the door.

"All right if I see him?" I said. He looked a lot like Spud, only instead of bales of hay, I suspect this guy loaded logs.

He shook his head. "Can't let anyone in."

"Too bad," I said. "He awake? I mean can he talk and all that?"

"He'll live."

"He's a friend of mine," I said.

A physical therapist walked up and asked the guard to help her walk Jules. I stepped aside and hung around. A few minutes later, Jules shuffled out with his feet shackled, his hands on a walker, a bright blue strap around his waist, and a pretty little lady with her hand holding on to the belt.

When he saw me, his face lit up. "How ya doing, Finn? No hard feelings, buddy? Your Dad all right?"

"He'll make it."

"We had a chance to talk a bit," Jules said. "You ought to give him a break. He's proud of you."

I let out a laugh. "Maybe I will."

I suppose I should have been furious with

Jules. Still, I felt for him. Easy for me to say, now that things had turned out all right, but I figured he was just along for the ride with Duke. When you're fresh out of prison after twenty years, there aren't many rides available.

The physical therapist instructed Jules to lift his feet. Jules reminded her that his feet were shackled.

"All's well that ends well, I suppose," I said. "How'd you know Duke anyway?"

"His father was killed by a Dink. After my father's shrimping business went bust, I got sent to prison for burning the boat of one."

"In Seabrook?"

"Yeah." Jules took a hand and reached up to where a shirt pocket would have been. "I sure could use a cigarette." The physical therapist shook her head. "I didn't know that anyone was in the boat, I swear. It was an accident. I just wanted to show the Vietnamese they couldn't do that to my father. Rossi was making money at our families' expense."

"So how did you find me?"

"Duke put the word out for the Bandidos to find someone in Polunsky that could get to Calvery. That someone happened to be you."

"It's a small world," I said. "Is anyone else after Chloe?"

"No," Jules said. "This was personal for Duke, with his father's death and all. He believed he was owed that money."

The physical therapist seemed to be enjoying the conversation as long as Jules kept moving.

"You think there's money?" I asked.

"Not money," Jules said, stopping to catch a look at me. "Jewels, and plenty of them. Duke thinks Rossi told Calvery where they were and told him to take them."

"Rossi was dead?"

Jules shook his head. "Dying maybe. Somebody told Calvery where they were. They weren't in the house when the police got there." Jules stopped walking to catch his breath. "I want you to know. I wouldn't have shot anyone, not you or your father."

I believed him. The story about Rossi was about how Broussard had laid it out for me.

"You haven't got a part in this," I said. "It's Duke who did the kidnapping. Chloe won't testify. You were just in the wrong place at the wrong time."

"Nice of you to say, Finn," he said, looking to the guard. "But it's a little bit more complicated than that. Anyway, there's nothing for me out here. To tell you the truth, I'm lonesome. What's a guy like me gonna do out here? That's why I got hooked up with Duke."

"You could work," I said, knowing how stupid I sounded. What's a fifty-year-old guy who's spent his life in prison gonna do?

"Naw. I'll just go home."

Everybody's got their own idea of home, I thought as I watched the physical therapist put her fingers on Jules' wrist. Her lips moved as she counted his pulse.

Jules smiled up at her. "How 'm I doing, darlin'?"

"You're doing just fine, Mr. Canfield."

"You could beat this, you know?" I said.

He shook his head. "I'm tired. It's not easy being free."

"No, it's not," I agreed.

"You still got that turtle?" Jules asked. "What was his name?"

"Sport," I said. "I gave him to Chloe."

"Well, give him a big head of iceberg for me. He always liked iceberg best."

"I'll do that," I said, thinking it was nice of him to think of Sport. "I guess I'd better get going. Think about it. You could beat this."

Jules shook his head. "Don't feel bad for me," he said, with a smile wide on his face and a nod to the therapist. "It's been a good run."

Chapter Twenty-Six

I convinced Chloe it was time to find the treasure. Still ecstatic from my visit with Dad, I figured anything was possible. A word of forgiveness, not to mention love, goes a long way toward healing the soul. Who wouldn't feel invincible and renewed?

Chloe for one. If you believed in being tested—which I don't, but if you did—you'd have to admit that Chloe's last few weeks were enough to try anyone's faith. And as far as I could tell, she didn't have much to start with.

Fortunately, I had enough for both of us, though I tried not to flaunt it.

The next day, Chloe and I drove down to Devil's Churn to check it out. The churn was a narrow inlet carved into the basalt shoreline by years and years of wave action. At the end of the chasm, we caught our first glimpse of the cave. At this hour, around eleven, the high tide covered most of the entrance. When the waves retreated, we realized an iron grate had been bolted over the mouth of the cave. For Chloe, it meant we couldn't get in. For me, it meant they were trying to keep people out. The place must look totally different at low tide. With the right tools, it wouldn't be that difficult to get inside the cave. First, we would have to climb down the walls of the inlet, then unscrew the bolts holding the grate over the cave entrance. We made plans to return later that day at low tide.

When I briefed Mother and Ovid about the quest for the treasure, Mother volunteered to distract the park ranger. In a month's time, I had managed to transform her into an adrenalin junkie.

An hour before dusk, outfitted with backpacks containing flashlights, a pair of vise grips, a hack saw and a rope, we descended the path to the ocean while Mother and Ovid engaged the ranger. I was confident they could keep him entertained for as long as it took.

A flock of sea gulls yakked above us as Chloe and I hiked silently down the path to the cave. When we reached the bottom of the trail, she took one look at the churn and said, “This is crazy.”

“It’s low tide. And look, there’s no water at the mouth of the cave.” I pointed to a tiny beach of coarse sand at the end of the churn and the opening of the cave. “We can walk right in.”

“First we have to get down there.”

The chasm walls dropped about fifteen feet straight down, not a bit of a slope, and the lava had dried to a spiny finish. The rock’s sharp edges poked out from the molten surface, creating excellent hand and foot holds for a rock climber. A noise swelled from the depths of the cave—echoes of an orchestra: the hollow sound of an oboe, the low blasts of a tuba. Above us rose the great mound of the Cape.

Dropping to the volcanic shore, I placed my belly against the black rock. Its sharp points jabbed at my rib cage. Extending my head and chest as far as I could over the edge, I examined the mouth of the cave. The opening appeared about six feet tall and four feet wide. At this hour of the day, the waves stopped several feet in front of the cave’s mouth.

My examination from this angle revealed little, but years of reading Stephen King and Jules Verne necessitated this procrastination. The cave, I feared, would be pitch black, can’t-see-the-nose-on-your-face dark, monster-jump-out-of-the-cave dark. Turns out, it was.

Climbing down, I positioned my hands successfully on several outcroppings of barnacles before grabbing hold of the body of an orange sea star. When I felt its live surface, leathery and prickly, I jerked away and almost fell.

Halfway down, I jumped out from the wall—it was a move I'd seen rock climbers do—and landed on the sandy shore in front of the cave's mouth. Chloe proceeded down in the same manner, except she managed to find an abundance of footholds. I marked them in my memory for a quick escape.

A patina of rust covered an iron grate blocking the cave entrance. Chloe and I tugged on it. As luck would have it, one of the upper bolts had loosened from the rock. I positioned the vise grips on the bolt just below it and hammered on the grips until the lower bolt twisted, and I was able to unscrew the lower bolt from the rock and the grate.

"Hurry." Chloe hovered over me.

"Give me some space. I don't want to catch you in the nose." She stepped back, pacing like a kid who needed the bathroom. "Don't worry. Mother will keep the ranger busy."

"What if someone comes down?"

"Tourist season ended a month ago, remember?" I loosened one more bolt, grinned at Chloe as I pulled grate away from the mouth of the cave. "You first."

She squeezed through the opening. I followed, cleverly pulling the grate back into place so no one would suspect anything. We stepped in, and I flipped on my flashlight and scanned the windless cave. Sand glittered on the floor. Long strands of sea grass swayed with the movement of the shallow water. All manner of sea creatures covered the rocks and walls: urchins with lavender spines, pink sea cucumbers with feathery tentacles, the hard nipples of barnacles, a glowing white nudibranch, and the shiny turquoise shells of abalone. As we stepped, the crunching of shells sounded against the walls.

Ten feet into the cave, the opening narrowed. "Turn off the light," Chloe said. Her voice bounced off the walls and repeated her words.

"Not on your life."

"It's okay. There's a light coming from somewhere." She grabbed the flashlight and turned it off.

Gradually, my eyes adjusted. It only took a few minutes—maybe seconds—before it seemed as if we had entered a new dimension. Great wells of blackness lined the cave, but we stood in light seeping from breaks in the walls of the caves. Chloe's face glowed bright as midday on Galveston beach. I kept my eyes away from the darkness and turned them to the odd music sounding from farther inside the cave. We crouched and belly crawled through a tunnel toward it.

A short distance later, we entered another room. It looked illuminated by moonlight, a silvery glow on the walls, the sand trembling under a thin layer of surf. We got to our feet and waded into it, neither of us speaking, the strange song still playing softly from somewhere in the depths of the place. Tiny fishes rushed away from our feet with iridescent flashes of blue and purple.

When I reached the opposite shore, I identified the source of the symphony. Piles of mollusks, conch, and clams had collected in heaps surrounding a crater a few feet in diameter. From inside it, the sea rumbled.

Rising out of the crater like fireworks, the sound of the Pacific erupted into the chamber with the guttural moan of a foghorn. The blast echoed repeatedly against the slick walls. At the same time, mounds of shells flared into the air, clattering in the rushing water with a crescendo of percussion.

It was a spouting horn, just like the one down the road, and it was amazing. Water had rushed into the lava shelf below the cave floor, and the pressure blasted the surf through a crack and up into the chamber of the cave.

Here in the cave, my mind filled with every word Calvery had ever spoken about truth, and deep inside I recognized this place, not visually, for I had never seen anything so incredible, but I knew I had been here at least once, maybe in another life, or maybe when time began, or maybe I was sent from here to Mother's womb.

Nothing seemed impossible.

Prison and all my mistakes receded from my mind and left me with the joy I had felt the first time I held Lacy in my arms.

And then Calvery appeared.

I was not at all surprised to see him. After all, I had completed my mission, a parting thank you was only fitting. His face took form, and its glow made me wish for a pair of sunglasses. I wondered where he'd been these last few months and, as soon as the thought left me, I had the feeling he'd been lurking around this whole journey.

Calvery smiled at Chloe.

I took the hint and backed away, allowing her to take an overdue turn with her father. After all, I had my own father now.

Chapter Twenty-Seven

Chloe edged between two columns of basalt, wet with sea sweat. Mist lifted from the huge pillars, and a diamond-white light streamed through it.

She followed the light to the roof where a gash in the earth allowed the sun just enough space to come marching through. She scanned the room, and in the time it took to take in the hovering cloud above the pillars, and the opalescent glow of the walls, Chloe the Captain of Perpetuity was gone. She was, instead, a different woman. The sharp blade of anger and dread she always carried with her, the one always poking and jabbing just below the surface, had disappeared.

Curiosity pulled her farther into the room, where tide pools rippled in the shadowy light and spotted the cave floor with violet and green. The air felt playful and fun like it had the day at the waterfall with Lucia and Finn when Lucia had wondered if every one of those drops of water were a living soul.

A tiny plume of light, like a match set to flame but not catching, flashed. She let out a cry of surprise. Wanting to hear an earthly noise, she shuffled her feet in the shells and rocks. The flame appeared again, this time brighter. It settled in the middle of a tide pool, its edges as diffuse as fog. In its center, a white swirl pulsed.

Standing inside the flame, she saw her father. He was no more than a fleeting image, like a reflection in a store window. A wind blew from the flame, nudging her hair, warming her chilled body. From the beginning, this had been the place her father wanted her to see, and she was finally here.

"Daddy?"

A sound escaped, first a whine and a whimper, then wailing. She grabbed her chest, pressing on her breastbone to calm its heaving. Nothing stopped it. She cried for his lost life, his senseless death, her loneliness. She cried for her mother and her years in the nursing home. She was content to cry. She would empty herself completely if the tears kept her here with her father. She tried to think of a time when she had ever felt so complete.

And then, this version of her father said, "I'll always be with you," and the tears stopped.

The flame changed to a thick mist, and shaped into a man's form. She glimpsed her father as she had always pictured him, the father of old photographs, always a handsome young man. She felt happy for him. He was young now, never to become a stodgy old man, and she was happy for her life, her boat, Jazz, even Finn.

As the flame melted into the tide pool, comfort spilled over her like soothing oil. The air brightened to a glow not unlike a sunset, then faded until the cave dimmed to the lowlight of evening.

Chloe wiped the tears from her cheeks. She heard Finn calling for her.

"It's getting late." He shouted from another room.

She stepped back through the basalt columns and into the other chamber. How had she ventured so far? She waded through the water toward Finn, filled with a new sense of peace.

"I saw him," she said, and wrapped her arms around Finn. "He was in there."

"I know." Finn said. "I saw him, too." He stepped back, took her hands in his and squeezed them, as if about to make a solemn vow. Then, he did. "He was innocent."

"Yes."

“No one would believe it.” Finn stroked her chin with his thumb.

“I wonder if I could come here again, and he would come to me,” Chloe said. “I could have a father.”

“I think you could.”

“What if it’s not too late? It’s like he’s not dead.”

“Whatever he is, it’s forever.” Finn said.

Silently, they worked their way back. She felt happy, pleased to be hand-in-hand with Finn. The splashing of waves grew louder. Five hundred or so feet in front of them, daylight streamed through the mouth of the cave.

“There’s the way out,” she said, pointing ahead.

“That was a helluva treasure,” he said.

“It’ll be hard to cash it at the bank.”

“Oh, well.” Finn repositioned his fingers between hers. “We could offer tours.”

Chloe stepped, and a foot collided with a rock. She fell onto the floor, cursing.

“You all right?” Finn squatted beside her.

She nodded, grimacing with pain. “Just give me a second.” She was wearing her Keens, so she stuck her foot into a pool of water. “This oughta do it.” Soaking her injured foot, she took one last look around the cave, then settled on the rock that caused her to fall. “Wait a minute. This isn’t a rock.”

Chloe and Finn dug furiously through the sand, shells and rocks until they uncovered a fiberglass box. She looked at Finn incredulously.

His fingers fumbled with the metal latch to the box, smearing rust on his hands. No way had anything remained intact after all these years in the cave. He knocked the latch with his fist, grabbed the vise grips, broke open the lock and motioned for Chloe to open the chest.

Her fingers trembled. A slick film of algae covered the fiberglass. She pulled away threads of seagrass and kelp and unfastened the latch. The chest sprung open. A pile of emeralds and rubies, some the size of knuckles, others as big as walnuts filled the chest.

"The Vietnamese paid him in jewels," Finn said. "Calvery said Rossi told him to take the jewels and here they are. That Calvery. I never should've doubted him." He lifted Chloe and twirled her around. "You're rich!"

"I was already rich," she said, squeezing Finn's hand.

A rush of water passed over their feet. "Your father was the richest man in the world." Finn said.

"Is," she said. "Thanks for finding him for me."

"No." Finn shook his head. "Thanks for finding me for me."

Chapter Twenty-Eight

After our adventure in the cave, things happened quickly. At my father's bedside, I told him about the thin place and the treasure.

It was not easy convincing him of anything, let alone thin places. I told him about the atmosphere turning electric, the air buzzing around me like birds before a storm. In my bumbling way, I described the first glimpse of the other side of this life: the rush of certainty spreading through me, the light bubbling around me like a river, the sudden joy of connecting. At first, I told him, I wanted to turn away, the light too much for earthly eyes. Then I explained how patience had paid off, about the angels all around me.

"Well, of all the tall tales I've ever heard, that tops them," he said.

How could my father know what I meant by such words when I have only just begun to comprehend them myself? After all, I didn't accidentally stumble on this new faith of mine. It was that pesky Calvery goading me, even after death.

"The truth is unbelievable," I said.

"Son, truer words have never been spoken."

"You agree?" I am sure I was unable to disguise the surprise in my voice.

He nodded, and I realized I wasn't the first or last person to have an angel watching out for him. I imagine there are plenty of them, all working overtime.

Dad recovered and flew back to Texas. On a breezy, blue day at the end of September, Mother and I left Washington. That is, Mother, Ovid and I left Washington. It is probably no surprise to learn he went with us.

On our last morning, we were standing outside Chloe's house, the Impala loaded for the trip home. "I don't want to go," I said to her.

"Yes, you do." She lifted her face to the sun.

She had changed after our day in the cave. Instead of always bustling around with a serious weight-of-the-world scowl on her face, she had slowed, as if just released from a spinning top onto a new and surprising planet.

"You'd like Lacy. She'd like you." I pulled her into my arms. "I hope someday the three of us might see the Cape together."

"Bring her to visit." She whispered in my ear.

"You mean it?"

"More than a visit." She lowered her eyes. In their beautiful green, our completely crazy adventure played out, even that twinkle she shared with me in the night.

"Don't tease me," I said.

"I'm not. You and I, we're not done yet."

With that, I kissed her, scratched Jazz on his chest, kissed her again.

Ovid had spread a road map over the hood of the car. He called out to me. "Averaging sixty miles per hour, it will take ten hours to reach the California border."

"Guess that's my cue," I said to Chloe. "Hold on," I yelled to Ovid. "Just one more thing."

I ran towards the house.

"What's the one more thing?" Chloe called after me.

I bounded up the steps, through the living room and into the mudroom off the kitchen. Behind me, I heard what I assumed were her footfalls.

I needed one last look at good Ol' Sport, living the dream in his terrarium, nibbling on a clump of clover.

"I'll never forget you, ol' buddy," I said, picking him

up with my hands book-ending the DCC that had led to the treasure.

I will admit my eyes welled up just a bit. After all, that turtle had seen me through some tough times.

Chloe caught up with me and stood beside me. “This is the one more thing?”

I shrugged. “Had to say goodbye.”

“You’re not going to cry over a turtle?” She rubbed a hand over my back.

“He’s not just your average turtle.”

“No, he’s not,” she said. “He’s Daddy’s turtle.” With that, I gave her one last, and I hoped unforgettable, kiss.

Chloe put her money to good use. First thing, she pulled her mother out of the nursing home. What a glorious day that must have been. It would have been worth waiting for, except I wanted to see Lacy in the worst way.

Next, she gave some of her money to help the Frees build a better school and maybe attract some tourists in the summer. Last, she fixed Perpetuity.

From the pictures, Perpetuity looked fine—a beautiful lilac and green paint job, shiny polished teak in the wheelhouse, a new galley, and the booths decorated with a seashell design. She painted a ring of shells, in honor of my vision, beneath the name Perpetuity. Chloe said when the sun hits it just so she sees the faeries dancing.

Just three months after we returned to Texas, Mother died. Death circled around her, relentless. Nevertheless, she and Ovid had a few good weeks. They even took a birding trip down to Aransas Wildlife Refuge.

Mother left this earth on Christmas Eve. Her body lingered between two worlds before stopping entirely. When her breath fired like a sputtering engine, just before her final gasps, I felt the weight of a hand on my shoulder and saw the curl of a hefty ocean wave coming to carry her across, just like Calvery's books had promised.

As for Lacy, God in his grace gave Brooke enough forgiveness to reinstate me as a father. In that respect, I am making up for lost time. First, I made good on my promise to myself and preserved that tiny sand dollar in glass. Lacy wears it on a gold chain around her neck.

We spend weekends down at Galveston where the Gulf looks the color of a root beer float. My daughter thinks the pelicans are cartoon characters and laughs as they bend their long beaks against their necks to sip the lapping waves. She points as they lift into the sky with a great flapping of wings and transform into feathered kites sailing on the wind. We ride the Dolphin Chaser with Jacob. Lacy applauds as the dolphins scoop the air in perfect arcs, squeals when they disappear under our boat, jumps up and down when they surprise us with a dramatic re-entry. Later, we fish off the pier until the sun colors the sky with hues gaudy as Dallas. It is a marvel Lacy loves, this time alone with her now-sane father.

Whenever I am tempted to head down to The Dive, I look over at her smiling face and out onto the Gulf. I watch the spray fly off the crashing surf like tiny leaping fish and wonder at the waves as they unfold onto the shore. Then, I breathe in the sky and think of my mother riding a whitecap or sharing a cup of heavenly tea with Calvery.

Sometimes Lacy places her little head on my lap, and we watch the seagulls circle overhead. I tell her how to find thin places and about the angels she will see.

And she believes me. She believes every word.

ACKNOWLEDGEMENTS

From the moment I burst into this world, the blessings of this life surrounded me. I am grateful to my parents, Durwood Owens, who believed in education and saving money, and said that he had never seen a more beautiful place than the Umpqua Valley; and Virginia Owens, who grew up in Lookingglass Valley surrounded by fir-covered hills. She always loved the Bible verse: I lift up mine eyes to the hills, from whence cometh my help? /My help comes from the Lord. I often feel both of them gather close to me when I stumble upon a thin place.

My sister, Jan, has always loved me unconditionally, cheered for me in my success and commiserated with me in my sorrow. When our parents died, she brought clarity to our new lives without them.

Thanks also to my first readers. For the last ten years, I have been blessed by my writing group—The Fabulous Writers of Austin. Their feedback and encouragement bolstered me through the years. Thanks to all of them: Gary Cooke, Pansy Flick, Nancy Gore, Gaylon Greer, Jim Hawes, Jacqueline Kelly, Kim Kronzer and Lottie Shapiro. Thanks also to Susan Jenkins and John Welsh for their technical guidance related to all things nautical. It was my pleasure to share this dream with many friends who always offered a listening ear and encouragement—Linda Olson, Meredith Shepherdson, Kathy Campbell, Sally Edgar and Suzanne Duncan.

I want to extend a special thanks to Jim Gingerich, the cover artist, who provided both literary and artistic guidance as I wrote this book. The cover pastel captures the action and mystery of my story, as well as the beauty of the Northwest.

I have known my editor, Pam Chaney Wilds, since the second grade. Over the years, we have shared the beauty of many thin places together, including a lifetime of trips to Cape Perpetua, Yachats and Devils Churn. Thanks to Pam's journalism background, she has given me the priceless gift of editing my manuscript. Grammar Greatness, the book she co-authored with Linda Olson, is an essential and practical resource for every writer. I also benefited from the counsel of editors J.C. Philips, Daniel Kalder and Billy Cotter during the writing of this book.

Most of all, thanks to my family. My husband, Ed, never seemed to tire of my droning on about the book. His patience, encouragement and enduring love sustained me for the five years it took to write this book.

For Lee and Cassie, my children, they've added spice to my prose and joy to my life. The legacy endures in Maddison, my granddaughter. She is a force not to be reckoned with, and I am certain that when the world opens itself up to her fully, she will understand what to do.

For my readers, may your eyes always be open, your hearts always welcome, and your joy always complete.

Thin places surround you. Believe.

www.ingramcontent.com/pod-product-compliance
Lightning Source LLC
Chambersburg PA
CBHW070607130626
46556CB00001B/293